Sarah's Home

by Connie Mikelson

Enjoy the story!

Connie Mikelson 2019

:

This is a work of fiction. The incidents, places and interactions of the fictional characters used in this work are a product of the author's imagination or are used ficticiously.

CreateSpace Edition

ISBN:1548322997
ISBN-13: 978-1548322991

for Julie.

Acknowledgements

Sarah's Home started as a thought and a challenge from my writer's group. As each draft was weaved, it became a difficult to keep from becoming part of the story. The project's completion soon grew into an obsession. However, with every good story, the vortex it creates can only be properly developed with help to see the forest through the trees. There are a number of people who helped, cajoled, encouraged, suggested, and even critiqued drafts after drafts after drafts.

I'd like to shout out to my local writing friends Mel, Patrice, Cathy and Ursula who gently helped open my eyes to the faults of the early drafts, and took the time to read through the potholed mess from whence the story evolved.

I truly appreciate my beta readers Gwen, Tanya, Sandy, Susan, Joan, and Lauren for their patience with my seemingly endless questions of what could be repaired and what should be taken out with the trash. I hope you all realize just how valuable your comments were to me.

Thank you, thank you, thank you to Scott, Nancy and Chris for your time spent injecting your thoughts that grounded the creative process and encouragement to continue despite how trying the remolding of Sarah's Home had become.

I would be remiss not to thank Susan, Bekki, Sean, Kristi, Mike, Nina, Scott, and Jamie for tolerating the moodiness and consumption of this self-flagellating process I profess to enjoy.

If I forgot anyone else, it was inadvertent.

Chapter 1

Carl Edwards combed through Sarah Tanchak's financial information, hoping he could find a hint at a hidden life insurance policy that could help Sharon keep her sister's house, or at least some way she could keep the house and avoid bankruptcy. He tipped his head back to focus more clearly on Natalie Gorman's scribbled notes through his bifocals. He had asked his co-worker to recheck the file to be sure he hadn't missed anything of importance on his look through. Losing confidence that there was one caveat that could provide a glimmer of hope, he studied all the way to the very last comment. After a few more minutes, he sighed and peered across the boardroom sized polished walnut table at Sharon.

"I'm sorry, Ms. Tanchak. Every penny is accounted for. I was hoping there was something about a secret investment, but there is nothing."

Sharon knew that if Carl Edwards' could not find anything in the financial statements that even addressed extraordinary expenses, the fact that she could manage the mortgage was irrelevant. She did nothing to hide her disappointment; her washed out face now wan by gaunt, sunken cheeks. Her reflection in the table showed differently and looked hauntingly like she remembered Sarah's.

Carl bowed his head, wanting desperately to help Sharon as a favor, since he had handled Sarah's accounting needs and had been a close friend both women through the years. "I understand your trouble, but there is nothing here."

"So there is nothing else? There is nowhere else to turn." Sharon thought aloud.

"There are quite a few payments made to Carolyn Appleton and the Conservatory. Have you considered talking with her directly? Maybe set up a charitable benefit?"

"I've tried. She won't even give me the time of day." Sharon rolled her eyes and shook her head. "She avoids my calls and refuses to see me when I go to the Conservatory. I could be President Clinton, but since I am not the virtuoso musician that my sister was, to her, I am not even worthy of being in her presence no less taking her time."

"Look, Sharon, I can try one more time to reason with her, but have to caution you, though; I am bound by probate law at this point. Unless I can convince Ms. Appleton to help with reconciling the medical bills, I'm afraid you will . . . well, you know."

"I understand. I've already made the arrangements. And I do appreciate what you've already done." Sharon stood, slipped on her fleece jacket, then headed out toward the parking garage.

As the conference room door closed, Carl slumped into his chair. He did not have a hard time imagining Carolyn Appleton talking down her thin, narrow, pointed nose at Sharon. Over his twenty-year career with the firm, she had been his most difficult client. They struggled through some huge disagreements since her portfolio was assigned to him three years ago, which was when she demanded Edwin, her fifth agent from the firm in four years, be removed from her case. What amazed Carl was that Appleton had still not "fired" him as well, since their disagreements seemed irresolvable, and only after some tough negotiation, they reached compromise. More often than not though, Carl felt he had only capitulated to her dark, cold-hearted whims. He realized her strong will probably made the Conservatory financially successful.

Carl finished cleaning up the conference room, throwing out the paper coffee cups and refiling the papers into the expandable brown file folder labelled "Tanchak." He secured the string around the round cardboard disc, closed the folder, then retreated to his cubicle, now as Spartan as it was the first day he arrived some twenty years ago. He laid the Tanchak file onto his desktop and sighed loudly, wishing he could have done more to resolve Sharon's dilemma before he retired. That, he resigned, was just not in the cards.

"I know that look," Natalie Bowman appeared at his cube entrance and leaned on the metal support. She was a very attractive strawberry blonde-haired woman with only a few freckles, stunning hazel eyes and an inviting smile. She was fifteen years younger than he was, but had proven repeatedly that she could handle the tough negotiations like a grizzled old salt. "Doesn't look like you found anything she could use either."

"Nothing. Absolutely nothing. Not even a rogue life insurance policy that could help her. I've never felt so frustrated."

"Rather hard leaving on that note, isn't it?" Natalie moved into the cube and sat down in his spare chair. She crossed her legs, leaned forward and placed her soft hand over his. "Maybe you need to stay a bit longer. I know you hate leaving things unfinished."

"I just wish there was some way of melting Appleton's heart enough to consider giving Ms. Tanchak a break."

"You'd need a blast furnace for that, I think."

"Well, I've got one more thing to try. I can talk with Carolyn directly and see if I can charm her into being a bit more understanding. There has to be an ounce of kindness in there, someplace."

"You are a glutton for punishment, aren't you? I'm thinking that effort is either impossible or improbable, but you may be the only one who could do it," Natalie chuckled.

"Well, what is she going to do? Fire me? On my last day?"

"You know, I'm going to miss you, old man. Always thinking you can right the world with your brilliant mind and golden tongue." Natalie stood up, opened her arms, leaned over and embraced Carl for a brief moment.

"As for the other side, is Ms. Tanchak handling it well?"

"To be honest, remarkably well. Oh, I've got something for you, young lady," Carl noted as he disengaged with Natalie. He picked up the Tanchak file and handed it to her. "Since I didn't tie this up in a bow, Joshua told me that you get this file to close up. The only thing left is to reconcile the house and the hospital bills, and Ms. Tanchak has done a great job preparing and arranging to sell. It shouldn't be more than a few minutes of work to clear the paper when that is done, so unless I can break through Dragon Lady's armor this afternoon, for all practical purposes, it'll be just a simple wrap-up."

Natalie's face cringed. "Joshua didn't give me the Appleton file too, did he?"

"No worries there. He wanted me to leave that for my replacement, you know, that young buck coming in from Chicago. He's a CPA and from what I hear a pretty savvy fiduciary. Those creds should make her happy. And since she's about gone through everybody else here, he thought a fresh face might just suit her fancy."

Natalie wiped her brow and left with the file folder wedged underneath her arm. "Glad I dodged that one. I could only imagine me and her getting into it."

Carl smirked. "That would be something to watch."

Natalie scowled, then added, "You are incorrigible," before she walked away.

Sharon sat on the front porch of her sister's house and set the framed picture of her and her sister down on the cold red bricks. She felt it was still Sarah's house, at least until she actually sold it. Cold seeped through her jeans and numbed her thighs. The March morning sun made little impact on the bricks or the patches of dead moss that spotted the stoop. She cinched up her brown fleece jacket as a light breeze tossed her shoulder length auburn hair about her face. Behind her, the front storm door squawked open, startling her.

"You've made some good progress," said Linda Beels, the local realtor, as she emerged from the house and let the storm door labor closed behind her. She was dressed more casually than most of the local middle-aged real estate agents, more down to earth and more like her, which made Sharon comfortable with Linda. She was easy to work with; direct, honest, and with that classic New Hampshire touch of dry humor. Her sales record was excellent as well, and she understood what would attract relocations and other out-of-towners to her operational base of Edenton. "That's probably all we can do for today, but at some point, we'll need to at least get the last of the furniture out."

Sharon glanced back at the house then back to Linda. "I know, I'm getting there."

"It's just my opinion, but in this market, the emptier the house, the easier the sell. People like to imagine how their things fit, and any clutter tends to confuse that."

"I know," Sharon mumbled.

Linda bent over and set a hand on her shoulder. "We should probably get the carpets cleaned as well. The dog didn't have any accidents, did she?"

"No. We cleaned the carpets after Cassie passed last year."

"Alright, but I still think one more good once over on the carpets couldn't hurt."

"Okay. I can arrange that."

"We need to focus on the inside since we won't be able to do anything about the dullness of the curb appeal this time of year."

That comment hurt Sharon. She glanced around the yard, still brown and compressed from four months of winter snow pack that had mostly melted off. She had taken great pride in her landscape artistry, something she had been recognized for in her work at Barrett's Farm and Garden. She had designed many of the showiest landscapes in the county, and she was proud at how well she molded Sarah's landscape — proud enough that she brought several clients out to see what she could do.

Linda was right though; the gardens showed only a faint hint of recovering from dormancy, looking now to be nothing more than a sad, mud-colored mural with little life. Once the leaves on the roses unfurled and the overgrown autumn clematis draping the fence pushed out its new growth, the front yard would again be vibrant and inviting.

"When do you think you'll be able to clear the rooms?"

"Maybe next weekend, if I'm not working," Sharon's tone was non-committal. "What if I just move it all to the basement?"

"And the garage?"

"Not sure. I guess I can take that stuff to the dump next week as well. That should be okay, right?"

Linda's scowl answered Sharon. "Do you want me to hold off on the listing until you can get all that done?"

Sharon knew she had to decide, sooner rather than later. Most of Sarah's stuff had been either donated, sold off, or given away so far, leaving just the few items still left in the house. She would rather not rent a U-Haul to remove what remained, even though her boss would most likely accommodate her with a small box truck from the store's fleet. What to do with what still remained left Sharon indecisive. The dump, or the recycle center as they called it out here, just didn't seem right, but she was starting to accept that it was really her only option since her condo was too small to manage it all.

"I still have another week after that, right?" Sharon looked up to Linda.

"Alright, then," Linda glanced at her watch. "My word, where does the time go? I have a showing on the other side of town in a half-hour so I need to be on my way. I can prepare the listing when I get back to the office, and hold off another week to post it."

"I'll do what I can."

"I know it's been hard, but you've done real well. Just remember, we are dealing with a narrow window if we want to take advantage of relocations. Most companies make their transfers in early spring." Linda cinched up her powder blue windbreaker over her white blouse, then headed through the latchkey gate, slipped into her white, late model Saab, and left.

Sharon stayed on the porch and looked down to the framed picture of her and her sister during their last hiking trip in the White Mountains. They looked like a pair of experienced hikers with well-toned bodies as they rested on the porch of Owens' General Store. Their sinewy legs stretched out from their cut-off jean shorts and hiking boots propped up on a long table crafted out of a split log of oak. Their shoulder length auburn hair framed their smiling oval faces while they clanked the tops of their Moxie soda bottles together.

She remembered that it took almost an entire week before she could even walk without something hurting. It was the first time she remembered ever being that sore, since she had always kept herself in shape. They spent hours on the phone just laughing and complaining about each other's aches and pains. The stiffness in her back was her worst, but her legs complained just as much, her thighs twitching in spasms while her feet throbbed. Sarah did not handle the daylong venture much better than she did, in fact, seemed much worse than just having overdone it. Sarah had always recovered quickly in the past. Now that

Sharon had some time to think about it, she should have recognized that clue of what was soon to consume their lives.

As she looked up, she caught a glimpse of the small cemetery across the road. It had been set off from the other properties across the street by an old rubble stonewall. It was an old historic, family cemetery, like so many of the other cemeteries in town, which few stopped by to wander through. Beyond the slightly rusting cast iron gate bolted into granite posts at the entrance, a flock of wild turkeys gurgled as they feasted on the acorns blanketing the centuries old plots, now revealed by the snowmelt. She remembered sitting in this exact spot with Sarah, watching the flocks root around for hours, undeterred by interruptions of an occasional pair of raucous ravens or skittish squirrels chattering for their turn at the nuts.

"Turkeys in the graveyard, picking at nuts," Sharon remembered Sarah starting to conjure songs about the birds as they worked over the plots in the spring. As spring moved toward summer and the weather grew tolerable, Sarah would sometimes play her oboe to serenade the birds. They would come waddling across the street, fresh new poults in tow, stopping traffic as they moseyed across before lining up at the fence to listen to the impromptu concert of Brahms melodies.

"Good afternoon."

Sharon startled at the gravelly woman's voice, realizing she must have drifted away in her thoughts. She looked up and noticed Esther Palmer, the elderly farmer's wife from down the road, moseying up the driveway to the gate. She and her husband, John, owned the farm that sat on a hill east of Sarah's house. Their daily walks up the hill brought them by the house, and Esther made a point of stopping in whenever they had seen Sharon and Sarah as they gardened or just puttered outside.

"Hello." Sharon smiled then pushed herself up to navigate the flat stone sidewalk and greet them at the gate.

"How are you doing, dear?" Esther offered her shaking, skeletal hand. She was a kindly, sensible woman that held no regrets about being a farmer's wife. Her children, both girls, had long since moved out, one for the city and the other a stone's throw down the road, homesteading on a piece of land they had cut out for her and her husband. Esther had taken a liking to Sarah and Sharon over the years they had been on Pleasant Hill, so much so that Sharon wondered at times if they had become subconsciously adopted as third and fourth daughters.

"I'm doing okay. Thank you for asking," Sharon covered the woman's hand with hers. Her shaking stopped, briefly.

Old man Palmer, as she and Sarah referred to him, lumbered up the driveway with his blind beagle methodically plodding behind on his leash, stopped to glance up at the two large pines that draped needle-laden boughs over the driveway. Sharon knew what was coming from his foggy-eyed glare that turned toward her. "Need to take those down," he mumbled, wagging his finger at the trees. "Damn things are just trouble, you know. Late

11

snows around here are heavy, you know. That'll make a mess to clean up."

"Oh, hush, John," Esther scolded and waved at her husband to mind his own business. "Don't mind him. He's obsessed with those trees," Esther added, turning back toward Sharon. She leaned against the gate to prop up her slight tilt.

"Oh, that's fine, Mrs. Palmer. I think I've heard that every time he's been up here."

"He's more obsessed with eradicating them than the pine beetles are," Esther giggled, politely covering her mouth. "We've had a lot of trouble over the years, you know."

"I know." Sharon was well versed about the invasive diseases and beetle blights that seemed to be spreading further north each year. Her fieldwork in college was on the impact invasive species had on the region. "It was something that Sarah was thinking about, but . . ."

Sharon stopped when the blind beagle waddled toward the gate with his leash dragging beside him. The dog sniffed at the pile of browned lily leaves, then looked up with his cataract-coated eyes. Sarah reached over and scratched the beagle's head, and felt a sudden jolt of sadness. Cassie always yapped at him from the front yard, running back and forth when he meandered by. She wondered if the beagle was still sniffing for Cassie.

"I know, dear," Esther comforted. "It will take some time to heal."

"I'm good. It's just a little tug when something brings up a memory," Sharon mumbled, recovering her mettle.

"And if you need something, don't be a stranger. We'd love the company, you know."

"I'm selling the house."

"That's a shame, but it don't matter, dear. You are always welcome to stop over for some tea. Or just stop in to watch the stars or the Northern Lights or whatever you girls watched those nights." Esther's lips twitched into a brief smile. "I know how much you girls liked doing that."

"I do appreciate that."

"And I know John didn't mind watching you two either," Esther winked and giggled like a schoolgirl before wagging her crooked finger at Sharon. "Now you don't be bashful. If you want to stop in and watch the show, just flash your lights. That way, I'll know it's you and I won't call the police."

"Thank you. I just might stop by for a meteor shower now and then."

"Oh, yes. You two enjoyed those shooting stars, now didn't you. The Almanac lists them now you know. It's in big print. It's about the only book I read now." Esther let go after a squeeze of Sharon's hand. She didn't have the heart to remind the elderly lady that the meteor showers had always been listed in the Almanac.

Esther took her husband's hand and started back out the driveway toward the road, leaving Sharon standing at the gate. By the time the couple and their beagle slipped behind a ragged stand of leafing out forsythia, Sharon noticed that Esther had again dropped off another pot of short, freshly sprouted leaves sure to be forget-me-nots in the front garden. Another pot. One she must have overwintered in her tiny greenhouse, that Sharon had helped her set up a couple years back. All during the fall, she had done the same to the point that the bare spot between the maroon and cream-colored mums had been completely filled in. Sharon just smiled and shook her head. She knew Esther Palmer was chuckling all the way home.

"Oh, crap!" Sharon recognized the time by the shadows creeping into the driveway. She glanced at her watch and realized her shift at her second job with Applebee's was starting in an hour, and it would take most of that time to get there. She had never been late for her shifts, and even though she was done after this week, she still wanted to leave on a good note. Vaulting up from her seat, she heard the Vicodin pills in her pocket jostle. Quickly looking around for a place to hide the bottle, she decided just slipping the bottle behind the storm door, figuring it would be safe enough for now. She'd be back in the morning before anyone else would be here and find another spot for them. After pushing the door closed, she climbed into her red Jeep Wrangler and headed out toward town.

Chapter *2*

Sharon rolled her Jeep to a stop in the driveway of Sarah's house on her way back home from her shift at Applebee's. She felt like she had hit a wall, burning candles at both ends, working all day at Barrett's Farm and Garden and then a waitressing gig in the evenings. Even with all the hard work, she still came up short, not being able to raise enough to reconcile Sarah's medical bills without selling the house. The administrators at the hospital had been more than understanding in the six months since Sarah's passing, but their patience had expired.

She had always been the strongest one in the family, the one that had, did and could summon the mental energy and logic to resolve and handle any issue, regardless of complexity or emotional depth.

She handled each of her parent's estates as they passed, methodically working through the long distance logistics. She helped Sarah through her phases of passion between music, food, and nature, as well as her mercurial hook-ups and the break-ups that followed. She supported her gloom when her beloved dog passed. She also stood by her sister's side as she wasted away from breast cancer that metastasized despite the valiant efforts of her surgeons. And so far, she had managed being the executor for Sarah's will, all the while believing she could somehow manage to keep the house. She wasn't used to giving in, but her limits had been reached; her stamina petered out, her tank on empty, and her confidence now caged and worn thread-bare like an old pair of jeans.

She flipped over the flat rock near the sad-looking Daphne, then picked up the key that she had squirreled away underneath. It would have to be handed over to Linda Beels with the other door keys once the house was sold, but for now, she was going to keep it hidden. She unlocked the outside door to the garage, moved through the small piles she still needed to clean out, and then unlocked the inside door to the foyer. There was a little bit of moonlight still eking its way through the skylights, but for the most part, the house remained chilly, dim and quiet.

She turned on the overhead kitchen light and stared at the stove, remembering the time that Sarah, so driven by her creative passion for good food, had given up her music career to attend culinary school. Sarah knew that irritated Carolyn Appleton to no end, but she was insistent that she needed to follow her passion. Sarah did decide to go back to the Conservatory when she explored her passion for cooking. Sharon understood why her sister did at the time. She was skilled enough to go free-lance and play for many of the local orchestras. She had played with the Boston Symphony, soloing at times. She was a virtuoso, no doubt but there was always that lingering desire to teach that brought her back into Carolyn's clutches.

Even as her cooking phase was brief, Sarah had learned enough that on some weekends, they created fabulous dishes together like her favorite ginger-rosemary pheasant in pomegranate sauce. Their visits to the World Grocery for supplies would last for hours, tasting the various spices for the perfect combination of flavors that would enhance the flavor of the dishes. Sharon's favorite was cardamom. Once she admitted that, Sarah always used it baking breads, leaving a rich, mid-eastern aroma lingering like incense through the house.

Sharon reached up and cracked open the spice cabinet. Inside, the collection of small bottles was still there, even the cardamom. She never did finish cleaning out the kitchen. It might have been that she couldn't bring herself to work through the cabinets. Maybe she figured it would be a nice welcoming surprise for the next owner to have something with which to start. It might have been that she knew each tape-labelled spice bottle would bring back some memory. Like now.

Therapy, she thought. Necessary, self-induced therapy. It was nice to remember the good times.

She stiffened, sucked in a strong breath, then took a small pot from the lower cabinet, filled it with water, then set it on the stove. As she waited for it to boil, which took no time at all, she filled a slotted tea spoon with a mix of rosemary and stevia. Grabbing one of the mugs she had left, she steeped the tea until it wafted wisps of aroma toward her face.

Darkness crept into the great room while she waited. With her drink in hand, she curled up in Sarah's favorite chair, a well-used armchair with stained, plain cream upholstery. Sharon never had a chance to clean any of the stains on the cushions since Sarah had spent most of her waking hours in this chair as she faded away. The chair remained facing the French doors overlooking the deck where Sarah could watch the chickadees and juncos battle squirrels for the sunflower seeds on the deck. Sharon always cleaned the mess of seed hulls and discarded millet every weekend to make sure no wandering rodents would decide to visit and party on the chaff, and then refilled the feeders with fresh seed.

Sharon took a sip of the tea and felt the warmth cascade down her throat while the steam helped clear her sob-swollen passages. She would have normally taken the tea out onto the deck, but the Adirondack chairs remained stowed away from the winter snow. She swaddled herself in the stained slipcover and nuzzled at her steaming tea as she stared out into the night where she was sure spotted fawns, coyote pups, and baby rabbits were starting fresh into a new world. Pulling her legs close and underneath her, she felt the day's frustration dissipate and exhaustion seep in. Eyes slipping closed as her head started to nod, she could not help but think about Sarah.

An oboe began to play Adagio for Strings with an exquisite, mournful quality and perfect phrasing. The crescendos were placed perfectly, rising with the higher notes, and fading as the scale moved lower in pitch. This had to be one of the most beautiful renditions of her favorite piece that Sharon had ever heard. Without opening her eyes, she listened carefully to the solemnness and timbre realizing there was only one person who played like that. Something was different, though. There were no breaks. No breaths. The music moved endlessly for five minutes before Sharon sensed she had to interrupt.

"How are you doing that?" she asked. Sarah sat in front of her on her music stool, wearing a delicate gown of beautifully patterned sheer linen. She had thinned a bit, but her breasts that had been cut away by surgery, were somehow back to their normal shape. Setting her oboe down in her lap cross-wise, she tilted her head and split open her lips, her teeth brilliant again, not like the sickened yellow she remembered from her last days. Her eyes sparkled as they did when she was young.

"Doing what?" Sarah's voice was hollow, but her gravelly pitch had vanished, and her face grew impish.

"You were playing without taking a breath."

"It only sounds that way, dear. Of course I have to breathe."

"Can you sing again? I mean, like you used to?"

Sarah started an open-mouthed scale. As she moved up in pitch, her voice grew louder. She added a vibrato as she moved into a second octave. Then she sang thirds and fifths in staccato before stopping. "Like that?"

"How?"

"I'm home, girl. You know I was comfortable here. The woods behind us, the farms all around, the birds in the air. You remember, it's like our childhood home in Indiana, except —"

"There are mountains, tall pine trees, and Northern Lights," Sharon finished for Sarah, as she had always done since they were toddlers learning to talk. It was an advantage or a scourge at times being close, identical twins.

"Oh, dear. Why are you so sad, Sharon?" Sarah's voice had lost the richness from her singing and returned to hollow again.

"I'm not sad. I'm over that. I'm just doing what I have to do. I have to sell the house, Sarah. There is no money left to pay the bills."

"There's no need to fret, Sharon. It will work itself out."

"Did you hear me? I can't keep the house."

"You can come and visit anytime you know."

"Sarah, listen to me. Someone else will be buying this house. I can't just drop in anytime I would like to."

"Everything will work out in the long run, dear. I know it will all be fine."

"How can you be so naïve? You gave away almost all of your savings to the Conservatory. What was even worse was that you had no life insurance."

"Not that I didn't try. No one would cover me after the first bout of cancer."

"You must have known there would be nothing left after all those payments to Carolyn. What were they for, anyway?"

"It's not something I would want to discuss at this point. Listen, Sharon dear. It will be alright." Sarah spread her arms open and drifted toward Sharon.

"How? Everything that you had here will be gone. No one else could understand the sentiment. To anyone else, this is just property. They'll probably throw out what's left, redo the gardens, till under your heirloom tomatoes, kill your currents, and uproot your peach trees just to replace it with a rickety old swing set where snot-nosed kids will pull each other's hair." Sharon stopped for a breath.

"My word. You are working yourself into a tizzy. Trust me."

"But —"

"Everything will be fine. Just be yourself. Be your old self again."

An empty dump truck crashed through potholes on the road, startling Sharon awake. The house was dark. Sarah was gone. The rumble and banging from a truck's empty box-bed grew louder and closer. It had to be Leo, the construction contractor that lived alone in the trailer down the road. The only time he ever slowed down was to ogle her and Sarah when they worked through the side herb garden in their bikinis and sun hats.

She cracked a grin remembering how Sarah would always blow him a kiss to get him to sound off his truck's obnoxious horn. She thought that was encouraging him too much, but even though he was a bit of a letch, he was harmless, especially since he had detoxed after his last DWI conviction. She then recognized that it must have been nearly dawn since that was when Leo left his trailer down the road for the quarry. As she worked the crust from her eyes, she realized that she must have fallen asleep, slept though most of the night, and dreamed about her lost sister.

Expected at work in a couple of hours, she still needed to get back to her condo to change into her work clothes. Flipping the slipcover off, she balled it up to take home and wash out the stains, then placed her cup into the deep sink. She'd clean it up before Linda had another showing she figured, then headed out.

Before closing the door behind her, she took a glance back into the house. For a moment, she imagined Sarah sitting in her chair again; watching the birds quarrel over the birdfeeder, tipping her head to one side, then slowly back to the other to see past the center doorframe.

"Be yourself," Sharon reminded herself as she thought she felt a soft touch on her shoulder and was flooded with a sense of comfort. After locking the door behind her, she placed the key back under the stone, jumped into and started her Jeep. As she pulled out, her headlights crossed the dining room window in the dim morning light. The curtains floated in the window, as if waving goodbye. She did a double take and stopped for a moment. The curtains were now as flaccid as they were when she arrived. She assumed the floating was more likely just her imagination playing tricks with her.

Chapter 3

Zachary Fields was comfortable enough; reasonably successful at work, condo just outside of the city, money in the bank, decent car, and a small number of close friends. Everything seemed headed in a traditional direction for him except that he was now single, or separated, or no longer committed, or whatever it was other than with someone. That wasn't much of an issue, since being single wasn't abnormal. At least that's what he convinced himself. It was the way it happened that haunted him. He totally missed the start of the downward spiral in his relationship with Brenda. It was too late when they had agreed to reconcile, and then never got around to it before the terrible accident on a rain-driven night that killed her, leaving him empty and their relationship unresolved. He figured it was a good time to head somewhere else when the company offered a transfer to Nashua from Chicago. A fresh start in a new place could be just what he needed to get out of his self-consumed rut. The salary increase and relocation bonus didn't cloud the decision either.

Until now, everything about the move seemed positive. It wasn't that there weren't houses available. There were. It was just that nothing seemed to precisely meet his needs, his budget, or felt right. His flight back to Chicago was tomorrow evening and striking out on finding a house at this point concerned him. Since he didn't want to settle for a condo or apartment in Nashua, stow his furniture, then look for something after he started his new job, he mulled over what needs and preferences to compromise.

Frustrated, he turned into a Shell gas station and pulled up to the pumps. As he started filling the tank of his rented Explorer, he mindlessly surveyed the intersection for a moment before looking back toward the convenience store. As he did, he noticed a very attractive woman exiting the store. Her self-assured air was radiant, from her long, leggy strides to the bounce in her shoulder length, auburn hair. As she headed directly toward him with her confident pace, he quickly estimated she was about his age. Her jeans and long sleeved, logoed t-shirt fit firmly to her shape, accentuated by her purse strap resting perfectly across the middle of her chest. A bright, inviting smile beamed from her face; he could not resist smiling back. He tried not to stare as she headed toward her red Jeep that was sitting across the island from him, then gave up and just tried not to let his jaw slacken and drop open. She turned briefly as she opened her door, long enough that he noticed her well-toned backside before she slipped into her seat and started her engine.

His gas pump clacked off, breaking his attention. From the time it took him to return the pump handle back into the slot, register payment, and then look back again, she had already driven off. He imagined it would be nice to catch up with her at some point, and to see if there could be more than just a casual conversation. There was something that was familiar about her that he sensed, but couldn't quite nail down.

Musing set aside, he finished at the pump, stepped up into his car, and then glanced down to what remained of his house-hunting list. He had whittled down his long list to one, a house that he penned in last night while he was browsing through the listings at the hotel. Conveniently, it appeared to be a short drive away. He punched the address into his Garmin then followed the directions. The route seemed longer than the ten minutes his tracker indicated, perhaps because of all the dips and turns in the road. The meandering did slow him down somewhat, but he wondered if the coverage out here in the boonies was limited. He even started to wonder if he was lost and had taken a wrong turn until he noticed a long bend in the road and something behind all the trees. He downshifted, and feathered his brakes as he surveyed the side of the road. There was nothing but a sprawling field behind a border of yet to be leafed-out hardwood trees along the fieldstone wall to his right. He glanced into his rear-view mirror and since he saw no one, he slowed further to be sure not to miss the driveway. After crawling for one hundred feet, he spotted an opening, pulled off onto the shoulder and stopped the Explorer just past the pebble-stone covered driveway. His view was unobstructed. In front of the garage and off to the side, a white Saab and a Subaru wagon sat parked. He slipped the gearshift into park and let the engine idle.

Behind a squat, New England style rubble-stone wall rested the "find," or at least it appeared that way. He immediately sensed this was the house. The listing indicated a Saltbox style, a design with which he had just started to become familiar. It appeared to fit perfectly with the landscape — a gradually sloping yard that disappeared into thickening woods, and a rolling horizon of hazy green mountains, probably miles away but close enough to border the blue sky. From his vantage point though, the house looked more like a small colonial, about half the width of most colonials he remembered from back home in the Mid-West, and those he had seen here. The tan colored siding, vinyl, appeared to be in reasonable condition, in stark contrast to the woodpecker-ravaged house on the north side of Manchester that he had seen earlier. Along the outside of the decorative, small, weathered natural cedar picket fence enclosing an area about the size of an English cottage yard were four, wild looking bushes, probably roses, their overgrown branches starting to show some green. A narrow flower garden, overgrown with well-nourished crabgrass lay underneath the sprawling shrubs and bordered a flat-stone walkway that led to a latched gate in the middle of the fence.

He tried to imagine how the yard would look later in the spring when all the ratty looking shrubs had blossomed and leafed out, but he struggled with that vision since he had no clue what the plants were, except maybe the roses. He also didn't know what would grow well in this part of the country. Knowing neither, he was unsure if the disheveled appearance was normal, the result of neglect, or actually deteriorating.

The house wasn't big by any means, Zach thought, but being alone, he didn't need more than a couple of bedrooms. The one-car garage would be adequate and from what he heard about the winters here, he was pleased it came attached to the house. From the side of the garage, another latch-keyed gate stood at the end of fencing that paralleled the face of the house, then turned south at a corner, where the fence panels disappeared underneath a line of draping boughs of old sugar maples.

He looked down again at the listing price, and although it was a few thousand over what he had planned to spend, he needed to peek inside to be sure it hadn't been trashed like others he had seen.

A young couple and an older woman, most likely the real estate agent by the way she was dressed, appeared from the side of the garage. Figuring he probably needed an appointment to see the inside, he realized he would need to talk to his agent about setting that up, hopefully for tomorrow. He shifted into gear and signaled to pull out, but before he could turn onto the road, a red Jeep Wrangler appeared in his rear-view mirror. He waited. The vehicle slowed, navigating the bend in the road. It slowed even more, then stopped a short distance behind him. In his rear-view mirror, he caught a good view of the driver. They exchanged brief smiles and made eye contact before she raised a finger in a mini-wave. He wasn't absolutely positive, but she did look like the girl at the gas station.

How many red Jeeps could there be, he thought as he checked behind the vehicle to be sure no one else was coming up from behind them. As far as he could see, there was no traffic, at least as far as the bend in the road. He carefully stepped out and approached.

"Hey. Weren't you at the gas station?" As he said it, he realized his line was lame. The woman turned and looked at him anyway.

"So, do you like the house?" she asked. His thoughts were derailed as he noticed her gaze shifting up and down, obviously looking him over.

"It's nice, at least from the outside." The words stumbled from his mouth. He swiveled his head around, watching for traffic, feeling vulnerable where he was standing and being distracted in the road. "Yard could use some work, but it's doable."

"You haven't seen the inside yet?"

"From what I could see, I liked it. I think it needs . . . wait. You pulled off the side of the road just to see if I liked that house?"

"Well, yes. It does have charm, doesn't it?"

"Do you do this to everybody that looks at the house?"

"Not really. You just looked like you were interested."

"Really? You know I could have been some whacko stalker who was casing out the house."

"You aren't. I can tell. Besides, I know how to protect myself so I'd advise against it. And I can tell you aren't from around here, are you?" she laughed, her eyes continuing to inspect him.

"No, I'm not. You can tell?"

"And I can tell I'm making you a bit self-conscious."

"Okay, I'm harmless." Zach stepped back and raised his hands.

"Well? Do you think it's charming?"

"Yes. It is . . . charming," he finally responded. He remained stiff, not wanting to chance getting any closer. "Do you own it?"

"No, but I know who does," she added. Her smile broadened. "If you are interested, I'll put in a good word for you."

"Well, I do appreciate it, but if you don't know who I am, that would be hard to do," Zach started to offer a handshake, but before he could, she shifted into gear and started to roll ahead. He stepped back to let her merge onto the road.

"I have my ways." She waved, released the clutch, and headed off.

"But I . . ." Zach just stood in the road, still baffled and weakly waving, and watching the tail lights of the Jeep disappear around another curve in the serpentine road. An odd chance encounter with a beautiful, nameless stranger on a back road in a town he knew nothing about. Twice now. He wondered what he was getting into if he did make an offer on the house. Collecting his thoughts, he climbed back into the Explorer, and headed toward town.

Zach merged onto the main highway, just in time to marvel at the sunset painting the western sky. The belly of the cloudbank roiled between pink, red and maroon with an occasional ray of light piercing through into higher cotton puffs. The tree line rising in the distance seemed to scrape at the bottom of the low cloud cover as it poorly hid the sun dipping below the ridge.

I could really get to like this area, he thought as a Vivaldi Oboe Concerto started on the classical radio station he found while scanning. New England was a little different than the flat landscape of the mid-west; rolling hills to the south, mountains to the north, and an intoxicating combination of expansive forests and open grazing fields where wild and domestic animals placidly moseyed along. The towns he passed by seemed quaintly smaller and more compact than the sprawling suburbs he had become used to. As he passed each one along the highway, he could see their greens lined by a mix of white clapboard houses, a spired church or two, and smaller two and three story businesses lining the two lane road that wound away from the highway.

As his thoughts melded into the music, the sunset-painted sky darkened, the road unfolded in front of him, and random ideas floated through his head as the road opened up like a ribbon between the hills before him. Leaving the comfort of the mid-west and starting a new life in this differently beautiful and exotic area, at least exotic to him, seemed impulsive. Brenda was the real reason he was escaping. He wanted nothing to remind him of his heart-wrenching past, since it seemed that at every juncture back home, something was there to remind him of Brenda. He met her when Kevin, an acquaintance from work and someone he considered his best friend, suggested a blind date once and Zach agreed on a whim. He should have realized Kevin's circles were a bit more gregarious then was his comfort level, but it was worth a shot anyway. Although a bit awkward at first, they eventually got along. He wasn't completely sure what Kevin noticed that made him think they would hit it off, but after that first date, the ice between them melted a bit and they seemed to grow closer. She was his opposite; quite attractive and socially active, especially in her circles, while he was an introvert and average — average height, average weight, not a first rounder for flag football games, but not the last one to be picked either.

They did well for about a year, and he did enjoy his time with Brenda, aside from the gala events, where she seemed more comfortable. He was more the brainiac geek who knew financial law and economics and pretty much a wallflower at the parties. It worked for a time, and things seemed headed in the right direction. She had moved into his condo and they were even starting to talk permanency. But someplace along the line he missed the signs that things were starting to unravel, and the downward spiral accelerated out of control before he could even find the brakes. Brenda spent more time on the road with the ensemble, or at least that was her cover story, as he discovered later. Her growing distance was concerning, and after some prodding, she admitted the reason — she was having an affair with another musician, a woman no less. The fact that she needed an affair hurt enough. Having an affair with another woman rattled his manhood even more. He buried himself at work to numb the disappointment, but that did nothing to resolve their issues. Spending nights and weekends in the office whittled him down mentally and physically. All work, no play and no time taken to hit the reset button.

Then came that devastating night when she had the accident. They were estranged at that point, but he was still the first one the troopers called. It had been storming heavily, and some people even swore they spotted a tornado. His own drive was as harrowing an experience he had ever been through —driving sheets of rain, hail stones at times pinging his car roof like stones, and a relentless wind jostling his car all the way home. His hands hurt from clenching the steering wheel so tight that he had left impressions. He wasn't home to take the call and when he did get home and played the message, he was stunned and paralyzed, so much so that he didn't return the call for almost two hours. Whether it would or would not have made a difference if he called back earlier didn't matter. In the end, she was dead and gone and they had not worked out their differences.

"Shit!" he cursed as he saw his exit sign. He recklessly crossed two traffic lanes to get off the highway. On Main Street, he dodged a wreck and just barely beat three yellow traffic lights before reaching his agent's office. Chicago city driving helped him survive this time.

He sucked in a deep breath as he turned off the car and realized that he hadn't thought about Brenda for over a year. Why she haunted him at this point bothered him, but right now, that didn't matter. Collecting his notes, he hustled inside before the office closed for the day.

"Hello, Zach. Any luck finding what you were looking for?" The receptionist, Cecelia asked, holding her hand over the receiver on her phone. Over the last couple days, she always seemed to be on the phone.

"A couple potentials. Is Maureen still in?"

"She's been on the phone for a while. I'm sure she'll be off soon, if you want to wait."

"I will. Thanks." Zach settled into a comfortable chair in the corner of the waiting area and glanced at the Home and Garden magazines on the end table. He picked it up and opened to the index, looking for gardening tips. Cecelia smiled and returned to her own phone call, all the while absently working her way through the stack of papers on her desk. Just as Zach started reading an article about soil amendments for brighter blossoms, he heard Maureen say goodbye through her open door.

"She's off. I buzzed her that you were here." Cecelia made eye contact and waved at Zach to head on in. He did.

"Hello, Zach. Anything pique your interest today?" Maureen looked up from her desk as Zach worked his way into the high-backed leather chair at the small conference table. She was middle aged and well kept. Her business acumen pleased Zach, as did her directness, although it had taken some getting used to. It was clear why she had been a top seller for years and why his firm used her for relocations.

"As a matter of fact, yes. I think it was in . . ," he stopped, opened his notebook and scanned the scribbled notes on the pages. "Yes, in Edenton."

"I know of a couple houses out there." Maureen turned her attention to her whirring desktop machine. "What's the address? I can look up some particulars."

"One-fifty-three Pleasant Hill, Edenton. Up the hill from the Smith Road house."

"Hmm. I don't remember that one." Maureen clacked at her keyboard, paused for a moment, then tapped the keys a few more times before stopping and staring at the screen. "Here it is. That's why. Just listed two days ago."

Zach nodded. Maureen continued. "A two-bedroom saltbox, one car, attached, full basement, five plus acres. A little over your price range, but not something we can't work with."

He looked at the makeshift schedule of showings he had scribbled onto an index card, and realized tomorrow was overbooked, and on opposite ends of his search area practically at the same time. Except for ten o'clock. If this worked out, it really didn't matter anyway. Cancelling the one on Beebe Road, since it looked to be more of a project than he thought he was ready for, would open a slot.

"This won't help. This listing agent is pretty tough to work with on price, but I'll do the best I can." Maureen started an instant message on her computer as she talked. "I am not supposed to say anything, but her agency does tend to overprice their listings. Not sure why but I'm thinking they haven't caught up with the drop in values throughout the state. Have you thought more about the Forrest Lane house?"

"Nice yard, but I think it's just too much house for me."

"I understand. Just a thought. Good value though. You could consider flipping it with a little bit of work. Prices are starting to creep up, you know. Especially in that area."

Kevin, who had grown up in New England, had warned him about two things when looking for a house in the area. Fixer-uppers were to be avoided, unless there was already a contractor doing the work, or you knew somebody who could do the work. The other was flipping houses, since there would be a lot of time wasted in playing the chess game of trying to figure out what buyers would really wanted in a year or two. Then there were the legal hassles of jumping in and out of mortgages. He was perceptive enough to deal with the financial part of flipping, but not knowing the contractors in the area left him wary of taking any additional risk. His information was convincing enough that he wanted to just buy a house in move-in condition and grow accustomed to the area.

"I thought of that too, but I think I'd rather find something I don't have to worry much about while I settle into a new position."

"I can relate to that. We just need to keep our options open." Maureen's computer dinged. She then called on her flip phone. After chatting for a few seconds, she looked up to Zach and covered the receiver. "These things are great. I don't know how we got anything done before these became available. Okay, how does ten o'clock sound?"

Zach gave Maureen a thumbs-up.

"Ten is good. Thank you, Linda." Maureen clicked off the phone and set it down on her papers. "Done. Meet here at nine, or would you rather meet out there."

"We can meet here."

"Good. That should leave us plenty of time," Maureen said absently as she scrolled though the listing details.

"You wouldn't happen to know if it is in move-in condition?" Zach turned around before leaving. Maureen looked up over her black-rimmed reading glasses and started a professorial squint.

"It looks like it. It's an estate sale. The owner passed away several months back."

"Is that good or bad?" he asked. Estate sales from what he remembered back in Chicago could get messy.

"Could be either. We'll have to look at it from the inside, since who knows how well it was maintained between then and now."

Maureen didn't say much to Zach on her way out to the house the next morning and as she suspected, the trip took about an hour. "The listing agent must be running a little late," she noted as she parked and started flipping through a notepad she had brought along. "With the sun being out today, we'll be able to see if this is as bright as Linda indicated.

"Hope she didn't get swallowed up by the potholes. These road are pretty rough out here," Zach chuckled as he looked in the rear-view mirror. He wanted more details about the house, but before he could start probing, a white Saab convertible pulled into the driveway behind them. A woman about Maureen's age stepped out and waved before reaching back into the car to fetch a pile of papers. Zach recognized her from the day before.

"Linda Beels. Most of the listings out here are hers," Maureen noted as Linda approached them. "She does have a certain air about her."

"Linda Beels," she bent over, reached into the car, and offered her hand.

"Zach Fields. Pleased to meet you."

"We can go in the front door," Linda noted before walking by Maureen's open window. "The garage hasn't been cleaned up yet so it will be easier to go in from the front." She continued over the curved walkway of flat stones set into the yard. Zach and Maureen joined Linda as she opened the storm door and fiddled with the lock box on the front door. When it opened, Zach noticed a dull brass key hanging inside.

Linda opened the door, revealing blue flat-stone inlays at the foyer entrance. Zach's attention was drawn to the openness of the floor plan and the brightness of the rooms. Two steps in, Zach could see all the way into the great room, where a cast iron wood stove sat on a charming, rounded, elevated brick hearth back dropped by a brick chimney where the stove pipe turned toward it. French doors stood to the east of the small dining area where an overgrown shrub reached over the small porch and feebly scratched at the windows. Tiny clusters of unopened purple blossoms sat on each branch, small and compact.

"Impressive," Zach mumbled to himself as he took measured steps into the house.

"This is the dining area, and over here is the great room," Linda led the tour. Zach craned his neck back, trying to absorb more details of the overgrown shrub just outside the door. He had wanted to learn more about horticulture before his mother passed and all her learned knowledge that made her gardens so special went with her, but never took the time. She would have wanted to know the shape of the leaves, the color of the bark, the light exposure, and the nearby trees that could influence the shrub.

"And this is the great room," Linda repeated, her tone disapproving of Zach's lollygagging. Zach moved forward to join the agents in the wide-open great room that spanned the entire rear of the house. A wide-planked, hardwood floor rested under a tightly striped woven rug. In the corner on the floor, a pair of framed paintings sat on the floor, as if waiting to either being removed or thrown out. The contrasting black, cast-iron wood stove rested at one end and a white baluster lined stairway rose at the other. The vaulted ceiling was whitewashed tongue-in-groove paneling rather than traditional ceiling wallboard. Spanning the walls, three thick, unfinished oak beams straddled the room, giving it more of an outdoor appearance than an indoor one.

"Nice touch," Zach thought as he tried to imagine how Brenda would have designed a house, and whether it would look anything like this.

"We haven't been able to get the house completely cleaned since it's been put onto the market. Settling the estate took some time," Linda made the excuse, paying more attention to her papers than Zach. "The owner passed away last fall. Wasn't sudden, but the long illness kept her sister from getting things settled earlier. When lawyers and fiduciaries are left to work out the details, it takes a while."

"I understand," Zach noted.

"The house was custom built for the owner," Linda noted. "Some nuances might be a little odd and might take some getting used to, but they are not so outlandishly unique like some musicians might have come up with."

Zach's attention was caught. The previous owner was a musician, like Brenda. But unlike Brenda, she had a sister. He wondered if that was what the girl in the Jeep meant by putting in a good word for him. This could be very interesting, he thought.

"I see," Zach realized he was lagging again and hustled to catch up and continue through the rest of the house. He was only half-listening to the agents chatter between each other about the nuances of this and a couple other houses in the area.

His decision though, was clear the moment he walked into the house. Actually, he made his decision the day before when he saw it from the outside. The rest of the walk though was nothing more than protocol for him. When done, Zach and Maureen exited the house through the garage and strolled around the wooden-fenced back yard. There were clusters of buds swelling on the fruit trees, some even hinting a blush of white and pink. Several small four-by-six foot raised beds lined up along the fence-line, overgrown with browned, winter wilted crabgrass and weeds.

"I'm sure I can get the rest of this cleaned out in a weekend or two," Linda noted as Zach stepped outside.

"Thank you," Zach replied. "This is a very charming house," he added, then headed toward Maureen's car.

"So, what do you think?" Maureen looked over to Zach as she waved good-bye to Linda.

"It is just right. Do you know if there is already an offer on it?"

"Not sure, but based on what I saw, I suspect this will move quickly."

Zach brooded briefly. "I thought I saw some folks here yesterday. With Ms. Beels."

"If this is your first choice then, let's get back to the office and put together an offer."

"Okay, I'm in."

"And I would suggest that you consider contingencies as well. I'm not sure if you are familiar with the kind of haggling people tend to do out here, but in the end, it is like the lottery anyway. If you don't try, you'll never know. But let's make sure we have a second choice prepared as well."

There is no second choice, Zach thought. As they backed out of the driveway, Zach looked down both directions of the road, disappointed that this time there was no red Jeep waiting along the side of the road.

❧❦

Chapter 4

"Hey, Linda, have any good news?" Sharon sat down in Linda Beels' office.

"I do." On the dark maple, polished working table, Linda had neatly arranged some folders that had papers peeking out from the corners. "We actually received three offers, all reasonable. I am not sure if another is coming, but they were aware that others had already seen the house and were considering bids."

"That was quick." Sharon felt relieved and disappointed at the same time.

"We only have a little time to decide, so I thought it best to sit down together so we can go over the details. I can help answer any questions you might have."

"I guess I can't ask which one you think is best."

"You can, but I'm not supposed to answer questions like that. I can provide some insight, though." Sharon leaned in to listen to what Linda could clarify. Linda took the first package and ran her finger down to the bottom line. "Full price offer, which is good. A couple from Rochester, contingent upon a radon test results and mitigation. You'll have to pay for fixing any problem the test uncovers before the closing."

"Pretty expensive, last I checked." Radon was something Sharon had already explored, but when Sarah's cancer metastasized, just about everything, including the radon evaluation, dropped off the priority list.

"Well, all sales now need to have this test done. Mitigation, if warranted, is to be completed as well. It becomes just a matter of who pays for it. And it depends on how elaborate you want to get for mitigation. Some people just have a fan system for the basement; others have a water treatment set-up. In any case, it is a necessary investment up here in granite country now."

"And if it doesn't fix it?"

"The right contractor will. Some are more expensive than others, like everything else." Linda handed Sharon a paper with several names and phone numbers. "Here. I hope you understand that I can't recommend anyone specifically."

"I do."

Linda looked back at the contract. "Oh, they also have a contingency about selling their house up in Rochester."

"And that means?"

"If they can't sell their house, this contract is voided. But on the bright side, houses up in that neck of the woods are moving. Slow, but moving."

"Are you saying then this process could linger for a while?"

"Maybe. Next one?"

"Sure."

Linda picked up the next contract and honed in on the bottom line. "A little lower offer. Single guy, I think. Can't tell. He's from out west somewhere, Chicago."

"Do you remember showing him the house?" Sharon perked up. She wanted to ask more, but she knew that would probably only lead to problems. If it was who she thought it might be, it could become quite interesting. Or complicated. Or both. There was definitely something about him sparked a sense in her to get a better look. When she happened by and stopped on the road, she took advantage of the opportunity. He didn't look too bad when she got that better look — neatly dressed, nothing outlandish, kind of average looking. He wasn't in the best of shape, but a few weeks in the gym would tighten that up. The touch of stubble wasn't all that attractive either, but that might have just been that he was on a relocation visit and didn't have time to shave. His demeanor seemed reasonable enough. She remembered that he didn't swagger when he approached the Jeep that day, like some macho guy would have. And he didn't try to hit on her either, which was refreshing.

"I think so. Rather quiet. Seemed nice enough. Relocation. And he indicates he'll take it as is. Just provide the results of the testing."

"As is means as it is, right?"

"And he wants to close quickly."

"I would not have to do anything more?"

"Other than the usual, like paying for the water and radon tests. You might be able to get away without moving the rest of the stuff out of there, if that's what you are getting at."

"That actually sounds positive." Sharon paged through in her mind what was left. The convenience not having to throw Sarah's stuff out would minimize her guilt.

"No contingencies. Looks solid," Linda noted as she examined the contract for any additional details. "If I remember correctly, I did a showing with Maureen out of Nashua."

"And?"

"Seemed quiet. Can't say much more other than he's a relo."

"And the last one?"

"A little bit lower still, but ballpark. Lady from New York, I think. Looks like she's looking for a summer place or something to flip. She did ask about town ordinances on renting. Sounds like she's done this before."

"Ok, what are your thoughts?"

"Well, I can't tell what to do, but they are all solid offers, so it depends on what is important to you. For the money, if the radon resolution doesn't cost too much, the couple from Rochester might be the best bet. They also are anxious to close, so that might be the quickest to resolve, unless they can't sell their house in Rochester."

"What's your thought on the others?"

"Not much difference between the two, although Chicago does specify that he will take it as is."

"Remind me again what that really means."

"First, anything that is there doesn't need to be moved out. The downside is that if there's anything left that you wanted, it might be too late to get. If you have second thoughts about anything, you might have to discuss it with him. Second, if the inspections, including the radon test identify issues, he is responsible for fixing them."

"And New York?"

"Don't think she really cared, and I didn't sense any urgency, so she might give you a bit more time."

"You did say I had some time to think about the offers."

"Some, but not much. I would say we would need to get back to them by the weekend."

"Friday?"

"The sooner the better, but if it takes you to Friday, that would be fine."

"Okay. Let me do some thinking and I'll get back to you by Friday." Sharon stood and offered to shake Linda's hand.

"One more piece of advice. If you have any questions, call me right away. Don't wait until

Friday. Things get confusing real fast when you're juggling three different offers."

"I will."

Sharon was back on the road in a few minutes and could not help but drive by the house on her way back to work. She slowed by the mailbox, now leaning to one side having been beaten up by the plows over the past winters. That was just something else she wouldn't get around to fixing. She pulled off into the rutted shoulder, then jacked up her parking brake and gazed at the house. Her shoulders alone bore the weight of this decision; one that would have been easier if her parents were still alive to at least talk over. For that matter, the decision would also be easier if she could talk to anyone. Anyone she really trusted. After one more longing glance at the shrubs struggling in the cold damp April afternoon to urge blossoms and catkins to wake from their winter dormancy, she dropped her brake, moved on and headed back to work.

Sharon finished her day at the store and headed home, exhausted. Travelling from work to Linda's office, then back to work had drained her, especially since the pace at Barrett's was non-stop. At closing, the predicted storm for tonight had everyone moving the tender plants around for protection. The storm forecast itself wouldn't have been too concerning except for the predicted hail and strong winds that could raise havoc with the latest arrivals.

As she drove into the parking lot, she noticed a white van parked directly across from and facing her condo. The shaded windows unnerved her a bit, but since the van's engine wasn't running, she figured it might just have been a new tenant. Once inside, Sharon locked her outside door before lighting the burner under her kettle and collapsing into her armchair in her small living room. After a brief rest, she dragged herself into the shower where the warm water trickled over her back and dissipated some of her soreness. As she stepped out, she wrapped herself in her green terry cloth robe, poured herself a cup of hot green tea, added stevia and lemon juice, then selected some Mendelssohn on her stereo to help her decompress enough to think. Curling up on her couch, she stared out through the sliding glass door into the dark night.

As she thought about the offers on Sarah's house, the first sips of the steaming brew drove her chill away. It would clearly take several weekends to finish cleaning what remained in the house, and since her boss, Rhonda expected everyone to work at least one weekend day with peak season upon them, her sense was that the decision was easier. The next few sips of tea chased some of the soreness away and relaxed her a bit more. Exhaustion took over, and she set the tea on the coffee table, wrapped herself in the quilted blanket, curled up and drifted off to sleep, coaxed on by the melody of A Mid-Summer Night's Dream.

"You know I never cared much for Mendelssohn." Sharon felt herself turn to the voice. Sarah's image was foggy and seemed practically transparent.

"I know. That's why I never suggested you play his work."

"You should really consider Mozart if you are thinking. His progressions are much more logical."

"You know I never cared for much for Mozart." Sharon sparred.

"The logical progressions of his works open the mid to clear thinking. There have been studies, you know."

"Maybe this isn't so much a logical decision. If it was, you know I'd be done by now."

"You are right. So why are you putting it off?" Sarah's image drifted about the room, stopping at every painting. "By the way, whatever happened to the seascape we bought in Concord?"

"I think I left it in the living room. Or maybe I moved it downstairs. I don't remember. I was going to pick it up this weekend when I finished cleaning up."

"I think you should give Chicago a try," Sarah's voice grew tinny and distant.

"The couple from Rochester actually had the best offer."

"Chicago's offer wasn't that far off." Sarah's image drifted toward the sliding glass doors that lead to a small deck outside just as lightning flashed nearby. "Oh that's a doozy brewing out there."

"How do you know?"

"The lightning looks angry, that's how."

"No, I mean the offers. How do you know?"

"Oh, you mean Chicago?" Sarah turned and floated back toward her sister, settling on the couch next to her. "He did say he would accept 'as is.' He wasn't a bad looker either."

"But how do you know about the offers?"

"And if I'm not mistaken, I saw a glimmer of a spark when your eyes met."

"You noticed?"

"How could I not. You went all googly-eyed at him when you first saw him at the gas station."

"I did not."

"You were hoping he'd say something, weren't you?"

"I don't remember."

"Really? I know you don't strut like that without purpose."

"I do not."

"Sharon, you know you do. Zach is his name by the way."

"I was just being friendly. He looked lost. I thought a smile and a friendly face would make his day. Wait, what? You were out there? You know his name?"

"I get around, girl. Nothing to really tie me down. Just the free spirit personality everyone loved."

"So what's wrong with Rochester?"

"They really don't want the house. They're just looking to get out of the city. Besides, they'll have a hard time getting rid of the place they have now. I've seen it. Too much work to be done."

"New York?"

"She doesn't really want the house," Sarah interrupted.

"Really?"

"You don't want to sell it to her. Trust me." Sarah's voice grew agitated. "She's buying it for someone else and then they are just going to flip the house anyway."

"How do you know that?"

"I just do."

"So you're telling me that I should take Chicago's offer?"

"You can do what you want. I'm just helping you make the decision. You did want the help, yes?" Sarah's image grew transparent. "Besides, he's got a nice ass, he's single and I have a sneaking suspicion things will work out between you two."

"How do you know that?"

"I just do."

Thunder crashed, loud enough to wake Sharon. The crack exploded outside, rattling sliding glass doors. A low-pitched rumble continued just before the sky lit up with a brilliant streak of lightning that forked behind the line of pines bordering the apartment grounds. Sharon reached a count of three before another crash of thunder shuddered the windows in her condo. Hail started pinging on the roof and peppering the vinyl siding as if a massive truck had released a bucket full of pebble stone. She was glad she put away the delicate plants before she left for the day.

She picked up her tea, now cold, and started nursing it as she watched the spring storm flash to life in the dark skies, realizing she would probably need to check on the house over the weekend when she had a chance to be sure she didn't have more to clean up. She also realized that she would need to get to the Conservatory to give Sarah's beloved vintage Bulgheroni oboe to Carolyn Appleton, since the witch insisted she had purchased it for Sarah. Sharon knew better, but like Mr. Edwards had stated, the will was the will and the law was the law, and the Buggy was willed to the Conservatory. As she looked over to the polished case now sitting in the corner of her condo, she resolved it was something she would plan to do next week.

Chapter 5

"You lost the bid on the house?" Carolyn Appleton glared over her black rimmed glasses and across her expansive oak desk at Judith Rhodes, her business advisor. Her jaw was clenched and her thin lips twitched into a tightly pruned scowl. Her voice echoed through the expansive, vaulted ceiling room, as if the acoustics mimicked the performance stage at the other end of the Conservatory. The massive gold plated chandelier over Carolyn's desk was filled with more than one hundred special light bulbs that glowed like rings of candles overhead, creating subtle shadows behind the exquisite, polished violins resting on the shelves.

"I did caution you that the odds were not good, Carolyn," Judith nonchalantly leaned back into the plush, high backed maroon leather chair situated in front of Carolyn's desk. "Besides, there was no real purpose to that purchase anyway."

"You should have counter offered."

"Look, Carolyn. I know real estate." Judith fondled a small, painted statuette of a conductor that sat on the corner of the desk. "I did tell you before this was a rather rogue idea. The asking price for the house was simply out of line, and my word, the agent is clueless about market process if she was really expecting that much for that house. It's just a shack in the woods, for God's sake."

"You said prices were going up. We could have held on to it until we could make a profit." Carolyn grew agitated as she opened her black leather bound ledger and noisily flipped pages.

"How much were you expecting to make? One thousand? Two thousand? That would take years to get that return. I had to consider what the house was worth and how low to bid to be sure we could get a good return on resale." Judith replaced the figurine, leaned back and shrugged her shoulders.

"There was evidence in that house. I just know that." Carolyn said under her breath. A wide-eyed anger etched her face.

"Evidence?" Judith raised her right eyebrow. "Overall, it wasn't a good deal. If someone else was foolish enough to bid any higher than what I had, then I wish them good luck in this market. It needed a lot of work to get anything worth the aggravation of flipping it as far as I could tell."

"I brought Sarah Tanchak here out of her mid-western wasteland to make her a star. She was my best hope to show those arrogant big city directors that I could find talent. Then she goes off to cooking school. Cooking school!"

"Are you forgetting that Sarah did come back?" Judith furrowed her forehead, clearly confused with sudden change in Carolyn's odd array of seemingly random thoughts.

"Her talent had been ruined. It's a wonder she didn't damage her hands any more with those knifes or burn herself taking biscuits out of some damned oven."

"But she didn't. She came back and became one of your best teachers."

"Let me make something very clear, Judith." Carolyn leaned forward and scowled. "It was not my idea to let her come back."

"Then why did she come back?"

"Vincent."

"Vincent?"

"He did it despite my objections since he was running the Conservatory at that point. I never forgave him for that. That move soiled my reputation."

"Really, Carolyn?"

"I thought you understood. In my circles, that embarrassment lives forever." Carolyn slammed her clenched fists onto her desk and glared at Judith. "Oh, that girl was talented. One in a million." She raised her hands toward the ceiling and shook her extended finger toward the chandelier. "And as her agent, I could have made enough money to move on to Boston or New York instead of staying in this backwoods town in a run-down Conservatory that still had to be saved from its own demise."

"You aren't making any sense, Carolyn. This Conservatory has a reputation of producing high quality musicians. The Boston Symphony calls you regularly, do they not? And Sarah had played for them. Often. Isn't that enough?"

"I get nothing from that," Carolyn slammed her ledger shut, stood up and started clomping about her office. She stopped in front of the large window overlooking the courtyard centered between the Conservatory halls and propped her hands onto her hips. "Sometimes I wonder if you really do understand the music business, Judith."

"As far as I can tell, the Conservatory is doing very well financially, Carolyn, so let me be frank. It's the management that concerns me. Perhaps you should square up with me. It's not really about the house or the money, is it?"

Carolyn spun around and speared Judith with her fiery stare. Her lips quivered as her entire body stiffened. Her face flushed as she chewed her bottom lip.

"It's really about Vincent, isn't it?" Judith prodded.

"I know he was going to see her that night he crashed into that tree."

"That was three years ago."

"I vowed that I would do everything I could to get back at her for stealing him."

"Did you forget Sarah is dead?"

"Not Sarah. Her sister."

"Really?"

"I know he was." Carolyn shuffled back to her desk and collapsed into her chair. With shaky hands, she pulled out a bottle of Gordon's Gin from her desk drawer and set it on the table while she fished around for a glass.

"I find that hard to believe. She seems a little flighty for Vincent."

"That's why he wanted to bring Sarah back. I know that." Carolyn filled her glass half way, then poured it down her throat and slammed the glass on the desk like a cowboy drinking whiskey.

"Is this the same girl you said had no clue what good music was? Sarah's sister?"

"He didn't know I was watching him, but I know what he was thinking. And she just flaunted her youth." She fumbled the bottle as she poured another half-full glass.

"So I assume you confronted him?"

"He would always avoid my questions. It was more than obvious. A woman knows these things, Judith," Carolyn finished that drink off as she did the first. Her eyes started to droop and work themselves closed.

"Listen, Carolyn. It's getting late. Why don't we close up shop and talk about this tomorrow with clear heads."

Carolyn looked up through bloodshot eyes and stared vacantly at Judith. Tears welled up in her eyes then trickled down her cheeks before dropping in spots on her desk. After taking in a big sigh, she agreed.

"I'll drive," Judith added as she softly placed her hand over Carolyn's, growing concerned something in her client's mind had snapped.

The following night, Sharon parked her Jeep in the office area parking lot of the Conservatory, took a deep breath, and glanced at the polished silver case in her passenger seat. She really didn't want to give up Sarah's beloved vintage Bulgheroni oboe, but as Mr. Edwards cautioned her, it was explicitly written in the will — the only thing specifically willed to the Conservatory. There were no cars in the parking lot that she recognized, stirring her thought that Carolyn Appleton would again not be around to accept the instrument. The window to her office though, was cracked open and the light was on, so someone had to be there. If it was not Carolyn, it was someone she trusted enough to use her office, which Sharon knew limited that to a handful of people.

Once inside the expansive Victorian style red brick building, she quietly worked her way down the long hallway toward Carolyn's corner office. The imposing ten-foot tall oak doors stood cracked open enough for her to see a woman working at the massive oak desk. There was no receptionist, considering the hour, so Sharon rapped on the door just hard enough to announce her presence.

The woman looked up over her small reading glasses at Sharon, smiled briefly and waved her in. As Sharon entered and sat down in the red leather high backed chair directly in front of the woman, she stood up and introduced herself.

"I don't know if you know me but I am Judith Rhodes, Carolyn Appleton's business advisor." Judith simply tilted her head and hooded her eyes momentarily.

"I know."

"Carolyn asked me to receive the oboe from you. She's not feeling well at the moment."

"The case is unlocked if you feel you need to inspect it." Sharon's words were measured. She skootched forward, enough to set the oboe case onto the desk carefully, then retreated.

"I know you and Carolyn have issues, but that doesn't mean we can't be cordial, does it?" Judith leaned back and gave Sharon a sideward glance. Her lips twitched a brief smirk.

Sharon squirmed, feeling uneasy in her chair.

"No reason to get defensive, dear." Judith raised her hands in surrender as she moved forward and faced Sharon. "But I would like to ask you about something that has been troubling Carolyn and me."

The words speared Sharon. She stiffened as she tried to imagine what else the two of them wanted from her. There was nothing left at the house that was of any value, at least to them.

"Is it about me or Sarah?"

"Mmm, maybe both."

Sharon sighed. She wanted to just get up and leave, but her curiosity encouraged her to stay.

"If I remember correctly, your sister was a real pip. You and she also held several dinner parties and invited several members of the Conservatory for wine and cheese or fondue or whatever, correct?"

"We did. They weren't raucous by any stretch of the imagination; in fact we were complimented by our neighbors that they didn't even notice a party was being held."

It was clear to Sharon that Judith was taking mental notes. "You do remember Vincent Appleton, don't you."

"Yes." Sharon's response was sharp. The man was as lecherous as anyone she had ever met. Flaunting his highbrow arrogance, he acted as if he was irresistible to anyone he laid his eyes on. He had tried to make a move on her once, cornering her when she attended a concert that Sarah was soloing in, but a quick knee backed him off. He never tried again after that.

"Did he ever attend your parties?"

"Never invited him and he never came uninvited either." Sharon's skin crawled at the thought of even telling him where Sarah lived.

"Didn't you find it odd that despite Carolyn's protests, Vincent did bring Sarah back after she left to attend some cooking school?" Judith twitched her eyebrows and leaned forward. She glared over her glasses and skewered Sharon's.

"I'm not following you."

"Let's just cut to the chase. You do remember that Vincent was killed in a tragic accident the night of one of your dinner parties?"

"That was three years ago." Sharon sensed a trap.

"Carolyn believes he went to see you that night."

"Why would he be coming to see me?" Sharon stiffened.

"Well, dear. I believe we both know the answer to that question." Judith tilted her head again as a knowing grin creased her lips.

Sharon retched at the thought of a romantic liaison with such a worm. "Is this one of those how often do you beat your wife questions? Has she convicted me already? Is that why her vitriol is directed at me?" Sharon gritted her teeth as she measured her words.

"Let's not get too defensive, dear."

"Let me be blunt, then. I despised the man. As did Sarah. And if he was willing to lie about cheating on his wife, he wouldn't think twice about lying as to who he was screwing?"

"If not you, then who would he have gone to meet that night? After all, he was headed your way."

"Someone who was naïve enough to believe Vincent was interested in something more than just a quick romp in the sack to satisfy his self-centered urges. Perhaps someone who just enjoyed sex and didn't care what the man was like. Someone who was looking to be showered with gifts and money. I'm sure you have watched him prowl like the letch he was," Sharon stood up and bit her lip hard enough that she could taste blood. She scowled at Judith for a moment, then spit out, "If you will excuse me, I believe you have insulted me enough tonight. I will not grovel for forgiveness for something which I had no part of, nor would even consider, if that is what you and Carolyn were looking for." She left the office and ran down the stairs, climbed into her Jeep and slammed the door hard enough that it echoed through the campus.

As Sharon shivered in her car, she felt vulnerable. And alone.

Chapter 6

As Zach crossed the state line into New Hampshire, the reality that he was now a homeowner started setting in. His first house. All through the flight out to sign the papers, he was nervous that he might have missed something that scared everyone else away from the house. He had hoped it was just his offer to take the house "as is", which in the end was Maureen's advice, that swung the decision in his favor. What still seemed odd though was how the estate's representative acted during the closing. Sharon Tanchak, as she was introduced, was in fact the Jeep driving woman. Her eyes remained fixed on him for what seemed the entire time, drilling into him as if she was mining his every thought. He didn't read anger, sadness, or pleasure in her eyes. Just focus. Her gaze broke only when the lawyer asked questions, and even then, she responded with nothing more than a nod or single word answer. He could not help but wonder if she really did follow through with her promise to sway the decision in his favor.

Over the two days that it took to drive the U-Haul truck from Chicago, Zach had plenty of time to think about how his life was changing. Getting out of Chicago with the U-Haul wasn't as difficult as he had thought it would be, and running across Ohio was as dull as ever, leaving him time for his mind to wander. The previous owner, Sarah Tanchak, was a single musician involved with a local orchestra. Like Brenda. But not like Brenda, Sarah spent more time teaching at a local Conservatory. And had a sister. A twin sister Sharon, the name he now knew as the girl with the red Jeep.

Getting through the rain in New York was a struggle. It could have just been showers, but it felt like a torrent with all the traffic splash around him. The radio in the U-Haul grew scratchy and more irritating as the lethargic flow bogged him down, requiring his close attention. By the time he worked his way out of the city and into the Berkshires, the weather cleared enough that he felt comfortable turning off the irritating, squealing defroster. Once in Massachusetts, the Turnpike continued upward, causing the truck's engine to labor and knock so much that he grew concerned that it might breakdown in the middle of mountains, in an area where he was unfamiliar, the next town was thirty miles away by the map and his flip phone desperately needed charging. With the truck shuddering at thirty-five miles an hour, he passed a sign declaring the highest point on the Turnpike and sighed, relieved that the truck could finally pick up speed and start heading downhill.

The last fifty miles toward New Hampshire seemed to drag on for more than the hour it should have taken. The next thirty after crossing the border seemed just as long. Once he got off the highway, the frenzied high-speed driving pace relented, replaced by slower but more challenging narrow, curvier roads that appeared to be plowed through thick woodland along the shoulders. He didn't remember the roads narrowing as much when he was here before, but the Explorer he had been driving was also smaller and more nimble than his present load. As evening moved in and the sky turned a deeper blue, he crossed the town line into Edenton, and then made the final turn onto Pleasant Hill Road. The truck again struggled to climb the one last hill before he turned into the gravel driveway.

Done. He sighed deeply. His nerves settled. Somewhat. The sky darkened quickly and evening arrived even faster than he remembered from back west. He stepped down from the cab and unhitched his Ford Explorer from the carrier, then parked it on the front lawn. He maneuvered the truck around with a rather lengthy but safe twelve-point turn, and then backed it in so unloading would be easier. He turned off the ignition. Now really done. Exhausted, stiff and sore, but done.

He rested his head on the steering wheel and felt his hands still trembling from clenching the wheel tightly over the last hour. There would be no unpacking tonight. The thought of digging through what he knew would be stifling hot, stale air in the rear of the truck to get to his bed frame was far from appealing. He had one more day's allowance on the truck and then the rest of the weekend to settle in before having to be at work. No need to rush, he figured. Morning would arrive soon enough, and he could start unloading then. Dropping out of the truck one last time, he stumbled at first on rubbery legs, but then straightened up and stretched with a loud groan. Instead of fighting off fatigue any further, he grabbed his sleeping bag and backpack with provisions that he had stuffed behind the seat then fumbled in his pocket for the keys to the house.

Instinctively, he locked the truck, although he had heard that outside of a stray moose or skunk, not much was out at night up in these parts. He pulled the latchkey string, opened the gate, then noticed a light on in the tool shed sitting in the corner of the yard. Or he thought he saw a light. Maybe he just imagined it, but exploring it would need to wait, he decided. He unlocked the door to the garage and stumbled inside the musty smelling single bay before opening the inner door.

Once inside his house, he smiled. His house. He dropped his backpack and ambled around the rooms that surrounded the center wall separating the kitchen and great room. In the naked great room, two piles of books sat on the hardwood floor where he had seen the framed pictures before during his walk through a month earlier. The pictures were gone. As he glanced through the titles, he noticed that several were about alternative medicines, a few about gardening, and one rogue title, a cookbook. He reckoned he had time to look through them later.

"Won't need that tonight," he thought as he noticed the woodstove at the end of the room, remembering the weather report said it would be in the forties overnight with clear skies. He went back to the door, locked it, picked up his bedroll and backpack, then stumbled on up the stairs and toward the bedroom. On the balcony overlooking the great room, dusk had started to roll in. Above, evening light seeping in through the open blinds fit into the row of skylights, providing enough light that he didn't need to fumble around for a flashlight. It would be a good night to sleep, even if it was on the floor in a sleeping bag. At least there was soft carpeting, he thought.

He opened the windows in the bedroom to cut the staleness. A fan to circulate the air in the room would have been nice, but the slight breeze slipping in through the open window started to cut through the musty closeness in the room. He untied his bedroll, stripped to his skivvies, then slipped between the down layers and without much encouragement, fell asleep.

It wasn't more than an hour before Zach sensed whistling. No, it wasn't whistling. It was singing. Not the kind of singing he listened to on the radio, but just vocalizations. Like a music scale. Soft vocalizations like a mother's lullaby; calming, soothing, an easy aria. It was just outside the window, or so it seemed, drifting in and out with the slight breeze. Rather than open his eyes and try to search for the sound, he remained in his bedroll, curled up on his side, eyes closed, and let the music drift him back to sleep and the breeze sweep by his face.

Zach woke early as sunlight peeked through the east window, then stumbled out of his bedroll and wiped the crust from his eyes. Having the window open through the night did cut the stale smell in the room somewhat, and chilled the room enough that he felt comfortable. He walked around the room for a couple moments, still a bit taken that the house was now his. He ran his fingertips along the salmon painted walls, feeling the smoothness interrupted only by pockmarks where pictures once hung. The closet doorjambs were next; he tested the smoothness of the white painted frames for the accordion doors that he left open through the night.

After a quick trail mix and Gatorade breakfast from his backpack, he wasted little time beginning the unloading of the U-Haul. As efficiently as he could, he moved each furniture piece through the open garage door, then arranged the tightly packed boxes in sections based on the room he thought it would go. It wasn't like he had a lot of furniture to begin with, having only a rather small apartment in Chicago, but once the truck was empty, the small one-car garage had surprisingly little room left to navigate. He finished with a rummage through the cab, grabbing what few groceries he happened to find on his rest stops on the way and set them at the only vacant spot next to the steps. He twisted open another one of the Gatorades, then sucked in a mouthful.

He tried to stretch out the soreness that had seized what seemed every one of his muscles. It was a soreness that rivaled his weekend warrior flag football escapades against Rocky from Security. Bending over, he straight-legged stretched his hamstrings, then stood up and caught a glimpse of the sun moving close to the western horizon. The day was spent. He needed to get the U-Haul back by five, or pay for another day's rent. Rummaging through the papers from the rental, he looked through the listed U-Haul dealers near-by and found what he assumed would be the correct one.

"Barrett's Farm and Garden Supply," he noted as he flipped open his cell phone and called, failing on the first try since he instinctively used the wrong area code. After a couple of rings, someone picked up.

"Barrett's, this is Sharon. Can I help you?"

"Oh, hi, Sharon. This is Zachary Fields."

There was enough pause on the phone that Zach thought he had been disconnected.

"Can I help you with something, Mr. Fields?" Sharon's voice sounded familiar.

"Yes. I . . . I need to return a U-Haul truck."

"Sure, let me get your file. Fields?"

"Yes. Zachary Fields, from Chicago." Zach heard keyboard clacking in the background.

Sharon was silent for a moment. Zach started to worry that the poor reception in the area might have disconnected them.

"It's right here," her voice broke through the crackling. "We are open until five, but you could just drop it off and leave the travel ticket in the night box if you can't make that. Do you need directions how to get here?"

"Probably. I'm new to the area."

"From your driveway, head west and turn left at each "T" in the road until you get to Route 23. Take another left and we'll be the garden center about a half-mile on your right, set back just a little from the road. You'll see the other trucks parked there."

"Ok, thanks. How do you know where I am?"

"Your contract."

"Really?"

"Yes, really. We normally have the contracts ready for the day to make it easier to process in. Like you just did."

"Oh, okay."

"And I know you bought Sarah's house."

"Hmm. Oh, one more thing —"

"Yes, I can. If you get here a few minutes before we close, I can give you a ride back. No charge," Sharon responded, quietly and warmly. As she disconnected, Zach started to wonder if Sharon was who he thought she was.

As Zach pulled up to the rustic styled porch at Barrett's Rental Office, he recognized the woman standing at the open door. It was Sharon. She retreated into the store as he parked the truck. She was efficient in processing the truck back into inventory, and in very short order, Zach was sitting in the passenger seat of her red Jeep headed back to his new house. She turned off Route 23 and headed downhill toward the narrow bridge on Hillcrest Road, a back way Zach figured he would eventually want to remember. The ride was a lot smoother than he thought it would be, considering the potholes in the road that had yet to be repaired. Zach held on to the roll bar with one hand as Sharon worked her way around the holes and through the curves and hills on the road.

"Did you get everything settled where you wanted it?" Sharon finally broke the silence.

"Well, I ran out of time. It's all stacked up in the garage for now."

"You should have started earlier."

Zach recoiled, not sure what to think about her comment, but when she winked, he relaxed.

"Are you a gardener?"

"Never really had the opportunity. Always lived in a condo or apartment. My mom always had a nice flower garden though, but I never really paid much attention. I guess I should have."

"I think you'll enjoy the gardens Sarah and I designed. She was an avid gardener. Nothing traditional for her, special colors, shapes, and sizes. She always had some new theme for the season. She pushed the limits of hardiness for some plantings just to have a uniquely spectacular show."

"I noticed some of the books left on the living room floor. Well used." Zach tried to keep up with the small talk as best he could, even though he sensed it was a feeble attempt. If nothing else, he felt he was doing better than he did when he first met Brenda.

"Sarah could grow just about anything I got for her. I never thought a musician could have a green thumb." Sharon said, but focused as she slowed the Jeep to make the turn toward the State Park.

"So Sarah was your sister?" He knew the answer, He was just trying to keep the conversation going.

"Uh huh." Sharon noted stiffly.

"Did you spend a lot of time at the house?" Zach asked but then realized by Sharon's silence that he might have been headed down the wrong pathway. He swallowed hard and regrouped. "Maybe you could show me around at some point, you know, so I can get a sense of what I am dealing with."

"Perhaps," Sharon muttered as she turned onto the road that cut through the middle of the State Park. She threw a slight grin Zach's way before focusing back onto the meandering road. Offering nothing more than sideward glances, she said nothing more as she continued to drive.

Zach could not help glancing at her as she drove, wind tossing her shoulder length hair about her face, a tight, confident smile etched on her face. She was even more attractive up close that she was that first time at the gas station. He sensed she noticed his glances, but she also didn't seem to mind.

As they neared the house, Zach worried his opportunity to get to know Sharon better was ending too rapidly for his social acumen to respond.

Rather than stumble through a stilted conversation though, Zach just clammed up and watched the trees lining the weaving road roll by until they reached the driveway.

"Well, here we are," Sharon slipped off the road onto the driveway apron. She let the jeep idle rather than turn the engine off, to Zach's dismay. "Were you able to get out and get something to make yourself for dinner?"

"Not quite. I ran out of time. Didn't think I had that much stuff," Zach noticed the sun had already dipped into the horizon and splashed the lower clouds purple and orange. "I had to get the truck back before you guys closed."

"You didn't have to."

"How else was I going to get home?"

"You did have a carrier for your car, if I remember correctly. You could have left it on."

"Well, I do appreciate you helping me out with the ride and all."

"No problem." Sharon reached behind his seat.

"Can I offer you dinner someplace? I can drive." Zack tried his luck.

"I really need to head out. Long drive home. Here." She casually handed him the paper — a tri-fold menu. "Check out the pizzeria in town. The bacon and pineapple is one of their specialties. And they deliver, so you won't have to go out and find the place."

Zach had hoped for something more than a fast-food menu.

"I will. Thanks." Zach tumbled out of the Jeep and into the driveway. He looked down at the menu long enough that he heard Sharon drive away. Zach simply waved, then turned and headed into the house. As he sat down on the garage stoop amidst his belongings, he went through the menu. He really wanted sliders, but he figured nobody here would have a clue what they were or how to make them the way he liked. He decided he would order some fried chicken instead of pizza.

Chapter 7

When Zach woke, he noticed a fog thick enough to obscure the cemetery just across the road had rolled in overnight. It wasn't a real issue for him, since he was not planning on doing anything but moving in. He figured he could explore the woods in the back when he was done. He headed downstairs, heated some water and spooned out some Maxwell House instant coffee. He didn't care much for the bitterness, but without his coffee maker available, it was his only choice. Once he had a cup in hand, he started moving furniture around.

By the time dusk had darkened the house, Zach had moved most of his furniture inside the house from the garage. He weaseled his way through the self-created debacle, found one lamp, and set it up on a stool in the great room. To his surprise, the bulb was not broken on the trip and it still worked. He looked around the room and noticed that the dim lamp light glimmered off the rheostats at each end of the wall separating the room from the kitchen.

Ceiling lights. He whacked his forehead for being so dumb not to look before digging out the floor lamp. He then panned around the room, still marveling that he actually bought a house. Not in Chicago, or the 'burbs where he expected, but in the New England countryside, with land and spitting distance from Boston. Smitten, he returned to his set up, moving most of his files up to the room he would use as a study, then brought up the pieces of his desk to reconnoiter how to assemble the room. The ceiling was not the typical flat, parallel to the floor construction. There was a bit of a mini-amphitheater feel to it, the angles just so to funnel the sound to the middle and out into the rest of the house. As he looked about the room he pictured Sarah weaving back and forth as she played her instrument, swaying with the feeling of the music. That was what most musicians did. That was what Brenda did when she practiced in their condo. He wondered whether Sarah would wear just a simple a pair of sweats and an oversized sweatshirt while she practiced, nothing fancy, just comfortable, like Brenda had done when she was home.

When she was home. Before the bottom fell out of his life. Moping now would not help, he thought and dug into the task of setting up his study. In a couple of hours, it was set up and a naked mattress covered by his dull gray sleeping bag lay on his bed. Sheets and blankets could wait for tomorrow. He dropped and melted into the bed. Prone and on a soft surface, he felt his fatigue cascade through his weary eyes, tingled down his neck and his back. It did not matter at this point whether or not the lights remained on downstairs. He did not remember, nor really care if he locked the door, too tired to get up and check. Within minutes, he drifted off to sleep.

The sun was out and a slight breeze mingled through Zach's hair. There was a light, sweet, floral bouquet. He was sure it was lilac. If there was one planting that he remembered and could recognize that was it; at least recognize when it was in bloom. His mother's garden had a stand of lilacs that would explode with lavender and white panicles, filling the yard with an intoxicating fragrance every spring. Along the driveway, he remembered were lilacs, but they had yet to bloom.

Had to be something else, Zach thought as looked around. Next to him, already in bloom was a sweet smelling shrub, teeming with tiny while fluted flowers. He took a mental note to explore that a bit later since a faint, mellow, woodwind sound drifted about the yard, muffled, but still skillfully articulated. Like last night. It was that same melody that he heard last night, except it was clearly instrumental — a solitary, sad oboe that he could not place where exactly it originated, but he was drawn to resolve.

A small tool shed in the far corner of the yard, painted the same color as the house. The small, four-paned window to the right of the door was fully open. The door was not. And the light was on.

That was it, he thought. The music was coming from there. As he approached the shed, crunching through what seemed a blanket of acorns on the gradual slope, he noticed an open lock slipped through the latch on the door. The music was clearly coming from inside this shed, but the lock hasp holding the door closed confused him. It was closed from the outside but there was something or someone inside. He carefully removed the lock and opened the door.

Stunned, he could only stare at the woman inside, sitting with her back turned toward him, in a flowing white, almost sheer, floor length dress, her auburn hair flowing over her shoulders, moving in time with the music.

"How did you get in here?" Zach stammered.

She offered no response and continued playing.

"Excuse me? Your music is beautiful, but how did you get in here."

She stopped playing for a moment and set her oboe down on her lap, but did not turn around. "I come out here to get away from the noises in the house. All that banging is so disruptive. Just can't concentrate." Her voice was as melodic as her playing.

"Banging?"

"The builders. I practice out here until they're gone, then I go inside. It is peaceful out here, don't you think?"

"But the door . . ." Zach pointed to the door with the lock in his hand. "But the door was locked. From the outside."

"I don't know what you mean," she replied. "I come out here so I can concentrate on my fingerings."

"But . . ."

"I lock it when I'm done."

Zach stumbled backward when he noticed that her chair started to rise from the plywood floor. It slowly turned toward him as if on mini-carousel. For a moment, he thought he saw Brenda's face. The image cleared more. No, it was not Brenda.

"Sharon . . .?" Zach whispered as the face sharpened, catching his blurt too late. She was wearing a pair of small, narrow, black-plastic rimmed glasses that slipped down onto the bridge of her delicate nose. It was the style that he remembered college professors wearing so they could show their consternation as they peeked over the tops.

"Sharon?" She cocked her head. "Oh, you mean my sister? Do you know my sister?"

"Sister?" Zach squeezed his eyes together then rubbed them clear when he opened them. She was still there. Her smile was as inviting as Sharon's. "You are Sarah?"

"Yes. I'm Sarah."

"But . . . you . . . you passed away?"

"Oh, my. Who told you that?"

"That's why I could buy the house. This house. It was up for sale. That's why I'm here."

"Oh, dear. I was just a bit under the weather. Just had to get more natural treatments."

"But I moved in last week," Zach stumbled through the words, confused. "They said . . ."

"Well, you aren't too bad looking. We might be able to get along if you insist on staying here."

"No, no. I moved here. I bought this house."

"I don't know if I believe you," Sarah was unfazed by Zach's protests. She simply cocked her head and smiled sweetly. "Do you like classical music Zach? Or is pop more to your liking?"

"You know who I am?"

An odd scream outside the front window woke Zach. It was hideous, like a baby screaming at the top of its lungs. He sprang upright for a moment and wiped the crust from his eyes before stumbling to the window. He looked out into the clear, crisp, moonlit night. A pair of green, glowing eyes glared at him from underneath the stand of already passed forsythia in front of the house, and then moved on. Zach heard leaves rustling as the animal appeared to move on out toward the woods. Fishers, it dawned on him. He remembered people talking about the nasty animals from back home; like weasels on steroids, complete with a hideous scream just as they pounced onto their prey and ripped them to shreds. The fisher must have found a sleeping chipmunk or maybe a mole.

He dropped back into bed and tried to get back to sleep but his eyes remained wide open, as if pinned in place staring at the ceiling. The dream, or what he thought was a dream disturbed him. She seemed as real and vivid as he imagined Sarah would have been when she was alive. The sense that she was visiting him from the other side sent a shiver down his back. He started to analyze his thoughts to resolve what he saw with what he believed. His feet were still dry and the grass had to be wet. It was dark, yet in his dream — yes, it had to be a dream — the sun was out. His eyes slid closed as he convinced himself it had to be a dream. The alternative was not something he wanted to accept. Drifting back to sleep, he wondered if the dream would return. It did not. Neither did the music.

Zach woke up sore. He lay in his bed as Saturday morning arrived, disappointed that a good night's sleep did not help. He could take it slower today, he reasoned and gingerly rolled out of bed. He grabbed a pair of gym shorts, pulled them up, then stumbled sleepily toward the stairs, thinking a shower would help. He tightly held on to the rail as he descended, concerned his rubbery legs would fail him and he would end up in a pile at the foot of the stairs, then changed his mind and figured coffee would help more. He rummaged through the boxes to find the one marked coffee, unpacked his drip coffee maker, and then hunted in the box for the coffee he had purposely packed with it. All of his boxes were like that. He found it easier that way. He recollected how his friends back in Chicago taunted him as being anal, but he defended it as just being efficient and practical. Maybe he was, but now it didn't matter. In a few short minutes, the coffee was brewing.

He rested his head on the table as the coffee brewed. He had two entire days left before he had to start work, and he figured he had about a day's worth left of unpacking the garage. The coffee maker hissed that it was nearing done; he had only made a half a pot to start. The last sloshes and pops of steaming water spit through the filter and he poured a cup, black and strong, then noticed that books were on the table. He didn't remember moving them there. Or maybe he did when he moved some boxes into the great room. But since they were, he sat down and grabbed the top one.

As he took his first sip of coffee, he opened the top book and noticed a newspaper clipping inside the front cover. "In Memorium," he started. It was Sarah's obituary. He took another sip and started reading. As he had thought, she passed away after a long and valiant fight with breast cancer. She had been an oboe player with several orchestras in the area, and had purchased this piece of property, specifically to build her sanctuary. This one. The one he had bought. The one that the girl in his dream insisted he did not. The only explanation for the dream, and it must have been a dream since the alternative was not something he believed in. He rationalized that the dream had to be his mind processing something he had already read about Sarah Tanchak, probably from the research he did on the property a few weeks back. The person in the photo seemed to stare at him with deep, dark eyes.

That was enough for now, he thought just as he singed his tongue after a bigger sip. He closed the book and decided to start in on the kitchen while the rest of his coffee cooled. He mixed his plates with all the other dishes that were still in the cupboard, oddly he thought, of similar design as his. Once the small box had been emptied, he returned to the table, sat down and returned to the article. As he nibbled on some dry, stale bread, thinking he should have toasted it, he flipped open the cover and read further.

Sarah was originally from the mid-west, Indiana, and coincidentally, they shared a birthday. She had taken to music at an early age, learning piano first, graduated to clarinet in elementary school, then to the oboe shortly thereafter. Even though she grew up in a farming family, music was always in the house. Her father played the accordion and she would play duets with him each night to the delight of the family. Her mother taxied her to the American Conservatory in Hammond for additional lessons, where she flourished and was heralded as a child prodigy for woodwinds. She enrolled at St. Johnsbury Academy, a fine arts boarding school in Vermont to continue her development and when she graduated there, returned home to become one of the premier oboists in the Mid-West. But while she studied at St. Johnsbury, she grew to love New England, enough so that when an opportunity arose to teach and perform near Boston, she returned and worked her way into the Boston Symphony Orchestra.

Zach mused over his discovery while he sipped his coffee. The several things that had been left were probably Sarah's, and with them were probably other stories, but he wondered if he really should paw through a dead woman's left-behinds. Maybe he could just return them to Sharon, which could be an interesting way to get to know her a bit more.

His first cup of coffee finished, he started back upstairs to get dressed, but stopped and stared out the French doors on the deck and spotted a shed, the small building nestled in the corner of the yard. After last night's dream, he wondered whether something was trying to tell him there was something out there he needed to see.

He slid on a pair of running pants, slipped on his sneakers then stepped out onto the porch and headed toward the shed, the film of dew on the grass squeaking under his shoes. The rusted lock on the hasp and the closed door were just as they were in his dream. He pried the lock off and when he cracked the door open, the acrid smell of dead animal smacked him in the face. It didn't take him long to spot the open D-Con trap on a corner rafter. The rest of the shed was dark. To his left next to the door was a switch. He reached over and flipped it on. To his surprise, the bulb lit.

Inside looked like a typical gardener's shed, reminiscent of his mother's. The shelves spilled over with leftover fertilizers and amendments. On the floor, empty flowerpots were piled in disarray. Oddly cut pieces of wood, most likely remnants from indoor projects, had been haphazardly stacked up in the corner. Partially used bags of fertilizer blends rested in between the pots and the wood and half-eaten acorns lay strewn across the plywood floor. On a wooden shelf near the tiny cracked open window rested a pair of glasses. Zach picked them up. They were the exact same ones he had seen in his dream last night. The lenses were dusty and smudged, but the temples were in fine shape.

"Good morning, Zach," Sharon's voice startled him. He stumbled back toward the open door, then poked his head outside.

"Oh, hi," Zach absently stepped out of the shed as Sharon let herself in through the gate. Odd, but convenient, he thought.

"I was passing by on my way to work and noticed this door open. Just thought I'd see if everything was alright."

"Yeah. Everything is fine, just exploring. I found these," Zach showed Sharon the glasses.

"Oh, my word," Sharon added as she reached out slowly with her hand. "Sarah said she had lost them a while back. I guess she just forgot they were out here."

Zach started to place the glasses in her hand, but Sharon withdrew, leaving him holding them out. She stiffly stood and stared at the glasses for a moment, then broke her gaze and looked up into Zach's eyes.

"You can take them if you would like," Zach offered but Sharon just continued her catatonic gaze. Her expression was different than what he had seen before. Zach read something more like a pained expression. Or confused. Something other than what he thought he expected.

"I really don't think so." Sharon shook her head and turned away.

"Okay, I'll just leave them here," Zach said as he ducked back into the shed. When he turned around and poked his head out, Sharon had already stepped through the row of sprouting lilies and the weatherworn cedar gate. As she closed the gate behind her, she weakly waved and called back, "I should be going before I'm late," before climbing into her Jeep and back out of the driveway.

Zach felt an opportunity slip through his hands. But he did have a long day ahead of him. He locked the shed and returned to the house to finish unpacking.

By late afternoon, Zach had moved the last pieces of what was in the garage into the house and arranged them in their respective rooms. The expansive great room, or so it seemed, was still a bit naked with the exception of a left-behind armchair. Maybe without specific wall boundaries, and opening up to a steep sloped cathedral ceiling made it appear more cavernous that it was. The beams that crossed the room between the French doors and the balcony, looking like heavy cribbing holding open a cavity, seemed naked and in want of something. They were wide enough for displays, he thought. Something that held memories from back west would probably look good. Maybe a baseball or two he caught at some old Cubs' game. His Little

League glove would look good on a stand. Plants would be a nice touch.

He thought about what was decorative enough to hang on the walls as he headed into the kitchen and slapped together a peanut butter sandwich. He warmed up his coffee in the apartment-sized microwave, then perched on the carpeted staircase to look over what he had left to do. If he had a list, like he normally worked from, it would probably be easier. He had accomplished quite a bit yesterday, but now that larger things were in and arranged, the emptiness was obvious. Maybe some small things, like end tables with plants or a small bookshelf, he thought. A poster or a painting. Maybe two. He thought he remembered some paintings in the basement, but couldn't quite recall their theme. They might just be the ones he saw in the great room during his walkthrough. That would be for another day, he decided. Today, unpack the remaining boxes and getting rid of the trash was on the docket.

Chapter 8

Helen Carter worked her way through the main foyer of the police station and into the detective's wing, a large open area with soft paneled cube walls. The desks were covered with piles of manila folders, some thick and teeming with papers, where others were thin and orderly. Against the far wall were four small rooms, set aside if the discussions needed a private setting. For a moment, Helen scanned the room, stopping when she saw Lieutenant Jack Bridges at his desk. His salt and pepper flattop, square jaw and slightly rumpled white shirt and rolled up sleeves reminded her of what was sure to be his rough and tumble past, where police work needed a bit of intimidation and physical conversation.

She had partnered with Jack on several other cases, but usually not one that was as close to blackmail as she was starting to think this one was. His intuition seemed to be clearer than most detectives' factual conclusions and she had always found him willing to help, except when there was encroachment on the fringe of the law. She understood her position as a lawyer was to ply the facts and find the ones that either exonerated her client or destroyed her client's adversary. Jack was honest enough and willing to make her aware when those boundaries were too close for his comfort. And she had never known him to cross them either. He was a good man.

"Hey, Jack. How are you doing?" Helen settled into the thin-cushioned office chair aside Jack's desk.

"Hello, Helen." Jack set his pen down and closed the report he was working on and set it on top of his manual typewriter. Despite the computers on most of the detective's desks, he preferred his old school Underwood. The machine precariously rested on a plain metal shelf that had been extended out above the side drawers of his gray metal desk. He reached over to the pile of manila folders in front of him, took the top one and set it down on the only empty spot on his desk, directly in front of him. "I'm not sure if I can tell you much more than you probably already know. This is a pretty severe charge Carolyn is considering, but I think you know that already."

"She's pretty adamant about it."

"She really thinks that that girl went fishing for her husband? Then killed him? For what?"

Helen nodded her head. "I'm not completely sure, but if nothing else, can we just look at the facts of the accident to see if there was anything that could be considered suspicious."

"You do realize if you were anyone else, I would just laugh your ass right out of here? This happened three years ago. Why the hell is she bringing this up now?" Jack furrowed his forehead as he flipped open the folder, which he had ready after Helen had called. He examined the first couple of pages, then some photos of the crash scene. He shook his head as he picked up the last photo, which showed that the entire front end of Vincent's Jaguar had been forced back into and through the driver's side of the vehicle. He handed it to Helen and added, "It was quite a mess to deal with at the time."

"So, it looks like he lost control. Weather?"

"Booze. Maybe drugs. Maybe both. It was a clear night. And dry. Skid marks would have been there if he tried to stop. When I got the results from the coroner's office, I was amazed he could even drive with that blood alcohol level. It was the highest I've ever seen."

"So you concluded that it was a case of drunk driving?"

"Alcohol and speed, the deadly combo. Pretty cut and dried case. I think the report identified a trace of cocaine as well."

"And the car?"

"Like I said, there were no skid marks. It looked like he fell asleep or spaced out at the wheel, failed to negotiate the turn, and plowed right into the tree. Based on the damage he had to be doing close to 80 miles an hour."

"And no one else was in the car that might have disappeared before the patrolmen got there?"

"No. He was alone."

"Could his brakes have failed? Or the car stalled and the steering locked up so he couldn't turn the wheel?"

"You're thinking somebody messed with the car?"

"Let's assume that if someone poured sugar into the gas tank, how long would it take before the engine would fail?"

"A few miles, depending on how long it sat and how much gas was being used."

"And if one brake line had been cut?"

"Maybe a few miles down the road as well, depending on how hard the brakes were used from the time the lines were cut. If you are headed down the sabotage path, I really don't know if I can help you. Those are hard facts to prove, and especially with no car available to dig into and being this long after the accident, it's all innuendo. I'm sure you understand that."

"I do." Helen leaned back in the chair, and felt the hard metal back support dig into her spine.

"Let me get his straight," Jack closed the file and turned to face Helen. The scowl on his face made it clear he was not interested in reopening a case that was pretty clearly resolved at the time.

"Ms. Appleton is looking to level charges against someone who she thinks purposely screwed with her husband's car to kill him? And with no real evidence? Three years after the fact? She does realize from a motive standpoint, she would be the most probable suspect, since I believe there was a hefty insurance payout."

Helen felt her stomach turn with discomfort, but she had to come ask the question since Carolyn was paying her to do so.

"Listen, Helen. I like you. We've worked well together on solid cases over the years and you know that if I try re-opening this case without adequate merit to do so, I might as well just drop my badge on the desk and walk out before I get laughed out of here"

"I understand, but I'm sure you also understand who I am dealing with here."

"I would suggest that Ms. Appleton stop watching cop shows, and have her see a shrink. Real soon. I think she's lost it, but I am not qualified to make that judgement. I am qualified to throw the BS flag on her allegation, though."

"I do appreciate your time," Helen said as she stood up and offered Jack her hand. I'll see what I can do to walk her back from the cliff."

Zach shuffled the piles on his desk, where he had been working through his company's transfer paperwork for what seemed hours. He had spent most of the morning working through certification paperwork, baffled at how much different the rules were between states. Above all, before starting to work with new clients, he wanted to ensure he was legal. With that completed, he started mulling over the insurance plans, which were just as convoluted, and were associated with some companies he had never heard of.

So focused on the paperwork, he startled when he was asked, "Are you about ready for lunch?"

Zach looked up at the very attractive strawberry blonde leaning up against the stanchion for his cube. She was well proportioned and dressed to finely accentuate her figure.

"Wow. I didn't realize I had been at it for that long," he finally replied. He could not help staring.

"Yes you have. I was going to ask you earlier when I walked by a few times, but you looked pretty consumed."

"Confused might be a better word," Zach noted, "but I'll get through it."

The woman straightened up and reached her right hand out to shake just as Zach stood up and stretched his arms upward. "I'm Natalie by the way. Natalie Gorman."

"Zach Fields. From Chicago." He shook her hand and stared at Natalie's sparkling hazel eyes for a moment before turning away to lock his computer screen before rolling his chair underneath his desk.

"It's nice to know I can still turn heads," Natalie winked. Zach froze, not sure how to respond. He stood slowly and glanced at the rather large engagement ring and matching wedding band. "I make it a habit to check out all the single guys that transfer in," Natalie smirked as she turned and started out.

"Sorry for staring." Zach swallowed hard, not sure how to read Natalie's intent.

"I'm not trolling if that's what you're thinking. I've just got some friends that have asked me to look out for them."

"Oh. Still sorry for staring." Zach relaxed, grabbed his keys and quickly caught up with Natalie. He wasn't sure whether he should be relieved or disappointed, although he had seen how ugly office romances got back in Chicago. People seemed to be very direct here and he realized it would take him some time to learn how to properly read the signs. Ultimately, it would keep him out of trouble.

"You didn't need to bring your keys. It's walking distance." Natalie said over her shoulder. After a few more strides, she added, "Besides, it's a nice day and this place around the corner has wicked good sandwiches."

Zach followed Natalie into the elevator and as the door closed, realized that he had become a focal point for the rest of the passengers. Rather than interact, he stared down at his shoes and noticed that everyone else, including Natalie, were wearing sneakers.

"New guy?" Zach heard someone ask.

"Hey, everybody. This is Zach, from Chicago," Natalie said as she pressed the button for the lobby. Silent, thin lipped greetings accompanied cordial nods.

"Did anybody come with you?" Natalie asked as the door opened. Zach waited to respond until everyone else had briefly waved, split up and headed in different directions.

"If you mean from Chicago, no."

"Anybody coming when you get settled?"

"No."

"Good."

They passed through the office building doors and stepped onto the street. The walk was short, as Natalie had promised. Within a few minutes, they had ordered at the counter, grabbed their bottled waters and then headed to one of the white metal tables nestled between a black wrought iron fence and brick porch. Zach sat down to Natalie's right and faced the narrow street so the bright sun wouldn't be directly in his eyes.

"I need some help. What did you do for insurance plans. I'm not quite familiar with the different companies and their plans. Is Anthem really as good as it looks?"

"Have you met anybody outside of work yet?" Natalie persisted her questioning and avoided Zach's questions.

"No. Only been here a few days"

"Good." Natalie studied Zach intently enough that made him self-conscious again, like he did in the elevator. Her face suddenly paled as her eyes widened. "Oh, you aren't gay, are you?"

Zach was stunned but realized it was probably just an inadvertent fishing question. "No, I'm not gay."

"Oh, okay." Natalie exhaled as if relieved. "Not that that's a problem, it's just that I wouldn't want to match you up with someone . . ."

"It's alright. Just caught me off guard."

Natalie took a breath, then added, "Go with Anthem. They're decent."

"But aren't most of the in-plan doctors down here?" Zach felt a breakthrough.

"Pretty much. How far out are you?"

"Edenton."

"Oh, that could be a problem for Amelia. Maybe just a small one though." Natalie flagged down what Zach assumed was their server, a high-school girl with a forest green apron.

"Who's Amelia?" Zach prodded as the girl approached them from street level, now a foot or so down from the patio, then cordially smiling as she passed a brown plastic cafeteria tray with their sandwiches up to Zach.

"Anything else I can get for you," the server asked politely. Her smile was cordial and sweet.

"No, thanks. We're good." Zach took the tray and set it down on the table, marveling at the size of the sandwich. The rye was warm, just the right amount of seeds, and freshly baked. The roast beef, rare and slightly marbled, was twice as thick as each of the bread slices. Tomato slivers topped the romaine leaves and chutney had been piled on the side since there really was no room on the sandwich plate. Before he started, Zach looked at Natalie and cocked his head. "So, who's Amelia?"

"Oh, just one of my friends I am looking out for. So, what do you think?" Natalie took a chip from her plate and waved it in the air.

"Glad I was hungry. I might need to take some of this home for dinner," Zach replied as he lathered a scoop of chutney onto the edge of his sandwich with his plastic spoon, still unsure of what Natalie's plan was for Amelia and him.

The afternoon passed quickly for Zach. He finished his indoctrination paperwork before meeting with Joshua Bengston, the department head, where he collected the list of clients that were being assigned to him. Joshua was tall, thin and looked all the part of a high finance boss; impeccably dressed in a tailored black pinstriped suit and wing tipped shoes. His long, narrow face had sharp, distinct edges.

Since his access to the company network had not yet been fully established, when he returned to his desk, he referred to a map that his predecessor, Carl Edwards, had left on his desk to help him locate each of his assigned business clients. Most of the addresses were north of the city except two in Massachusetts; those he assumed were just across the border. From what he remembered, they would take a bit more research based on the difference between the state tax laws. The desk calendar his boss provided to him was appointment sparse, at least for this week, for which he was grateful. A quiet week would give him some time to confer with his clients and set up appointments for the following week.

The client files here as back in Chicago were considered confidential, and because of that, security protocol restricted them from being on the company network. File folders filled with paper were locked away in a secure, alarmed vault. It seemed a bit over the top to Zach, but he understood that this was Nashua's way to meet the corporate security standard. It was something he would just need to get used to. He wanted to do one quick review of his client's folders, so he prepared a list by hand and headed down the corridor of cubicles. He stopped at Natalie's cubicle, politely knocked on the metal support and popped his head into her space.

Natalie raised her index finger to let him know she'd be off the phone in a minute.

"So, tomorrow at three will be good for you? Perfect. See you then," he heard Natalie close the call. She then turned toward Zach and asked, "Hey. What's up?"

"Client list," Zach pointed to his list. "Looking to do a little homework on them so I know what I am dealing with. I assume you know . . ."

"You're in luck. I'm headed there now." Natalie grabbed her access badge and pushed back from her desk. She slipped on a pair of flat-heeled shoes that were sitting under her desk next to her brown high-heels and sneakers. "Badge?" She held hers up.

"Just got it," Zach stepped back and to the left of Natalie's cube.

"Not bringing your keys again, are you?"

Zach rolled his eyes.

"Just kidding. The vault is over there. " Natalie pointed over a set of cubes to the corner of the floor and started in that direction. Zach caught up as they turned the corner and headed toward the darkened end of the floor.

"I assume you are familiar with biometrics?" Natalie asked as they stopped at the door.

"We had hand scanners in Chicago."

"Seven second delay, here."

"Same."

"We can go in at the same time as long as you badge in within seven seconds. You know your ID number?"

"Got it." Zach remembered the protocol from his introductory meeting. He had added the number to the top of his client list. He readied his badge as Natalie presented her badge to the card reader and placed her right hand onto the platen. After a moment, a green LED light replaced the red one, followed by a buzz signaling the door was unlocked.

"Natalie Gorman, access approved," a computerized voice mumbled as she pushed the handle down and opened the door. Zach badged in as Natalie held the door open. "Zachary Fields, access approved."

Once Natalie closed the door behind them, Zach gaped at the wall-to-wall files, none of which had key locks, only keypads and small readers above narrow handles.

"The files are arranged alphabetically, starting from this side and working around to the other." Natalie pointed to the east wall. "The microchip in your badge will unlock the file drawer as long as you punch in your employee ID. If you take out a file, the computer to sign it out is over there. Each of the files is bar-coded to make it easier to keep track of them. If you are only checking a few facts, you still have to log the file out, but it's probably easier to just validate here rather than take the file back to your desk."

"Appreciate the tutorial." Zach checked his list, relieved he had alphabetized the names.

"And don't forget that last one. Security is a bit touchy about that. You will only forget once, believe me."

"Speaking from experience?" Natalie pruned her lips. Zach was already familiar with that expression. "I'll try to remember."

"And if you are thinking about a little romp in here with someone, well, let's just say that's not such a good idea." Natalie cracked a wry smile.

"Watched a few friends get gigged in Chicago. Not something I would want to get involved with," Zach admitted, wondering if there was some history that Natalie was hinting around.

"And there's the badge reader for when you leave." Natalie pointed out the exit reader. "Any other questions?"

"I'm good," Zach nodded as Natalie headed over to the east wall to obtain her own client's file. He took note of her performing the process, scanning into the file, then scanning the file out.

"Last chance," she said as she looked over her shoulder. She flipped her hair away from her face. Zach just nodded as she processed out. The vault door locked behind her.

Zach looked down his list and looked for the one he had check-marked as most important. Thompson. He walked along the wall of files until he found the T's, then precisely followed the process to access the cabinet. Flawless. He heard it unlatch. With a slight tug, he pulled the drawer out, then flipped through the files until he saw Thompson written on a yellow coded paper slipped underneath the clear Penda-Flex tab. He slipped the marker in the slot, but as he started to close the drawer, he noticed another name.

Tanchak. It was an orange tab, which meant it was closed.

He stopped for a moment, staring at the name he didn't expect to see here. In the old office, he would probably know who had control of this file, but here it was a different story. Resolving he would explore that one later, he took just the Thompson file out, finished processing it as Natalie had done with hers, then headed back to his desk.

As five o'clock approached, Zach finished reading through the last few papers in the Thompson file, satisfied he understood his client's position and needs and concluded it would be a relatively easy case to discuss and lay some ground work. There were only a couple of loose ends needing follow-up before he would consider it in maintenance mode, only requiring periodic check-ups as the market moved. After writing a few comments on his legal pad, he closed the dark green folder and figured he could get an early start tomorrow on the other clients on his list. He grabbed his badge and the file, but as he stood up, he noticed that Natalie was standing at his cube's entrance watching him. She had slipped on a windbreaker and her Nikes, clearly set to leave.

"If you are trying to be the last one out, you win," she grinned.

"Lost track of time, I guess. Just wanted to get a jump on things," Zach noted. "Still have a few more to get up to speed with, but tomorrow is another day."

"Well, you need to get that file back in the vault or you'll have to deal with the night shift security. They are not pleasant to deal with, especially the night shift Lieutenant. Nice guy most of the time, but he's a bit over the top, if you know what I mean."

"Got it. On my way," Zach started down the corridor, but then stopped and asked over his shoulder, "By the way, do you know who has the Tanchak file."

"Had and yes. It's closed. Why do you ask?"

"I might have bought her house."

"That I know. Anything else?"

"I guess." Zach sensed Natalie was being furtive for some reason. "It caught me off guard."

"We can talk more about that tomorrow, but I will caution you that there isn't much I can tell you other than what you probably already know."

"I know. Confidentiality." Zach nodded. Now that he knew that the file was hers, his curiosity was going to make it difficult to stay away. "Well, have a good night," he added and continued toward the vault to put the Thompson file away.

Chapter 9

Sharon worked her way through the rows of the newly arrived perennials, making sure that each of the plants got a healthy share of nutrient-laced water. She knew that getting the solution on early helped each of the newer plants toughen up to survive through the week and the coming weekend when spring gardeners pawed through these new arrivals. The last pallet that she worked on was the special double order of Clethra, which Rhonda Barrett ordered on her request since last year's shipment had been sold out as soon as they arrived. She wanted to set one aside for Sarah's garden, but never had the chance. These plants didn't look like much now, just a bundle of soft twigs with fragile, practically microscopic buds, but once they emerged from their dormancy, with the help of the special nutrient spray she had developed, she knew that they would surely be fabulous. The showy pink and white racemes flowers carried a heavenly scent, and the plant was easy to care for and a pleasure in anyone's garden. Hummingbirds and butterflies could not resist the fragrance. And what a fragrance, Sharon thought. Just a single one-gallon plant could produce enough scent to fill at least a quarter-acre.

Sharon had worked at Barrett's for years, almost as long as she had been in New England, and the establishment had developed a reputation for top grade, healthy perennials. Rhonda and Jack Barrett enjoyed the accolades awarded their family owned business. It was publicized in the papers as the top nursery for miles around, and their reputation was enhanced by the advice provided by the well-versed associates that the Barrett's hired, like Sharon. She had been a major part of that crew for years and the owners recognized that she had a special talent for mentoring new associates.

"Those are some great looking plants. I'm glad we ordered them. I suspect that they'll be gone in a week or so," Rhonda noted as she finished the inventory from the delivery. She was petite and wiry with straight, blonde, shoulder-length hair, but could hold her own with the heavy work as Sharon had seen many times. Most of the time toward her, Rhonda's aura was more a mother's than a boss's was.

"I'm sure they will move quickly, like they did last year," Sharon commented as she turned the plastic knob on the nutrient supply off. She then turned off the mister and let the hose drain a bit before letting it retract into the overhead. As she sat down on a bench in front of the plants, she brushed her hands through the twigs and let them scratch at her hands. She sighed heavily.

"Don't take this wrong, but you look terrible," Rhonda said as she pulled up a folding chair and sat down beside her. She placed her arm around Sharon's shoulder.

She was right, Sharon thought. She had still not fully recovered from her moonlighting effort to make enough money to pay off Sarah's medical bills. She knew she had deteriorated into a physical wreck. She still felt weak and feeble all during the day and every joint ached. The bags under her eyes had darkened to the point that they looked like sagging half-moon shaped skin flaps. Despite her exhaustion, since the spring thaw, she took on any extra hours here that she could and worked every weekend, partly to keep herself busy, partly to escape from the reality that she failed to keep Sarah's house, but mostly to escape the reality that she was now alone.

"Anything you want to talk about?" Rhonda added.

"No, I'm fine. Just catching up," Sharon lied.

"I don't believe you," Rhonda noted. Sharon stared off into the table in the center of the greenhouse where the geraniums had opened their scarlet blossoms. Rhonda squeezed her shoulder. "It's the house, isn't it?"

"No. Maybe. I'm not sure. Sometimes I need to stop and think about what's real, what I am imagining, and maybe even what I really want. I'm not even sure at this point."

"Why don't we take a walk." Rhonda motioned to Amy to manage the counter as she offered her rough, calloused hands to help Sharon up from her seat. They meandered out back to the pathway they all used for summer break strolls behind the long rows of mulch and peat moss.

"I'm worried about you, Sharon." Rhonda's eyes widened and her tone softened. "You look like a mess, you've lost weight, and you aren't as quick as you used to be.

"I guess I've been kinda down."

"It's not drugs, is it? I pray you didn't get messed up with that."

"No, no. Nothing like that."

"It's Sarah, then, isn't it?"

It was, sort of, Sharon thought. It was more herself. She was disappointed in herself. Hard work had always paid off in the past, and she was always able to rebound from disappointments. Getting back into the swing of her life had never been an issue. This time it was different. Maybe the hours she had spent, trying to earn enough money to pay off Sarah's bills and keep the house that she loved had just frazzled her. Maybe it was that she had spent so much time with Sarah as she passed away that that time was now lost. Her life was on hold, her relationships put off, and places she wanted to go forgone for time with her dying sister.

For the first time in her life, she felt alone. No parents. No siblings. No close friends. Her circles were Sarah's circles, and without her sister, she felt a separation from them. Maybe she did finally need someone in her life; someone close enough she could confide in and lean on. She wondered if this was the creeping depression people had talked about as her melancholy just seemed to linger like a spring cold.

Then there was Carolyn Appleton's sudden accusation for Vincent's drunken death, which wore on her like an anchor. She had no idea who he was sniffing after, and since it wasn't her, it really wasn't her issue anyway to resolve for the witch either. She had delivered everything that Sarah committed to her and the Conservatory, regardless of whether or not Sharon felt it was deserved. Her business with Carolyn was complete as far as she was concerned.

And then there was the white van with the dark windows that started showing up at her condo's parking lot. Since it looked out of place with all the smaller fuel-efficient cars her neighbors drove, Sharon grew more nervous each day it was there.

Carolyn's rage was probably her biggest worry at this point, especially since Sharon knew the old woman was unstable. Rhonda's conclusion though, did provide a convenient out for the moment. A touch of guilt crept into her heart at not being completely open with Rhonda, but she realized the basket of disheveled laundry in her own head was something she had to deal with. Sharon nodded her head as she lowered it to her chest, and took the out.

"I know you've been through a lot with Sarah's passing, getting the bills settled, and selling the house. I'm not a twin so I may not know exactly what you are feeling right now, but I also lost a sister who I was close to. I dwelled on it for a while, and I did the same thing that it looks like you are doing now."

"Wasn't Jack there to help?"

"Oh, sure, but men don't understand the bond sisters have."

"It is something special."

"And from what I remember of Sarah, I don't think she would appreciate you being all glum about her passing away. I think she would want you to cherish the time you spent together, not agonize over it, and go on living your own life and share it with her in your dreams."

Sharon mulled over Rhonda's counsel. She had thought about heading back to Indiana for a week or so, but since her parents had passed a few years back, there wasn't anyone else there to help sort things out. And there had simply been no time to get there, between getting the estate settled, getting the house cleaned up as best as she could for showing, and working. Here, there wasn't anyone other than Rhonda that she felt comfortable enough to talk with and help sort things out either. Sometimes just a willing stranger's ear was the best sounding board, she had found. Or a shoulder that she could lean into and just rest for a moment or two; a shoulder and chest to rest her head on and feel the warmth emanate and comfort her fears.

Sarah had tried to help her with that while she still could. She did coerce a few of her musician friends to ask Sharon out for a dinner or a movie, but Sharon never accepted or even followed through. She had always had an excuse — had to get up early; too tired from a long day. In reality, she was simply not interested in highbrow discussion of the differences in interpretation between European and American conductors without Sarah. Or was it just that she just didn't want to start a relationship while the emotional roller-coaster she was on continued on its raucous ride and scrambled her senses. Men always seemed to be looking for something more than conversation and friendship. Especially at her age. Dating seemed to have turned into a race for the sheets rather than a stroll to get to know each other. Maybe she was just too old school when it came to relationships. And not having gone out in years, she was concerned if she even remembered or could recognize the signs that the relationship was headed in the wrong direction.

Now there was something more tugging at her lonesome heart. A stranger from Chicago waltzes in at just the time she feels most vulnerable and seems interested. She sensed something more than just a Saturday night fling. Even with the brief encounters she had with him, Zach seemed different that most men her age she knew. He seemed sensitive and caring. And thoughtful enough to offer her back some memories of Sarah, like her glasses, but she clutched, wondering if she was just jumping at the first opportunity that came along after her emotional trial. "Maybe you're right," she finally relented.

"Of course I am," Rhonda smirked briefly. "By the way, I do know that you have not taken any time off for yourself recently?"

"Huh?"

"Didn't think so." Rhonda squinted assuredly. "You need to get away. Relax a bit. Maybe spend some time up in the mountain air to cleanse out what's troubling you now, since I can tell that there is something more you don't want to tell me. You always enjoyed your trips up there as I recall."

Sharon spun her head around and stared at her boss and her friend. Rhonda just squeezed her eyes together and let a knowing smile slip.

"Didn't you?" Rhonda added.

"Yeah, but when —"

"This weekend."

"This weekend? Memorial Day weekend?"

"We know that, but we can handle it.´ Rhonda waved her off. "You've done a wonderful job mentoring Amy, and she has already agreed to fill in for you."

Sharon scowled, but time in the fresh air of the mountains could help free the caged bird sense she felt encircling her. Sarah was gone. Cassie, Sarah's little white Cairn Terrier, had to be put down a year earlier when she had developed an inoperable tumor. The house was sold and now in someone else's hands. Even the enjoyment she got from imagining new blends of plants and shrubs had dulled and grown mundane over the last few months.

Sharon looked at Rhonda's eyes and read her motherly concern. She always seemed to come up with just the right thing to say at the right time. Sharon knew she was very fortunate to have Rhonda as a boss, a friend, and a confidant. Her scowl eased into a brief smile. As Rhonda pulled her close, Sharon whispered one of Sarah's favorite phrases. "So what can I do, but laugh and go?"

Chapter 10

Sharon woke early enough to grab a quick breakfast of black coffee and toast and be on the road headed north before the sun breached the eastern sky. She had packed the Jeep the night before with her hiking gear so that she could get an early start, hopefully to beat the holiday crowds. As she headed out of town, she thought about her favorite bed and breakfast near Franconia Notch, an old restored mansion that felt like an eccentric relative's house when she and Sarah stayed there. The rooms were filled with a blend of antiques and modern collectable odds and ends, each that had a back-story that Ed and Alex, the owners always enjoyed sharing. They also served a hearty mid-day meal for hikers that traipsed through the area. It felt like a distant relative's house; a restored old mansion, With her trip being spur of the moment, though, she wouldn't be staying there, but she figured she could stop in for lunch and a brief chat on her way back.

Looking east from the highway a hint of fog rested over the White Mountains like a layer of cotton candy swirled on top of a green paper cone. Fresh, crisp air squeezed through her cracked open window, enough to toss her hair about her shoulders and occasionally tickle at her nose. By the time she reached Conway, the sun peeking above the mountains to the east had burned off the cloud cover. She turned off the highway and onto the two-lane road that wound toward the Notches. Just off the exit was a country store she remembered which like most shops up here, catered to hikers and campers. She and Sarah had always stopped there on the way up to fill their bag of provisions for their daylong hikes in the mountains. Their selection of trail mixes and homemade power bars made it the perfect place to forage before a weekend hike. It was better than sunflower seeds alone, and better for her teeth, not having to crack the hulls. After parking her Jeep in the rutted dirt expanse that doubled as a parking lot, she clomped up the old warped wooden steps connected to a wraparound porch, where a line of Adirondack chairs sat against the grayed clapboard siding. Strewn about the porch were small tables, each a cobble of a wide diameter slice of a maple tree trunk with whittled legs doweled in underneath. On one table, a pair of coffee cups sat empty, she figured where Jack and Jill had started their day.

"Well look who's here." Jill Owens beamed a wide smile from her perch behind the cash register, as Sharon opened the screen door and stepped into what felt like a wall of smoke-tainted heat. "Jack, come see who's here," she then crowed toward the back room.

"You're not saying! I know only two people that come up here this early," Jack Owens grumbled as he emerged out into the congested main floor of the store. He habitually rubbed his heavily calloused hands on a towel stained with cutting oil before tucking it into his pocket, more out of habit than need. His brown checked flannel shirt hung loosely over his torso, tucked in place by fire engine red suspenders holding up worn bib jeans. Sharon held back a chuckle, finding it funny that the owner's names were Jack and Jill Owens, and their store was at the foothills of the White Mountains.

"Well, well, lookie here," Jack said as he wiped a spotting of white ash specks from the lenses of his black plastic framed glasses. A smile creased his stubbled cheeks. "Come back to do some hiking, are ya?"

"Yes, sir. It has been a long time. I'm pleased you two are still here." Sharon opened her arms and let Jack shuffle into them for a friendly hug. When he stepped back, he kept hold of her arms and examined her through his smudged glasses.

"If I told you once, I've told you a million times, young lady, don't call me sir." He weakly shook her arms.

"Just being polite, Mr. Owens," Sharon joked with the old man, her heart melting at his grousing.

Underneath his gruff, gristly, woodsman exterior, he was as lovable as a teddy bear.

"Eeh. That's just as bad." He playfully wagged his finger at Sharon. "Can't you kids just call me Jack, like everybody else does?"

"You still have those special hiking bars, don't you?" Sharon leaned over and whispered through his nest-like whiskers.

"Sure, sweetie. Still have them right where they've always been," Jill chimed in, pointing her crooked finger toward the back of the store. Jack winked at Sharon before releasing her. "Now don't you go chasing her back there, dear. She's too young for you," Jill warned.

Sharon found the shelves that had a menagerie of different granola, trail mixes and power bars, some homemade while others more mainstream commercial, precisely where she remembered, stacked haphazardly alongside boxes of plaques that Jack made in his wood shop. Drawn to the boxes, she absently started flipping through the signs, carvings of mountain animals, and other nick-knacks stashed in the special corner of the store, where day-trippers usually migrated while waiting for the single restroom to be vacated. Sarah would always giggle at the odd quips Jack would carve in wood plaques, some that might even have been original. What caught her eye, though was an ornate woodcarving of a moose and her calf sitting by itself in the corner.

"You didn't get lost, did ya?" Jack called back, still working his way through the myriad of shelves.

"No, sir. Just admiring your work." Sharon picked up the small, varnished statue along with the trail food, and a small bag of Jack's homemade jerky.

"You like that?" Jack smiled with a toothy grin.

"It's got character."

"Good. Tell the old woman up there I said it's a gift," Jack leaned in and whispered, waving his liver spotted hand.

"Oh, I couldn't."

"Eeh," Jack croaked as he waved his hand before shuffling back deeper into the store. Sharon figured he had another door he had put in on the far end of his shop that spanned the store. With her supplies in hand, Sharon headed to check out up front and set everything down gently on the yellowed, Plexiglas counter.

"I'm sorry about your sister, dear. Last I knew she was dreadfully ill," Jill noted.

Sharon stiffened. There was no way Jill should have known,

"Thank you."

"It was that damned cancer, wasn't it?" Jill's eyes were wide with empathy.

"Yes, Ma'am." Sharon dropped her glance.

"You alright?"

"I'm better, thanks. It was a bit rough at first, but things have finally settled down a bit."

"Well, you know what the mountain air will do for you. It's like a revival, my Daddy always said." Jill's mouth turned up at the corners as she worked through the merchandise. She leaned forward and added, "Might even have a chance to talk to the spirits up there, you know. Some people mistake them for UFO's and such, but I know better."

"That would be interesting," Sharon said as she watched Jill pick up the moose carving. She grimaced as she turned the wooden animal's face toward hers, inspecting the carving, then scoffed at the finely tooled antlers.

"Ten dollars," Jill said after totaling the merchandise in her head.

"Did you count everything?" Sharon frowned.

"Don't you go questioning my math, young lady." Jill scowled back for a moment, but then both started chuckling like a pair of schoolgirls.

"Thank you," Sharon mumbled as she dropped a twenty on the counter. "It's at least worth ten dollars, isn't it?"

"I won't tell the old man," Jill whispered as she flashed a toothy grin. Sharon stepped out onto the porch, the lack of a full breakfast gnawing at her gut. It was still early enough that even if she just took a moment to drink in the view of the mountains in the distance and devour one of the small bars, she figured she could make the head of the trail before anyone else considered heading out. Plopping herself onto the red paint stained chair, she took out one of her nut bars and started to nibble through the gooey goodness.

"Don't mind company, do ya?" Jill asked, standing in the doorway, holding two large ceramic cups with moose painted on them. Steam rolled up from the hot coffee.

"Not at all," Sharon replied.

"Well, even if you said no, I'd still join you." Jill chuckled as she set the cups down on the small table in front of them. "So, you wanna talk about what's got you twisted up, or not," she then asked.

Sharon tilted her head and studied Jill, surprised she had landed the perfect word for how her head felt right now. There was an impish curl to her lips as she brought the coffee closer to them, wisps still weaving upward in front of her eyes.

"Don't be so surprised. Your face gave you away. It's all pruned up, you look like you need a good cleaning out," Jill added.

"Now that's something I haven't heard in a while. Are you sure you aren't my mother's twin?" Sharon felt a weight release from her chest.

"So, spill it out. What's nagging at you? I can play twenty questions and keep you here all day or we can just get to the point."

Sharon sipped at her coffee, thinking it was going to be a bit strange spilling her problems out to a perfect stranger, but Jill Owens wasn't really a perfect stranger either. The old woman seemed more like a combination between a bartender and a long lost aunt than she was a storekeeper to her and Sarah. She did seem to help sort out life's conundrums for them in the past.

"Well," she started as she set her coffee down and looked out over the mountains. "It's complicated. I think I'm over Sarah's passing, that was tough. Having to let go and sell her house wasn't the easiest thing to do either. But here's where it really convolutes. I never did hook up with any of the musicians Sarah tried to match up with me. And you know my parents passed a while back, so all we had was each other."

"I remember you two were worked up about that."

"Well, after Sarah's passing, I had to sell the house. Some guy from out of town buys it. Single, at least I think he's single. Not bad looking, and seems to have some interest in me, maybe Sarah, maybe both of us, but I'm not really sure. Seems to be a nice enough fellow. And I don't understand why I can't pass by the house without stopping in and poking around. Even if it's the long way around I find myself driving by. Maybe that's just a habit I got into when Sarah was alive, Sorry to ramble on so, but —"

"And you've had dreams about Sarah and him, I suppose," Jill took the advantage of Sharon taking a breath and a sip of the coffee.

"I know this sounds hinky and all, but yes, I have. Not really of him, but the topic always seems to come up with Sarah."

"So what does she tell you?"

"You know, that's kinda weird, too. She seems to know a lot about him, more than I know. And that's got me all confused. How does my dream know more than I do?"

"Well, dearie. I think you know the answer to that one then." Jill's mischievous smile was back. She took another sip of her coffee.

"Huh?"

"Well, this may be Sarah's way of finishing what she had started."

"You think she's visiting me?" Sharon tilted her head and stared at Jill. She remembered that Jill did believe in ghosts and spirits, and as Sharon thought about it, her visions did seem to be a touch more ethereal than a dream would have been. She didn't think she believed in spirits, but so much seemed to be pointing in that direction.

"All I'm saying is that it's a matter of what you want and don't want to believe. Personally, I think it's quite cute." Jill leaned forward. Her eyes twinkled. She took Sharon's hand in hers and added, "Did she convince you to take after this boy, or is she stealing him for herself?"

Sharon frowned. "Now that's weird. Do you think Sarah's is trying to pick him up? That's a bit out there, don't you think."

"Well, Sarah was a bit free-spirited, but to be honest, I don't think that's her plan."

"Plan?" Sharon asked, feeling Jill was getting a bit obtuse.

"I think more she's trying to play matchmaker now that this guy has shown up. You been thinking about him, haven't you?"

Sharon's eyes widened. It seemed odd that someone Jill's age would be talking about spirits and the supernatural. But what she said sort of make some sense.

"Looks like I've got another customer. You headed out?" Jill asked as she stood up. Sharon noticed a car turn into the dusty parking lot, a cloud of dust growing as it trailed the truck.

"I think so," Sharon said as she stood up from her chair and gathered her forage. As she started down the steps, she turned back and added, "And thanks."

"Just trying to help."

"You did. Oh, I'm sorry, the cup." Sharon started back up the creaky wooden steps.

"Just leave the cup there with the others. I'll get them all later. Next time, maybe bring that boy of yours up here." Jill winked as she headed back into the store.

That may be a bit premature, Sharon thought as she waved and headed out for the short trip to the parking area at the head of her favorite trail. Within ten minutes, she turned off the road and noticed a car already parked there. Not being the only one there really did not matter at this point, since whoever it was had probably already headed out and was far enough along the trail that there was little chance of bumping into them. She slipped on a dry pair of socks, her hiking shoes, stuffed her snacks into her pack, grabbed her hiking stick, and headed out.

Rhonda was right, Sharon thought within the first couple of minutes of being on the trail. The twists in her mind unraveled as she wound up the path, a little slippery with scattered, damp leaves that had overwintered, but manageable. Paying close attention to the roots breaching the surface along the trail, she maneuvered the curves methodically while drinking in the sights and sounds. Whippoorwills had tired from their morning song, leaving the twittering for the warblers and tanagers as they flitted through the dense pines forest. When she passed the mile marker along the trail, Sharon thought she heard the tinny mooing of a young moose. As she grew closer to the sound, she recognized that it was not a nature call in the distance, but the mellow sound of a muted French horn. She remembered a fork ahead, which led to a clearing where Sarah and some of her fellow musicians sometimes came to practice. The acoustics of their instruments as they played outdoors was much like Tanglewood, and even though the hiking up into the woods with an instrument was difficult, the practice out here provided valuable insight for their repertoire. Stumbling down the winding pathway, Sharon caught herself before face planting into the single huge white birch that marked the end of the trail. In the clearing ahead was the horn player she heard, Liza Schumann, sitting on a stump, working through passages of what sounded like a Hayden piece.

Sharon remembered when the three of them would lounge around on the deck of Sarah's house on weekends in the summer, drinking wine and eating small bits of sharp cheddar while Tchaikovsky played on the stereo. Sometimes they would dabble into salsa and chips for variety, and of course then play some of the Spanish Classics.

Liza was as typically eccentric as any musician she knew. She had played for years together with Sarah in the New Hampshire Symphony and while they taught at the Conservatory. Her long, straight, jet-black hair had been wound up on the back of her head and then trapped in a floppy brimmed hat. She was not thin by any means; but Sharon did not consider her overweight either. Husky was the term Sarah always used to describe her friend. She stopped playing and knowingly glanced over her shoulder.

"You can keep going. I didn't mean to bother you," Sharon said, sitting down on the stump next to Liza. Since the stump was wide enough to accommodate, she pulled up her sinewy legs and crossed them.

"That's okay. I was just finishing up, anyway," Liza noted as she pulled out the mouthpiece and turned the horn over a few times to clear out the spit that had collected in the tubing. After carefully wiping the moisture off the brass with a chamois cloth, she put her horn away then closed and latched the case. "Haven't seen you out here in a while."

"It has been a while, hasn't it," Sharon said.

"I presume you were here for a hike?"

"Well, that's what I was thinking by getting here this early. I suspect there will be people all over the place in a few hours."

"I have an idea. I need to stretch my legs some. Why don't I put my horn away and we could walk the trail together, you know, up to the waterfalls? It is a nice morning and I know that not many people are out yet."

"Sure, I'll wait here," Sharon said. Liza's expression brightened. She lifted her case and headed back to the parking lot to store her horn.

She was right, Sharon thought. It had been a long time since she had been up in these parts. Sarah and Liza did seem to spend a lot of their free time up here when the weather accommodated, to the point where Sharon fleetingly wondered if they had something more than just music in common. She never got as close to Liza as her sister did, but they still considered each other friends.

"Let's go," Liza prompted when she returned.

"I've got some trail mix here if we get hungry." Sharon undid her legs, rose from her seat, and the two women began trekking up the winding, gentle incline that led to the top of a hidden flume. For the first half-mile, they were silent, focusing more on the roots that rutted the incline and the squirrels rustling through the leaves than to talk. As far as Sharon was concerned, that was fine. Her anxiety dissipated with each pace.

In the distance, a woodpecker pounded away in staccato on an old, decaying maple while a hawk screed as she circled, probably looking for a mouse or if she was lucky, a baby rabbit. Once the women reached a point where the trail turned to a lookout over the waterfall, Sharon, now out of breath and struggling to keep up, stopped and leaned against a tree. Time seemed to stand still as they looked out over the running and falling, spring melt-gorged river as it splashed and rushed over the rocks and downed trees in its way. Liza though, seemed a bit more aloof than Sharon remembered.

"I was curious. Are you all headed back to Tanglewood this summer?" Sharon knew that Liza had always been involved with the summer arrangements as she recalled. She also remembered that she headed up the post-performance parties that left so many musicians in twisted piles on the lawn of the Briarwood Inn.

"We've been talking about it, but nothing solid at this point." Liza bowed her head as she loosened the laces on her boots.

"It would be nice to head up there for a concert in the woods. And those parties were something else."

"I don't know if Director Appleton has made inquiries to the BSO or not. She's been a bit out of sorts lately."

"Out of sorts is putting it mildly." Just the mention of Carolyn Appleton spiked Sharon's anxiety. She thought dropping off the Buggy would be enough, but now it seemed to have done the exact opposite. Sharon knew Carolyn had some cockamamie scheme brewing, but could not quite figure it out.

"There is something we should talk about, Sharon." Liza's mood seemed to shift from distant to frightened, and her face twisted a bit, as if etched by concern. She turned and headed toward a fallen log, sat down and invited Sharon to join her.

"Okay." Sharon joined her on the long, thick moss covered oak.

"Did you know Carolyn's got a real inquisition going on at this point?" Liza's voice trembled more than Sharon ever remembered it doing. Sharon noticed she was slowly digging a hole with her shoe.

"When I returned the Buggy, her business agent practically accused me of trying to steal Vincent from her. I guess I should have read something more in her questioning."

"She believes that you know something more about that night he had the fatal accident."

"Three years ago and just now bringing it up?"

"I'm not saying it makes sense, but she's been dragging most of us into her office and questioning if we had seen him with you."

"He tried to corner me at a concert once, but I'm sure my response was very clear. That was the last time he forced anything with me."

"She thinks he was coming to see you the night he had that accident. You had a dinner party that night, right?"

"We had several parties before Sarah's cancer took over. But there was no way either of us would have invited him, not that he wouldn't have tried to invite himself, as arrogant as he was. But I know both Sarah and I would have sent him away, and Sarah never said anything about that."

Liza leaned forward and dropped her face into her palms. She brooded for a moment before looking up to Sharon with tears in her eyes. "I know he wasn't there either, Sharon, but Carolyn's gone off the deep end and believes you and he were having a liaison."

"That makes me puke."

"He did make a pass at you once didn't he?"

"Oh, God, once. That was so nauseating."

"I think he set you up. I thought I remember him talking about sneaking out to see you. I didn't think anything of it until after the accident."

"He was using me?"

"To hide who he was really seeing. And while Sarah was alive, Carolyn wouldn't come after you."

127

"Any idea who?"

"I have my opinions, but I need to do some poking around. That might be the only way to bring her down."

"Is there anything I can help with?"

"I don't think so. It is probably best you keep your distance and let me see what I can figure out from the inside."

"Will you let me know if you find out?"

"I will, Sharon. I will." Liza leaned into Sharon and they hugged.

Rhonda Barrett recognized the woman slowly working through the gift shop corner of the store, surprised that Carolyn Appleton would even consider shopping here. Clearly overdressed for perusing through a garden shop, Carolyn's gaudy string of pearls and white heels stood out from all the blue jeans and dull plaid shirts the rest of the patrons wore. After a moment of sifting through artisan carved signs and homemade jams, she looked up. After Rhonda made eye contact, she headed in the direction of the counter with a very unsteady gait. Rhonda figured she'd had a few drinks already.

"I do not see Ms. Tanchak. Is she working today, or is she off gallivanting with someone's husband again?" Carolyn's voice was as condescending as Rhonda had ever heard.

"Well. Good morning, Carolyn. Rather nice spring day, wouldn't you say?" Rhonda remained calm with her immediate response, but inside the innuendo angered her. Despite her desire to spit reflexively, she remained cordial and made mental notes.

"Enough of the niceties, Rhonda. My time is precious and limited."

"Sharon is not working today. Is there something I or one of our associates can help you with?"

"No, that will not be necessary. I came to settle some unfinished business with that girl." Carolyn grew more cross as she opened her handbag and fished around for a minute before pulling out a business card to hand to Rhonda.

"I thought the estate was settled?"

"We have some unfinished business."

"I will have her call you on Tuesday. Monday will be a very busy day for us. And you don't need to leave that since I know she has your phone number. She has tried to contact you, you know. Several times."

"Perhaps I had missed those calls." Carolyn demurred with a head twitch. "Nonetheless, you will have her contact me as soon as possible? We have some business we need to attend that needs to be settled."

Carolyn dropped the business card on the counter and snapped her handbag closed. Rhonda steeled and turned away as Carolyn strutted out to her silver Jaguar, wanting to spit out at her, but knowing it would benefit nothing. Instead, she took the card, slipped it into her jeans pocket, and sighed the acrimony out from her veins before tending to her next customer.

⊱⊰

Chapter 11

Zach woke to a crisp, dry and comfortable Saturday morning, groggy from long hours during his first week in the office. After pulling on a pair of gray sweats, he stumbled his way downstairs to the kitchen and started his Mr. Coffee. As the water heated up then dribbled into the carafe, he wandered to his front window and surveyed the cottage-sized yard between his house and the street. The stand of roses in front of the fence had greened up and each shrub was starting to push out clusters of small, white tipped blossoms on top of tall, leggy branches. They all looked more like wild, tall lollipops than the compact rose bushes he remembered from his mother's garden. He surmised the brutal task of pruning was in his future, but since he wasn't sure when to prune and train the branches, it was something he was just going to put off until he was sure he wouldn't kill them.

The weekend could not have come any sooner. Each day seemed to end later than the last; and by Friday, he could only muster enough energy when he got home to microwave a couple hot dogs, catch a baseball score or two, and then crawl into bed, exhausted.

His house on Pleasant Hill was now his escape from work and the city and there was plenty for him to explore. He had never been much of an outdoors person, but he did remember enjoying summers at camp up in the U.P., as the locals called the upper peninsula of Michigan. Now, with several acres of woods and fields spread out on either side of him, he had a chance to dig into nature again. The land around him stood mostly undeveloped; a working hay field for a couple that were subsistence farming down the road, and a paddock for a small stable of horses on the other side. Behind the house were several hundred acre plots, full of wildlife he was sure, considering how expansive they were.

Across the road was a cemetery — an old cemetery with broken, slanted and deteriorating slate and granite headstones. He had discovered that there were quite a few cemeteries in town, and each of the plots had at least one fascinating story rooted in the rich, long history of the area. He had enjoyed history in high school, enough that it had sparked an interest to read about the westward American expansion, the nuances of the Civil War, and how groundwork had been laid post-Antebellum for the Civil Rights movements in the 60's. Being raised in

Chicago though, his American history wasn't as much focused on the colonialization of America or the Revolutionary War as it was westward expansion and the growth of the mid-west. Here there were so many historic sites within spitting distance of each other and each providing a fresh opportunity to explore.

The coffee maker spurted out the last bit of water, hissing as the carafe's moisture evaporated on the warming plate as his thoughts drifted, mesmerized by the blossoms on the shrub outside the French doors until Sharon Tanchak crept into this mind. They had seen each other so rarely that he didn't think he was infatuated already. She did stir something that he could not easily pin down, whether it was that she randomly appeared or if he couldn't separate her from her sister's house and the dreams or visions he was having about her. Each time he saw Sharon, feelings suppressed since the deterioration of his relationship with Brenda kindles back to life. Maybe it was more the intriguing coincidences between her, Sarah and Brenda that were teasing and twisting his emotions to the surface. Sarah and Brenda were musicians, but Sharon and Sarah were also twins, and he understood that twins maintained a spiritual connection from birth to death, and sometimes after. The whole swirl that the three of them presented had scrambled his thoughts and led him to believe he was becoming unraveled.

He got up, poured coffee into his well-used 1985 Chicago Bears Super Bowl Champions mug, and then resettled at his small dining room table. It appeared a lot smaller now than he remembered from his condo; it was adequate though. He didn't need much more for himself, and when he did finally make a few friends here, it would be big enough for a few buddies for a round of cards, beer, and chips. Nursing the first few sips of hot, black and bitter coffee, he peered through the overgrown shrub at the edge of the small deck, and saw a small garden at the edge of the backyard fence. It was overgrown with weeds and grass, disguising whether flowers or vegetables had been in the rows. Maybe an herb or vegetable plot, he thought. Further out, at the edge of the tree line he recognized a compost pile, contained on three sides, obviously built from pallet lumber and wrapped in chicken wire.

He swallowed another mouthful of coffee and decided to take a closer look. Outside, the sun had already moved up over the horizon but still hid behind spreading oaks. He navigated the steps of the six-by-six side deck, an interesting feature he mused, then continued down the hill to the weed-filled garden. The first row looked like a mass of spent strawberries where intermingled mint had overgrown. He bent over, slipped his hands through the tri-leafed plants, picked a sprig of the mint and chewed on the leaves. There was a lemony taste to the leaves. At the end of each of the rows were foot tall mounds of fine leafed evergreen, half-dead with browned spires poked up through the center. It was a familiar aroma, but for the moment, he could not put a name to it, even after weaving his hands through the stout branches.

With not being sure which plants might have been weeds and which had been planted, Zach grew unsure of what to pull out and what to salvage. To him it all looked like a hodge-podge of green and gray shades emerging from amidst brown winterkill, with stems and flowers peeking out at random locations. Growing more confused where to start, he decided he should get help from someone who probably knew.

He meandered back into the house, found the phone number for Barrett's, and after checking the time, called. It was after eight, so they were probably open.

"Barrett's Farm and Garden Supply. This is Amy," she answered after a couple of rings. "What can we do for you today?"

"Hello. I was hoping to speak to Sharon. Is she in today?"

"No, sir. She took the day off. Is there anything I can do for you?"

"Just looking for some garden advice. Sharon had indicated she could help with that a week ago."

"Is there something in particular that I could answer? Sharon did train me."

"No, not really," Zach was disappointed.

"Would you like me to leave a message for her that you called? Your name again?"

"Zach. Just let her know Zach called. Thanks."

He hung up then picked up one of the gardening books that had been left in the house and started reading while he finished his now cold coffee. When his cup was empty, he decided to head back outside and see if he had learned anything.

By the time evening darkened the sky, he was exhausted, having walked most of the cleared property, poked through the weed-filled gardens, and inspected the fruit trees. He tried to identify some of the tall trees that shot up around the wide reaching maples and oaks, but the intriguing mix of fragrances, lilac and rose, kept drawing him back toward the house. There was little more he could accomplish, so he dragged himself up the stairs to his bedroom, peeled off his clothes and dropped them on the blanket chest he had placed at the foot of the bed, then slid open the east window to let the cool breeze dance through the sheer curtains still hanging over the opening. They looked a bit feminine, but changing them out now would be too much of a hassle. They would have to do for now. He had no one to impress. He flopped onto the bed, face down, then reached over and turned off the light. It did not take long at all for him to drift off to sleep.

The music started again. It was a haunting melody this time; a slow, drifting melody he had heard before, but something about this one was different yet familiar. He strained to remember which classical music composer it could be. Not Mozart. Not Beethoven. Not even Mahler. Then it struck him. Barber. Samuel Barber. It was Adagio for Strings, the melancholy music from The Elephant Man. This one though, was being played by an oboe rather than violins, and it sounded like it was coming through duct work. He didn't remember any ductwork here. The heating was baseboard. The music was coming from inside the house, though.

He drifted out of bed and peered into each of the rooms upstairs. Nothing. The melody continued, louder and softer like the crests and falls of a lazy, lumbering tide. He headed downstairs and circled through the rooms. Still nothing. The music still wafted up into the house. When he reached the cracked open basement door, it was clear that the music was coming from downstairs.

He slipped through the door and navigated down the dark, narrow wooden stairs toward dim flickering lights. The stairs turned and continued down for three more steps. He stopped. There she was again. Sarah. Her back was turned and she was swaying as she played her way through the score. Small, lit candles rested near the open window, their flames melting rose-scented wax and emanating a fragrance that overpowered the musty smell he remembered.

She stopped playing. Smoothly and gracefully, she rose from her chair and turned to face Zach. "It's raining outside. You don't expect me to ruin my instrument, do you?" A wry grin slipped across her blanched face.

"No, no. Of course not." Last that Zach had remembered it was clear and dry outside. He glanced out through the small casement window and was baffled that it was indeed raining. "That's not what the weather report said."

"You didn't believe me, did you?"

Zach turned back to Sarah and with measured words, added, "I . . . I just haven't heard that particular music played with an oboe."

"So you are familiar with Adagio, then? It is my own rendition."

"It's lovely," Zach mumbled as he sat down on the step and stared at the beautiful woman in front of him. Or was she an apparition? Her sheer white gown left little for his imagination, except where her dark hair rested over her shoulders just above her shapely breasts.

"I found a Bulgheroni in Philadelphia. I fell in love with it as soon as I picked it up. It was perfect." Sarah presented the oboe in her open hands. Candlelight gleamed off the silver plating on top of the silvery, nickel-plated keys. The wood was rich, deeply stained mahogany. "My Buggy fits my hands perfectly," she added, lifting her hands above the floating instrument.

"Can you play more for me?" Zach was mesmerized.

Sarah brought the double reed to her lips and resumed playing, this time just a simple scale. The voice from the oboe was pleasant and mellow as she swayed her head slowly with each changing note. "What do you think of the sound? Isn't it just rich?"

Zach could not help but stare at both the instrument and Sarah. He started to move toward her with measured steps, but she seemed to remain out of reach as her smile turned coy. She then stopped, lowering her instrument from her thin lips again, revealing a wide smile and bright white teeth.

Zach moved closer until he was near enough to reach out and run his fingers through her silky hair.

A loud bang, or what sounded like one, startled Zach. He sat up. He was awake; groggy but awake. It was dark. He was in bed. Sarah's image had vanished. The entire house rattled again for a moment, then it settled. It was silent for a few seconds. A pair of slight rumblings followed. Then nothing more.

He caught his breath, dropped his feet over the side of his bed, and went to the window. Pulling up the blinds, he scanned outside for something that might have explained the noise. The light from a full, bright moon streamed through the tree boughs, shedding beams that glowed on each of the headstones across the street. Nothing more. No fire, no sirens, no commotion, no car wrecks, and no storms brewing. Just a quiet, moonlit night under clear star-filled sky. Nothing fell inside, or at least nothing that he could see that had fallen. The clock read a bright, steady red two-thirty. The power was still on. Could have been thunder, but the skies were clear, stars were shining and it was not raining.

An earthquake? He wondered. When he was growing up in Chicago, there was the same kind of loud boom once, like a sonic boom, followed by some low rumbling. The house shook a little, no windows broken, nothing like what he learned about what happened in the big one out in San Francisco, or the New Madrid quake that rumbled all the way up to the lakes. That made the most sense to him. He was in the foothills of the mountains, and he did know that where there were mountains that there were bound to be many, small earthquakes. And there were plenty of maintains nearby.

Tectonics, mountain ranges, and earthquakes. He shook his head and realized these were topics too heady to think about in the middle of the night. Especially while he was tired, and his eyelids feeling like they were heavy shades. He lay back down as a slight breeze, cooling and comfortable, meandered through the window.

Drifting off to sleep, figuring Sarah would return.

She didn't.

Zach listened for a moment as he lay in his bed, waking up slowly. As sunlight crept through the sheer curtains in the bedroom's east window, the sounds of woodpeckers hammering into hollow trees resonated like competing snare drums in the morning silence. He realized that there had not been a single night that he hadn't had at least a brief sense that Sarah was there, whether it was just some musical passage or actually dreaming about her. A chill tingled across his neck as he started to rationalize that what he had been seeing might not be just dreams. He had heard stories about haunted houses, where people that died miserable deaths, returned in a paranormal state to their homes, taunting those who dared invade their sanctuary. He had always passed them off as stories of wild imagination, convolutions of odd, explainable physical phenomenon. But the last few nights made him question if Sarah had indeed come back to the home she built as her personal resting place. Maybe she never really left. But that would mean that she was a ghostly apparition.

No he didn't accept that. There had to be some other explanation. Zach scoffed that his imagination that seemed to be running off in some fantasy. Maybe it was actually Brenda's memory and his fogginess at night was confusing him. They did look similar, but Brenda had turned cold before the accident, and Sarah, or at least he figured it was Sarah, was warm, cordial, and inviting.

He hadn't studied dream interpretation in school even though it was offered, since it wasn't something that he felt salient, but he did think there was some significance to dreaming about Sarah. Maybe he was actually fanaticizing about Sharon, and Sarah's image was acting as a surrogate. He started to think that he might just be making too much of it.

He shook his head again. Confused with trying to try to tease out feelings from dreams and from thoughts, especially early in the morning when he was foggy brained anyway, he set his thoughts aside, rolled out of bed, and gingerly walked to the closet. Each step was painful; the bottoms of his feet still sore from walking the whole property in sneakers rather than hiking boots. He grabbed some clothes, dressed and headed downstairs, figuring coffee would clear his head.

Coffee started, he logged onto his computer and pulled up the Manchester news station's web page. One story reported a two-point-two tremor centered in Suncook, just a few miles away. Several people had described just as he heard it — an explosion like bang, then some light rumbles that followed. No damage reported in the area. He figured it would be wise to see if there was any structural damage in the basement, just in case. Since the coffee was taking it's time brewing, he stepped down the narrow staircase into the chilly basement, cold from the concrete floor seeping through the callouses on his bare feet. Enough sunlight spilled in from the east casements that he didn't need to turn on the lights or head back upstairs for a flashlight. On the sill of the small casement window was a box of matches, three used ones placed into a shot glass and several drops of wax. Nothing else. No candles from where the wax could have dripped. Just like last night, but without the candles. He shook off his imagination.

The south wall was clean, no cracks. But as he started toward the east wall, he passed through a spot next to a chair practically in the center of the basement that felt warm. It was exact spot in his dream where he saw Sarah. He did not recall ever seeing a chair like this one before. The chair was weaved of yellow dyed cane, with a narrow, high back that made it look more like a shrunken throne than a chair. He walked through the spot again. It was still warm. The chair was probably here during his walkthrough, but he just never noticed. It was strange though that it was the same chair Sarah, in his dream, had been sitting on in the shed.

Thinking that there had to be a reasonable explanation, he scanned the walls and spotted an opening in the concrete blocks covering the furnace and wood-stove flues. From that opening, a slight breeze pushed a cobweb, coaxing it to sway in response to the flow. When he reached over and felt the breeze, it was warm.

Question answered, he resolved, relieved he had found a physical reason. The east wall was intact, but the north wall had a narrow crack in it that ran from the sill to the floor. It didn't look like much and seemed to follow a seam where the forms used to set up the walls had been matched up. It did not look big enough to cause a problem, he figured, and if it did show any signs of leaking, he could always run out and get some waterproof cement to seal it up.

Near the crack on the floor was a pair of framed paintings. He recognized one as an overhead view of a mid-western farm. There was no signature so he wasn't sure what is was other than a simple farm landscape. He recognized the flatness of the fields as mid-west, but nothing more distinct.

The one behind it was more intriguing, though. It was a painting of an old sail ship caught in a raging storm. In the corner was a dated signature — Campo, 1750. He was not sure if this painting was worth anything, but that really didn't matter. It was an interesting scene, though and would provide some ambiance to the great room. He carefully slipped the painting under his arm and started upstairs just as he heard a car horn outside.

Before he could get to the front door, the horn blared again.

"I'll be damned," he mumbled as he opened the front door and saw Sharon's red Jeep in the driveway.

"Hey there." Sharon waved and dropped out of her red Jeep. She was dressed for work — her forest green, long sleeve t-shirt with the Barrett's logo fit perfectly, her capris fit her legs very nicely and showed off her well-toned naked calves. Her demeanor, though seemed reserved.

Maybe relaxed, Zach wondered. Sharon pulled the sticky latchkey on the gate and stepped into the yard. "Pleasant surprise seeing you," Zach realized her gaze settled on the roses along the fence line.

"You really need to do something about these. May be a little late for this year, but you should prune these girls back. They are getting quite leggy."

"Been meaning to. I think I need to get some shears, though." Zach lied. He had no idea how to prune roses, other that it was something that his mother dreaded every spring.

"Oh, no worries. We've got them at the store." Sharon smiled enough to narrow her eyes.

"So, you got the message?"

"Message?"

"Oh, I thought that's why you stopped by."

"I was up in the mountains. I heard about the earthquake last night. Shook me a little where I am. Any problems here?"

"No. No problems. Maybe just a small crack, but not anything I can't handle on my own."

"I'm sure we've got some waterproofing cement at the store if you are looking to pick some up, just in case. Hardware. Should be pretty cheap."

"I'll keep that in mind." Zach sensed Sharon inspecting him, which was a little unnerving. If she was showing interest though, that was fine with him.

"So you said you called?" Sharon tilted her head and smirked. A lock of hair teased her forehead, melting Zach.

"Uh, I . . . I guess I was looking for some advice on the roses."

"Oh, okay. Well, was that enough that I just gave you?"

"I was thinking . . ." Zach started. "Pardon my poor manners, Sharon, but would you like to come in for some coffee? It's about all I can offer at this point."

"Sure. I've got a few minutes," Sharon agreed, checking her watch. She followed him into the dining room where he had placed the painting.

He headed into the kitchen and poured up some coffee. "Anything in it?"

"Black is good," Sharon absently replied as she ran her delicate fingers along the frame and then over the ship.

"Found it downstairs. Looked interesting."

"There's a story behind it." Sharon's gaze fixed on the painting.

"Maybe you can tell me about it, if you've got the time." Zach placed the coffee on the table next to her.

"Alright," Sharon closed her eyes and nodded before sitting down. She sucked in a deep breath and started. "Well, I think it was a couple years back, just before the leaves started changing colors. Sarah and I went to Concord to do some shopping. She wanted a picture that reminded her of how powerful the sea can get. She would get like that at times. She would chase some random thought for months until she found what she wanted. It seemed like we had looked for hours . . ."

As Sharon talked about that day with her sister, Zach could not stop himself from staring at her every feature, feeling fortunate that she seemed lost enough in her thoughts not to notice his gaze. She looked hauntingly similar to the image of Sarah he had seen in his dreams through the week. Her almond shaped eyes smiled as she reminisced about her sister. Zach restrained himself from reaching out and running his fingers through her wavy auburn hair, unsure if his advance would scare her off.

". . . and in every antique and collectible shop on Main Street until we saw this little shop on Pleasant Street. In the window was this painting. Sarah immediately said that she had to have it. Cost was no object, she had said and fortunately, it was not expensive. I think I remember her even working the price down more. I think she loved to haggle just for the principle." Sharon stopped for a moment, looked toward the ceiling, then took a sip of her coffee.

"So this painting has some sentimental value?" Zach pried.

"Sarah had it up in her studio for the longest time. I know I took it down last winter when the pipes burst so it wouldn't get ruined during the repairs. I was going to take it home, but — " Sharon stopped. Her fingers froze mid-stroke on the canvas when she turned and looked at Zach. It wasn't the same look from last week with the glasses. This one was a more curious one.

"Do you want it?"

"I couldn't."

"Would you like to have it?"

Sharon remained silent.

"What if I offered it to you? It sounds to me like you might have some attachment to this painting," Zach pressed.

"I would feel bad about taking it. I should have removed it before —"

"Would you like the painting?" Zach asked insistently.

"Well, if I may ask, what were you going to do with it?"

"I just found it this morning. Probably hang it in the living room, maybe over the wood stove."

"You could put it back where it was. I am sure Sarah would like that."

Zach wondered what Sharon meant, then assumed that it was simply an off-the-cuff comment. He tried to read her face, now fixed on the painting, curious as to whether or not she knew something more about Sarah. And if she did, perhaps she understood that those were not dreams after all. In either case, he wasn't ready to spook her away. "You mean back in the basement?"

"Really?" Sharon grimaced for a moment before an elfish grin turned the corners of her mouth up. "That's not what I meant. Do you want me to show you?"

"Be my guest," Zach replied, opening his arm as if inviting her to show him where she was thinking. Without hesitating, Sharon got up from her seat, scooped up the painting and headed directly upstairs. Zach followed, catching up with her in the study. She reached over one of the foldaway tray tables that Zach had covered with a couple books and papers, then touched the wall.

"Right here. This is where it was. You can see the hole where the hook was."

"I don't have any hooks, though," Zach mumbled before glancing over to his desk. On the edge was the right sized hook for the painting's weight. He didn't recall taking anything out of the wall, but maybe he did and just forgot. "Well, I didn't think I had any," he added, picking up the hook and handing it to Sharon.

She slipped the hook into the wall and mounted the painting. With a little nudge at the bottom, she straightened it and stepped back. She cocked her head right, then left. She took another step back, close enough that Zach picked up the smell of her soap. It was Irish Spring. No surprise.

"Yes, Sarah will like that," Sharon added as she turned and looked at Zach. Their eyes met. It was that same look he saw in Sarah's eyes last night. It was a deep, sensitive, wondering look. A fleeting thought crossed his mind to inch closer. He remained locked in an adoring stare into her green eyes instead.

For a moment, her eyes caught his gaze. He wanted to ask what she meant about Sarah, but words were vaporizing before he could say them. Before he could finally muster a word, Sharon inched closer, reached over and touched his nose with her forefinger.

"Not now. Maybe later."

Zach stiffened and wondered if she was reading his thoughts. Before he could assemble a coherent thought, Sharon turned around, headed out of the room and down the stairs. She called back over her shoulder, "Gotta run. See you later, okay?"

"But —" Zach took one step toward her and stopped. He wanted to offer breakfast. He wanted to ask if she would give him some help with the garden. He wanted to spend some time with her. Mostly, he wanted to hold her close. Instead, his hesitation failed him. Sharon was out the front door and into her Jeep before he could even get any words out. Rather than heading downstairs, he walked to the window of the small middle bedroom and watched as Sharon pull out of the driveway, waving goodbye.

๑๖๑

Chapter 12

Sharon drove her Jeep into the parking lot at Barrett's, later than she normally started work, but since she wasn't expected to be there today anyway, she didn't think it a problem. She felt guilty taking the first part of the Memorial Day weekend off, but the day in the mountains did wonders for her psyche. With a bright sun and cloudless sky, she was sure that the extra hand would be more than welcome. She swung around the back of the lot near the hay and feed barn where all the nursery's employees normally parked during the busy times. She used this spot for down time as well, since it was out of the way and had an open view over the spring fed duck pond. It helped settle her mind and tease though the roller coaster ride she felt like she was on.

Being with Zach eased her and scared her at the same time. She was unsure why she felt she had to check on him this morning, but she did. Earthquakes were quite common and never caused any damage. But she did, and when the opportunity presented itself, she couldn't quite bring herself to make that move one step closer. With the whirlwind that Carolyn was spinning her through, it would have been comforting to rest her head on his shoulder and let things happen. Instead the sense spooked her. Maybe just unsure. She couldn't pin-point what she felt. It seemed each time they met, something tingled inside a little bit more.

When he offered Sarah's glasses and caught her off guard, she recoiled. She probably should have just taken them. It wasn't that big of a deal to have to run away from. And she had forgotten about the painting until he showed it to her this morning. She sensed safety in that, but just couldn't tell why.

And then there was Carolyn Appleton. She fretted about what the old lady was up to. She never expected that the deep ill toward her could be because of what Judith Rhodes and Liza Schumann revealed. There was probably some validity in Carolyn's anger if in fact her philandering husband was chasing someone younger associated with the Conservatory, and then lied to her that it was Sharon. But why the confrontation now? That her anger had boiled over now rather than three years ago before seemed peculiar, unless Sarah's death relieved something — some secret that she had sequestered until Sarah left. But it could not have been Sarah. Not Sarah. That didn't even sound right. They were too close and she would have known. It had to be someone else that Sarah was protecting, but she was at a loss as to who. She had to keep her faith that Liza would follow through.

"Well, hello, stranger. I didn't really expect to see you today." Rhonda's voice interrupted her thoughts. Sharon startled, then looked up and saw Rhonda standing by her open window, a hand truck stacked with three bags of horse feed next to her. There was haggardness on her face she had only seen before when all hell was breaking loose.

"Couldn't stay, no room at the inn. I guess it was too much of a last minute decision for this weekend." Sharon smirked as she slid out of her Jeep. "But when I drove by and saw the parking lot full, I figured that you might need an extra hand."

"And you just happened to have your work clothes available this morning?" Rhonda scowled for a moment.

"I felt like I was letting you down. It looks pretty busy." Sharon winked and cracked a grin.

"Well, I do appreciate you looking out for our business, and I'm not going to turn down the help today, but we should talk, sooner than later."

"Am I in trouble?"

"Not in my eyes. Let me get this going." Rhonda's deep brown eyes morphed from pleasantness to dire concern, a look Sharon had only seen that look a few times before. Rhonda waved Ted over to take the feedbags over to the blue Ford F-150, indicating that it was already paid for. As he took control of the handcart, Rhonda placed her arm around Sharon's shoulders and they walked out toward the pond and sat down at the picnic table.

"Carolyn stopped by yesterday."

Sharon immediately tensed up. "I did run into Liza Schumann up on the trail. I think I might know what Carolyn's digging at."

"Don't take this wrong, but I do need to hear it from you."

"I understand." Sharon looked out over the water for a moment then tilted her head back and sighed. "She's accusing me of sleeping with her husband, isn't she?"

"That's what I gathered."

"I wouldn't touch that man." Sharon dropped her head and stared directly into Rhonda's eyes. "He was as vile as they come. I get it that he would lie about me being his conquest. I am having a hard time placing who would have lowered their morals far enough to even consider that."

"I believe you, but there is another issue. Do you know what this is about?" Rhonda gave her an empty prescription bottle. "Carolyn dropped this off."

"That's Sarah's, but she hadn't used Vicodin in years — since her first bout of cancer. She preferred natural treatments." Sharon opened the bottle and noticed powder on the inside. "Where did she get it?"

"Carolyn said it was in the case with the oboe."

"You have to believe me. I have no ideas how they got there."

"I believe you. I just had to hear you say it." Rhonda appeared to have a weight lifted from her shoulders. She reached over and squeezed Sharon's shoulder, then sucked in a deep breath through her nose. "I know you've had a rough time with Sarah's passing, and this doesn't help, but we'll get through it. I will deal with Carolyn."

"Thank you. I really appreciate you being there for me."

Rather than head directly home that evening, Sharon decided to head up to Portsmouth for a relaxing walk in Prescott Park to clear her head. The workday had been unexpectedly exhausting, but the revelation of the Vicodin pills shocked her even more. She agonized at the thought that Sarah had been lying to her and had been giving her drugs to Vincent. None of the whys made any sense to her.

The evening was much cooler than the day had been, and the breeze slipping off the bay helped relieve her tension. When the mountains were not available because she didn't have the time, she preferred a walk along the park's pathways, where the breeze swept through and moderated the heat of the day. The crabapples, cherries and flowering plums were all in full bloom. The colorful annual beds this year were as fabulous as ever, even under the dim light of the street lamps that spotted the brick walkways through the park. She was partial to the arrangements since the city had contracted Barrett's as their landscaper.

Lighthouse horns out in the Piscataqua River moaned in the light fog, singing their melancholy announcements to evening boaters while overhead, the light cloud cover let some stars sparkle through.

At the end of her walk and at the edge of the park, she caught the aroma of wisteria blossoms drifting in from one of the adjacent side streets. Drawn by the sweet bouquet, she wandered into a section that felt and looked Victorian. She followed the fragrance for a few city blocks until she happened across the source — a single colonial with lavender wisteria wrapped along the eaves, and a small, simple shingle posted in the front yard.

Inga. Medium.

Nothing more, nothing fancy, just the sign that swung gently from its perch. Sharon stopped, cocked her head, and stared at the dim yellowish light seeping out through sheer curtained windows under the porch canopy. Wisteria vines twisted their way through ornate gables. Centered between two brick chimneys rested a cupula, barely illuminated with a small yellow light at its center.

Sharon was not sure why she felt drawn in, but she wandered along the walkway and onto the porch where an old, bent woman sat in a throne-like chair, smoking a pipe. She stared at the woman, whose head was down. She seemed to be moaning. No, she was chanting in a low growling tone. Her black silk gown flowed to the floorboards; its hemline swirled next to the chair.

"Sit next to me dear, you look bothered."
Inga's voice was gravelly but oddly welcoming. She tilted her head up and peered at Sharon through cloudy gray eyes. Sharon inched closer and sat down in the wicker chair next to Inga at the round, tablecloth covered table. The old woman sighed,

craning her neck from side to side, as if inspecting Sharon. "There is someone here for you, Sharon."

"How do you know me?"

"Sarah wanted to talk with you. Give me your hand," the woman said as she laid out her skeletal hand, palm up. Sharon tentatively placed her trembling hand onto the spooky old woman's hand, more curious than scared. She felt light-headed as the woman's gaunt fingers curled over hers. The wisteria's intoxicating scent wafted down from the eaves and onto the porch, accompanied by a vague image shimmering across the table from her. It was an older woman — a woman who she imagined she had seen at Barrett's looking over fuchsias that afternoon at the store. But when she turned to grab a radio while being on the floor, the apparition was gone. She figured she was seeing things.

"Excuse me," the older woman's image mumbled. Sharon dropped her jaw open as the dream, or what she thought was a daydream was unfolding before her eyes. She was back at Barrett's, standing at the counter like she had been. "Could you be so kind as to help me with those over there?" The woman asked as she turned and pointed to the row of cascading fuchsias hanging on a long suspended rod. Sharon stared at the rows of color underneath the glass greenhouse ceiling.

"Listen to her message, Sharon." Inga interrupted, demanding focus.

"Message?" Sharon mumbled as she felt herself drift over to the hanging plants. The fuchsias were gorgeous; their red, pink and blue petals flowing along the sides of each plant, like a rainbow waterfall. Sharon combed her fingers through the branches of each of the plants. "Was there one in particular you were looking at?" she asked.

"The one on the end," she pointed to the last one with her crooked finger, then revealed, "It reminds me of an old boyfriend."

"Really?"

"Oh, it's a long story, dear," the lady said.

"Well, why don't you tell me while I get it down? You did want this one, didn't you?"

The woman grew glassy-eyed as she tipped her head and stared at the plant. "Well, dear, years ago, I was paying too much attention to my fuchsias and never noticed this young man trying to win my heart. He was aloof and I paid him no never mind. I thought he was odd, but I found out from a friend that he had been hurt by someone before. Since I ignored him, he just faded away. I never met anyone like him again. So now it's just me, my plants, and my cats."

"That's so sad," Sharon said as she carefully unhooked the plant and brought it down to the woman's cart.

"Listen to the message, Sharon," Inga croak reminded her.

"Now these have just been watered, so they should do fine on their way home," Sharon noted.

"Thank you dear."

"And they like a good amount of shade." Sharon mumbled. "So why this color in particular?"

"It's the only one with only lavender, red, and white. It's not like the other ones. Like Harold."

"I see. Can I help you bring it to the car?"

The old woman did not respond. Instead, her face shimmered and started to change as if layers of chiffon were peeled away. The image transposed from the old woman into Sarah.

"You know, he's not such a hard luck case. In fact, I think he's reasonably cute."

"You mean Zach?"

"You seem to be thinking of him quite a bit."

"It's only been a couple of weeks."

"Probably long enough."

Sharon noticed through the corner of her eye that Inga's head swayed slowly from side to side about her shoulders.

"I've been busy," Sharon demurred. Sarah's image shimmered and started to fade.

"You always were, girl." Sarah's image faded.

"He's probably given up on me." Sharon stammered for an excuse.

"No, he hasn't," Sarah said as Sharon could hear the distant strings of Adagio.

"How do you know?"

"Been there. He is attracted to you, as you are to him. That's what you are feeling, Sharon." Sarah's voice grew tinny. "Listen to the message. Give him a chance."

Sarah's image shimmered, blurred then started to fade, but remained a translucent fuzzy image above the table.

"Wait. The pill bottle. What about the Vicodin."

"Tell dear Liza to talk to Julian. And don't fret about Appleton. I will take care of her." After her final words, Sarah vanished into a wisp that swirled away into the wisteria boughs.

Sharon turned to Inga who was now regarding her through opaque eyes. The corners of her mouth had turned up into a quivering but distinct smile. "I think your sister loves you, dear."

Sharon withdrew her hand and closed her eyes, trying to make sense of the visit. As she started to dig into her wallet, the old woman said, "Your happiness will be payment enough for me, dear."

Chapter 13

Zach felt good about trueing his fifth case on the day, even though he had stayed a couple hours later than he had planned. The lack of office distractions and no one walking by helped him concentrate and tie up the loose ends. The Carsen case, in particular was convoluted, rampant with more tangled webs between claimants, long lost relatives, and descendants than the first four cases combined. He had spent most of the afternoon in the company lawyer's office, which had helped a great deal, and allowed him to finalize his accounting piece.

But the day was finally done, and he felt he was ready for his morning appointment with as he understood, his most challenging client, Carolyn Appleton. There were some interesting notes Carl

Edwards had left in the file, and he wasn't quite sure what to make of all of them, other than a cryptic note about helping Sharon. He was sure he meant Sharon Tanchak, but he wasn't positive what he meant by helping her.

Zach turned off his desk lamp and leaned back in his high-backed leather chair. After tomorrow, it was the weekend. He closed his eyes and wondered if this would be a good weekend to head up to the White Mountains to explore around a bit. A hike in the mountains would certainly help end the week on a positive note. He thought he might see if Sharon was interested a taking that trip with him. That way, he was sure not to get lost.

"Working late again. Mr. Fields?" a deep voice interrupted his thoughts. He looked up and saw Ben Parker, the black night shift sergeant standing at his cubicle entrance. Since Zach had been working late more often than not, he was getting to know Parker and the night shift Lieutenant better. Neither of them were as bad as everyone had led him to believe, but he had to admit that Parker's linebacker physique was a bit intimidating. As scary as he seemed to everyone else, Zach warmed up to him quickly, especially since he always seemed to stop by to offer snippets of fatherly advice.

"Yeah, a little. Seems I can get more work done when nobody's here to distract me. I've been thinking about using ear plugs during the day."

"Don't know if that's wise. You might not hear the fire drills," Parker sighed heavily as he settled into the chair in Zack's office. His blood-shot eyes locked laser-like onto Zach's. "Let me give you some advice, son. Your work will be here tomorrow. And the next day, and the next day after that. If you spend all your time here, you'll burn out, or worse, have a stroke."

"I know. Been there, done that." Zack tried to joke, but Parker was having nothing of it.

"It seems to me your clients create enough stress for you, especially that Appleton lady. She's as crazy as a bed bug. She's been the ruin of many well-meaning folks here."

"I guess I fell off the wagon of recovering work-a-holics."

"I wasn't there personally, since this job is a bit less stressful, outside the hours. But the gentleman you are replacing practically drove himself into the ground. Don't know what he was trying to do, but he almost killed himself before he had a chance to retire. Stress raises hell on a man's body, son. And once you lose your health, the mind starts going. Then there's no turning back once you start getting mashed potatoes up here." Parker tapped on his closely trimmed graying hair.

"I do have quite a bit to catch up on, Sarge," Zach noted.

"Really? It may not be my place, but sometimes lack of sleep will just jumble things up and maybe even give you some visions you might not want to see."

"I do have my first real meeting with Appleton in the morning."

"I hear you there, but a good night's sleep will serve you better," Parker's voice firmed up, more than Zach really wanted to hear.

"I heard she's a real piece of work."

"Did you hear me, son, or am I wasting my breath. For your own good, I suggest that you pack up that file, put it away in the vault and be on your way. I don't think you want to be explaining to the Lieutenant that you were tired when you mess up the codes in there. He might not be as understanding as I am."

"I'm listening," Zach noted as he stood up at his desk and collected up the files.

"Have you been listening to any weather reports while you've been holed up in here?"

Zach's eyes widened.

"Didn't think so. There's a nasty storm brewing out there. You best be on your way before getting swallowed up in that mess. May not be like them tornadoes I heard you folks get out west, but these here can still raise some holy hell."

"Okay, you win."

"Heard that before, too, but I'd prefer you listen and take my advice to heart." Parker rose from his chair and towered over Zach, arms crossed over his huge chest and a scowl that could scare off the sun. "I've got some rounds to take care of, and if I have to wait much longer for you to start heading in that direction, I'm going to be late. That will not sit well with me or the Lieutenant."

"Yes, sir," Zach eked out a smile. He started to march to the vault under Sgt. Parker's escort. Once the vault was secured, he accompanied Zach to the exit doors.

"You have a good night now, Mr. Fields. And drive safe out there. It's supposed to be getting fierce." Parker disabled the door alarm and let Zach out.

"Thanks, and you too Ben," Zach waved and headed out into the parking garage. He heard rain trickling through the garage drainpipes. Once he exited the garage and turned onto the city street, his wipers streaked the dust from the parking lot across his windshield. The rain did nothing more than just make it worse as it grew heavier and harder. The sky seemed to open up and pour as he turned onto the highway's entrance ramp.

Zach slowed once he merged to split his attention on the road and his radio. He flipped through the stations hoping to find a public radio station, knowing those were consistently good all over the country. The clear stations all seemed to be playing country, though. Not his favorite. He left the radio on scan and it finally tuned to a news station that was finishing the international news of the day. He listened carefully, thinking the local weather was next and tried to focus on the oncoming headlights shimmering through the pine tar that had streaked across his windshield.

"Rain, heavy at times. Local flooding possible . . ." The station faded out.

"You could at least tell me where," Zach mumbled as he leaned forward to get a better view of the road. Traffic was heavier than he had remembered it being late on a weekday, but then remembered Natalie mentioning that some people usually left early for the weekend in the mountains. Rather than fight with reception, he switched back to an oldies station he had found and sang along for the rest of the ride.

It seemed that it had taken twice his normal time to reach his exit, but once he got there, he maneuvered through the water collecting on the two-lane road that crossed between the highway and Pleasant Hill. Blinding sheets of water cascaded off his windshield, convincing him he needed to slow even more. Puddles crept out into the road, looking more like an incoming tide. As he drove through them, the splash hammered his undercarriage. He slowed at his turn onto Pleasant Hill, then leaned forward, as close to the windshield as he could without fogging it up with his breath, concentrating to ensure he wouldn't fall off the edge of the road. It wasn't that the drop off was steep, it was more that there was no line along the side of the road marking where the hard macadam ended and ooze of soft mud and running water started. As he rounded one of the last bends in the road, he slowed to a crawl, noticing something ahead.

No, it was someone. Someone in a hooded jacket was walking along the side of the road just ahead of him. Underneath the jacket, a street length dress swayed with the wind, as if untouched by the rain. He flashed his high beams and slowed even more, but there was no response — she continued moving up the hill. As he drew closer, he pulled off to the side of the road right behind the walker, hoping not to get stuck in the saturated mire that was now the road's muddy shoulder. He reached into the glovebox for his flashlight, but it was dead.

"Hey! Do you want a ride?" he called as he stepped out into the pouring rain. No response. She kept walking. She didn't even turn around. The rain came down harder, in sheets, pelting his face. She kept moving. He walked faster, but as he reached the extent of the light beams from his car, she was gone.

Where could she go? Zach thought as he looked around. There were no driveways to slip into. The rain obliterated his vision so much that even if there was a pathway, he would not be able to see it. Whoever it was had just vanished as quickly as she appeared.

He returned to his car, soaked, chilled, and spooked. He was sure there was someone there, but as he wiped his face, he wondered if he was just imagining the figure in the road. It was a night like this that Brenda had her accident. He did have as difficult a time getting home that night as well. He never got further details from the police as to whether she survived long enough to get out and walk in the rain as did this woman.

Maybe Ben was right, he thought as he wiped his face with a towel from the back seat. With all the hours he was putting in, he was starting to hallucinate. The alternative of what he was seeing gave him angst.

It didn't matter now, he thought as he wiped his face again. He put the car into gear and slowly worked his way back onto the road from the soft shoulder, spinning his tires just a little to get out of the mud. He peered through the rain beating on the passenger side window, but there was nothing to see without the direct beams of his headlights.

Only a few minutes passed when his headlights flashed over the red and blue reflectors on his tilted mailbox. As he pulled into the driveway, it became obvious why the darkness along the road seemed blacker than normal —the power was out. The motion sensing floodlights over the driveway did not flicker on. As his headlights swept across the front of the house, he thought he saw a figure in the house. He stopped, backed up and turned slightly enough that his headlights swept across the window.

"Can't be," Zach mumbled when he saw what looked like a figure in the dining room window. Maybe he was just imagining it. He was exhausted from the harrowing drive that had drained him. As he pulled in close to the garage, he hit the door opener out of habit, but nothing happened. He turned off the car but left the lights on so he could see the garage door lock. Heavy, cold rain stung his face as he keyed into the lock and lifted the door before heading back to his car to turn his lights off.

Inside, the house was quiet, with the exception of the rain beating on the skylights and pelting the east side of the house. Eerily quiet. Only his squeaking shoes on the kitchen floor disturbed the silence. He fumbled for a flashlight, turned it on, then swept the beam across the front window. The sheer curtains in the dining room were tangled and waving in the breeze. He did not remember leaving the window open. For a glancing moment, he wondered if someone had broken in, but since there was no other evidence; wet tracks on the floor, stuff rearranged or strewn around; he realized there was no one else here. And if they were, they were gone now. He sighed and closed the window. He was cold, soaked through, exhausted, and without power.

A branching streak of lightning lit up the living room through the skylights. Just as Zach sensed the sizzle, he braced himself for a loud crash of thunder. It was going to be close. And loud. He was not disappointed. It was enough to make him jump. The weather cell must have settled in directly over-head. Another flash lit the whole house, brighter than any lightning show he had ever seen in Chicago. Each successive rumble rattled everything, from the windows to the floors, and even a few plates when the louder, throatier thunder claps rumbled on for close to half a minute.

On the stove was a pan of water that for some reason he had left partly full. He must have been rushing in the morning, he figured. With the power out, he realized for once, not cleaning up worked out for the best. Fumbling for matches, he found a pack in the cupboard and lit the gas stove to heat the water for some tea.

As he stood at the stove, another streak of lightning lit up the room behind him. He swapped out the wet shirt on his back for a sweatshirt he had left on a chair next to the kitchen table, hoping it would warm him up as the streak's rumble rattled the windows. He swept the flashlight beam across the counter top and spotted several homemade boxes he remembered had been left. He stepped closer and read the label on one of them. Peppermint-Rosemary. Hand written. No brand.

Interesting combination, he thought as he grabbed one of the hand folded tea bags and dropped it into a wide, white mug. He turned off the stove's burner, and then poured the hot water from the pan over the tea bag, taking care not to overfill the mug. Settling in with the steeping tea in the living room to warm up while he waited for the storm to calm down, he hoped the power crews would get out and fix whatever problem caused the outage. He grabbed a towel and set it down on his new leather couch before sitting down on it with his wet pants. He squirreled his feet underneath his legs while he started prodding his phone to life. He poked through the phone numbers until he found the power company's emergency call number.

Another lightning bolt hit nearby. At least it wasn't on top of him this time, Zach thought as he punched the phone number. A low rumble from the thunder started to build, like a bowling ball headed his way.

The line connected. The recorded message started.

Scattered outages in the Edenton, Bow, Contoocook, Suncook and Merrimack areas. Most of the outages due to trees falling over power lines, uprooted by the flash flooding. One sub-station has sustained some damage. Crews were on the scene and are waiting to make repairs when deemed safe for the workers. Estimated return in areas where the storm has subsided is four hours.

Zach wasn't sure if he could believe that or not, since the estimates he recalled that Commonwealth Edison touted were always woefully wrong — storm damage repair always seemed to take longer than they professed. And it was very dependent on the weather clearing. Right now, though, it didn't really matter. The tea had started to whittle away his chill, and he needed to get some rest since his meeting with Carolyn Appleton was in the morning. Natalie had already primed him that she could be his most challenging client. He grabbed his battery-powered alarm clock, set it a half-hour before he normally got up in the morning, and settled in for a quick nap on the leather-covered couch. Within minutes, he was asleep and felt like he was drifting.

Zach felt an odd stroking on his legs, like a daddy longlegs working its way up. When he rolled over and sat up, the sky lit up with distant lightning, enough to shed light through the skylights and into the room. It wasn't a spider at all. It was Sarah, again. She was holding a small, shivering dog in her arms, he recognized as a Cairn Terrier. The poor thing nuzzled so deep into her chest that he could barely see the dog's nose nestled in her cleavage. It must have been the dog's tail that was tickling his ankle.

Small votive candles ringed the room; all of them lit and perched up on shelves so they would be safe from a scrambling, frightened dog. And there was an aroma in the room, like tomato sauce cooking down. Pungent. He struggled to place the aroma, but all that came back to him was the smell

169

of one of his high school friend's kitchen when his mother was cooking. He thought oregano since his friend was Italian, and his mother always seemed to be cooking some tomato based sauce.

"She doesn't like storms," Sarah said as she slowly stroked the dog's wiry gray hair.

"Are you cooking?"

"Oh, no. I'm not cooking anything. It's the rosemary in your tea."

"Rosemary?" Zach sat up and tried to rub the crust from his eyes.

"Your tea," Sarah's smile seemed to light up the room. Another flash in the distance lit the room overhead and highlighted Sarah. She was very pale skinned, but her smile was inviting. As were her brilliant green eyes. "Do you like my blend? It's from the herb garden. You had walked through the garden last weekend, yes?"

"But it smells like an Italian kitchen. A traditional kitchen."

"You don't do much cooking, do you," Sarah giggled this time as she stroked her shivering pet.

"I do cook, but for survival, not entertainment."

"Italians use rosemary for that special, homemade sauce taste."

"I didn't know that." It didn't dawn on Zach until Sarah mentioned it. There was a distinctly different aroma at Anthony's house as compared to the Italian restaurants.

"I learned that in cooking school," she added.

"Were you on the road? When I was coming home, was that you?"

"No." Sarah mouth curved into a smile as she stroked her pet.

"Someone was on the road, in the rain. Wearing a hooded jacket."

"It wasn't me. I've been here. It's rather frightful outside. Are you sure you were not just seeing things?"

"I saw something — someone, I'm sure. She was on the side of the road just down the hill. Wandering, as if she was lost."

"Why do you still think about Brenda?"

"Was it Brenda? Do you know Brenda?"

"Why are you still obsessed with her?"

"How do you know Brenda?"

Sarah tilted her head and hooded her eyes.

"Some things you will just need to find out for yourself."

The entire house lit up, followed by a crackling thunderclap. Zach startled. There was a nagging beeping coming from somewhere. He reached over and hit the snooze button on his alarm clock to stop the noise, but it continued.

He sat up, opened his eyes and realized that the power was back on. The alarm clock indicated 12:30 in red, He realized the incessant beeping was coming from the kitchen — the stove. He turned on the spotlights and looked around the room. Sarah was gone. There were no candles in the house. There was no dog. He picked up his mug and inhaled deeply. He remembered the smell from Anthony's house when his mother was cooking. Yes, that was the smell. The rosemary aroma was from his tea. He took a sip of the now cold tea and thought about his vision. Or his dream. Or something else.

The storm had passed. Morning was going to be here too soon. He needed sleep. He stumbled out into the kitchen, turned off the beeping and returned to the couch. After resetting the clock's alarm, he pulled up the blanket, then rolled over and went back to sleep.

Chapter 14

Sharon arranged the forms at the rental counter for the expected returns, filling in for Ted who had called in to take the day off and handle storm related damage to his house. The store didn't get much damage from the storms the night before, and neither did her condo. That was the primary reason she decided against buying her own house here. So much of her spare time was spent helping her sister that she wouldn't have the time to work on her own. She heard reports of trees and power lines down in the surrounding towns and started to wonder if the pine trees she never got around to cutting down did any damage at Sarah's house — no, Zach's house now she corrected herself.

As she logged onto the computer, which was slower than usual this morning, she wondered how

Zach made out in the storm. She hoped he didn't run into any problems, and figured she might just drive by sometime this weekend when she wasn't working to see how he was doing. He hadn't called since she had dropped by on Sunday but she didn't find it all that unexpected. He was probably busy at work and getting home late. He probably had to find some things to get settled in the house. He did seem like the workaholic type; a business professional in meetings all day chatting about finance and mergers.

She was busy as well. The counter was nothing more than one of the jobs at the store. Since she knew what had to be done, and could do it as well as Ted did, she didn't mind volunteering to fill in. It was not the most enjoyable assignment, but she didn't mind doing it either, since handling the rental returns helped keep things fluid around the store. It also saved Rhonda from having to tend the counter. She knew that Rhonda disliked the desk since it made her feel trapped, and then she would be irritable for the entire week that followed. She also knew there would be long stretches between calls, so with the portable phone at the desk, she could manage getting some time in the greenhouse.

It would be a busy day, she noted, looking over the number of agreements she had pulled from the file. The weekend promised to be busy as well, since it was the unofficial start of the summer. Memorial Day had passed and everyone was now on the move for summer vacations. As she sorted through the contracts, it crossed her mind that the last time she filled in for Ted was when Zach called about returning the truck that he drove from Chicago. She remembered that her first impression was that he matched her stereotype of an accountant; dull and not very interesting. But when she went to check in on the house a couple times, especially after the earthquake, something about him was different.

She picked up the phone, turned it on, and headed into the greenhouse. As she worked her way through the geraniums, picking at the wilted leaves and leafless branches, Jill's comments from last weekend kept surfacing like an itch that wouldn't go away. All week long, Jill's thoughts made her think about Sarah's appearances as to whether they were dreams or visits from the other side. Inga solidified in her mind that Sarah was something more than just a dream.

The phone rang. Answering as she headed back to the desk for better reception, she realized that on the other end was the man from Rochester that had bid on her house. She heard they had bought something else in the next town over, and now that they had finished moving, were returning the rented truck. She filled out the necessary papers and after a cordial conversation on the condition of the truck, she disconnected and headed back to the greenhouse.

As she returned to sprucing up the geraniums, she felt disappointed that the call was not Zach. It would be nice if he called just to say hi, and maybe even suggest a dinner date, she thought.

"Hey, there." Amy slipped into the greenhouse for a moment. Although she was a several years her junior, she and Amy had developed a decent friendship. She would have liked to be closer to Amy, but there was enough gap in their ages to stilt their conversations. "Hadn't had a chance to ask how your weekend in the mountains turned out. This week has been crazy, hasn't it."

"It was actually just one day, but it was nice for the most part. But you know me, anytime in the mountains, even if it is pouring, is a good time."

Amy came close and whispered, "Anything you want to share?" She twitched her eyebrows as the corners of her mouth turned up. Sharon stared at Amy with hooded eyes.

"Something in particular you are interested in?"

"Perhaps how a mountain rendezvous went with a certain someone?"

"I went up alone. I did run into Liza Schumann while I was there."

"Oh, I see." Amy recoiled, then perched her eyebrows. "So you didn't meet up with Zach Fields? Really?"

"Why would you think that?" Sharon tilted her head, curious at Amy's comment. She turned sideways toward Amy and buried her hands into the geraniums.

"He called here last Saturday. I just figured that he was calling to . . . I guess not, huh?"

"Oh, that answers that."

"Huh?" Amy's eyes widened as she stared at Sharon

"I stopped in to see him on Sunday before coming back to work. He asked if I got the message."

"You did?"

"It was just a quick visit. No kiss and tell, sorry." Sharon winked. "Oh, excuse me, duty calls," Sharon tapped her headset, then answered, "Barrett's, this is Sharon."

As Sharon headed back to the counter, Amy caught up with a customer who was picking through the kalanchoe plants.

Zach woke to the irritating buzzing of his alarm clock. He rolled off the couch, stumbled into the kitchen, and then poured himself a bowl of Shredded Wheat. While the coffee pot gurgled with his morning brew, he tried to remember anything from the rest of the night after the power came back on. Nothing except that Sarah did not return. While he worked through his breakfast, he listened to the morning news on his radio, hoping to get more information on the damage caused by the sudden spring storm in the area. No road blockage at this point, but the main transformer down the road was struck by lightning and was the cause for the outage. He finished his breakfast, quickly changed into a fresh shirt and trousers, then headed out.

The drive into work was tricky; fresh leaves and small branches scattered along the highway. No delays, though, which was good. Once in the office, he prepped his talking points for Appleton, headed downstairs and made a quick check of the conference room he had set up for the appointment. He did not have to wait long in the lobby for the tall, thin, well-dressed, older woman to step through the front door. She seemed a little unsteady with her approach, but Zach passed it off as unbalanced with her heels. Her salt and pepper hair was neatly tied back in a bun, no rogue locks brushing at her forehead.

"Good morning," Zach approached. "Are you Carolyn Appleton?"

"Director Appleton, young man," she turned toward Zach. He felt her eyes scan him from his mussed hair down to his casual shoes. He grew self-conscious as she focused on his pant cuffs, worried he may have slipped on the ones with frayed edges.

"Zachary Fields." He offered his hand. She did not reciprocate. He felt flushed and a building pressure that usually ended with a sinus headache. "Pleased to meet you. We are set up in the conference room over there. Would you care for some coffee?"

"I was expecting someone a bit more . . . experienced." Carolyn Appleton stiffened and perched her eyebrows in disapproval.

"I just transferred in from the Chicago office and took over from your previous account manager, who retired about a month ago. I thought it best to have a discussion with each of my new clients to make sure I fully understood their goals." Zach bit his lip, sensing the trouble Natalie had warned him about Carolyn Appleton. She was demanding, at times rude, and never pleasant to deal with.

"And how long did you work in Chicago, young man?" she asked just as Natalie walked through the front door. Natalie winked and smiled as she walked by, her laptop case slung over her shoulder.

"Good morning, Ms. Appleton," Natalie smiled widely. "I see you have already met our new fiduciary, Zach Fields?"

Carolyn broke a thin-lipped smile as she leaned toward Natalie. "Is he as good as he says he is?"

Zach started to mouth that he said nothing of the sort, but the watchful eye of Carolyn stopped him.

"We only hire the best, Ms. Appleton. I am sure Mr. Fields will be able to manage your account as well as, if not better than Carl did."

"I will be the judge of that," Carolyn narrowed her eyes and turned back to Zach as Natalie continued into the office area, and once the doors closed behind her, the woman asked, "You may enlighten me about your experience, young man."

"I spent ten years in Chicago and handled over one hundred clients over that time period. I am bound to confidentiality, however I can add that I have managed several high profile clients like yourself."

"And before that?"

"College. Northwestern. MBA. Internship in Atlanta."

"So why are you here. Were you fired for improprieties?"

"No, Ma'am. I needed a change. I heard there was an opportunity here in Nashua, so I requested a transfer."

"Well, young man, time is precious so we should get down to business."

"I agree. Coffee should be in the corner." Zach smiled as politely as he could, all the while thinking, "I thought you'd never stop the inquisition." With his outstretched arm, pointed toward the conference room. Carolyn's thin lips twitched at the corners. As she started in that direction. Zach sighed with relief and followed her into the room.

Zach crashed into his chair at his desk, exhausted from his initial meeting with Carolyn Appleton. The hour discussion felt more like it had consumed the entire day. He closed his eyes for a moment while he tried to squeeze away the throb from his exploding sinus headache.

"Tough discussion, I see?" Zach heard Natalie ask.

"I don't think I have ever dealt with someone like that before," Zach muttered as he squeezed the bridge of his nose.

"She didn't fire you, did she?" Natalie asked as Zach cracked his eyes open.

"No. Or at least I don't think so."

"You would know if she did. I'd rank that as a success, then. She's fired seven agents before you, three before they even sat down with her.

"And what about Carl. Did she fire him?"

"Oh, no, but . . ."

"But what?" Zach asked as he leaned back in his chair and glared at Natalie.

"Well, rumor has it that she was a large part of his decision to suddenly retire."

"You could have told me that before I went in there against Dragon Lady."

"And miss the fun? Nah, I couldn't do that. Besides, I wanted to see if you could handle her."

"Thanks for your confidence," Zach squeezed the bridge of his nose and hung his head.

"Are you alright?" Natalie leaned over.

"You wouldn't happen to have any Sudafed, would you?"

"I do. I'll be back in a jiffy. No charge."

Zach squeezed the bridge of his nose again, trying to relieve the sinus pain.

As morning moved into the afternoon, Sharon was pleased that most of the contracts had been resolved in the morning, for both trucks heading out and those being returned. The afternoon promised to be calm, so she could spend more time in the greenhouse nursing some of the more challenging plants. She felt like the flower whisperer, working on diagnosing the issues with each plant that had been put into the triage ward, as she called it. It bothered her that she could not save all of the plants, but she knew that sometimes, all that could be done was to turn a plant into compost or throw it out altogether.

"Barret's. Sharon speaking. How can I help you?" Sharon answered.

"Sharon, dear, I am so glad you answered the phone," a familiar voice noted.

"Mrs. Palmer? Is that you?"

"Yes, dear. I am worried about John. He is insisting that he has to get some plowing done this afternoon so he can plant tomorrow, and he's having a devil of a time getting his tractor started."

"Do you know what the problem might be?" Sharon had helped John Palmer many times in the past, as a neighbor and as a customer. It was always an adventure when he shuffled into the store, cantankerously grumbling that one of his machines had broken. Of course, everyone directed him to Sharon when he came in, which settled him down some.

"I think it's the battery. I told him to get a new one last year when he had trouble with it, but he insisted he could make it work."

"I remember talking to him about that."

"He probably didn't want to admit you were right. But he's out there swearing his fool head off. I'm worried he's going to have a heart attack over that damned tractor."

"Give me a minute," Sharon figured she could bring a new tractor battery and put it on their credit if the portable charger didn't bring it back to life. They did carry the old style batteries that the long timers in the area still used. She put Esther Palmer on hold and paged Rhonda.

"Right here," Rhonda said as she leaned into the counter. "I was taking a walk to stretch my legs and I was just coming to check on you. What's up?"

"It's my old neighbor, Mrs. Palmer. The old man is out fiddling with his tractor and she's worried he might work himself into a stroke." Sharon said as Rhonda scanned the building, and then peeked out into the plant shed, where Amy had started the afternoon watering rounds. "If I could bounce out there for an hour or so with the portable charger, I think I can take care of it," Sharon added.

"Shouldn't be a problem," Rhonda said as she looked over the desk. There was only one contract left for the day, and it looked like traffic was slowing down. "The charger is in truck number three, so why don't you take that one. I'll take the desk until Jack gets back."

"Thank you. I'm sure Mrs. Palmer will be very appreciative."

"So anyone due in this afternoon?" Rhonda glanced over to the desk.

"Just a couple from Rochester."

"Got it. Drive carefully."

By the time Sharon arrived at the farm, John Palmer had the cover of the engine of his faded red International Harvester tractor propped open like wings while Esther sat on the bench close to the house, fretting as she knitted the arms for another sweater. She waved as Sharon pulled up in the forest green pickup with the Barrett's logo on the doors. With charger in hand, Sharon dropped out of the truck and headed toward the quiet tractor and the grousing that spewed out from John Palmer, now buried up to his waist in the engine compartment. She knocked gently on the front of the tractor, hoping not to startle the old man into bumping his head.

John's legs twitched before he slid out of the engine. As he turned and faced Sharon, a thin smile creased his face briefly before it soured. He tugged at his hat to keep it from slipping off. "She called, eh? Six or twelve, then?" He growled and glared toward Esther, who wagged her finger in return.

"I know you didn't convert this old horse," Sharon pointed to the switch on the charger, which was already in the six-volt position.

"Eeh." Palmer waved at Sharon. "Not changing this one. These things last forever you know." He grunted, then winked at Sharon before shuffling toward the battery compartment on the tractor. With a deft twist of his screwdriver he pulled from his bib jeans, he popped open the box exposing the terminals. He stepped back and let her unravel the cables and connect up to the battery.

"It might take just a bit to juice it up," Sharon noted as she worked the grips to make sure they were secure.

"Eeh. We'll see." Palmer grumbled again. Sharon just tipped her head and headed over to visit Esther, who had already set her knitting aside. She started flipping through her Old Farmer's Almanac, then handed the book to Sharon, opened to the astronomy page.

"Last one before summer starts," Esther said as she looked up with wide, cloudy eyes. An impish grin creased her lips.

"Let me think about that. It might be nice to take an evening out to watch the shooting stars."

The tractor sputtered to life, catching Sharon's attention as a cloud of blue smoke spewed out its rusted stack and through the exhaust cap. She handed the Almanac back to Esther and hustled over to help. Before John could work himself out of the metal seat, Sharon reached into the engine compartment and disconnected the charger clips. Under his watchful eye, she sealed the battery box, closed the engine compartment, then tapped it closed before saluting the grizzled old farmer sitting high on his tractor. As he clutched the tractor into gear and headed out to plow the fields, Sharon wrapped up the jumper cables and returned them and the charger back into the truck cab.

A flock of turkeys, flushed by the tractor heading toward them, hustled their way out from the field then regrouped and formed a parade line next to the road, hens in front, poults bring up the rear, struggling to keep up. The line started to cross the road, but then the hens stopped as if waiting for the little ones just as a Ford Explorer rounded the corner and started up the hill toward the turkeys. Not sure if the vehicle was going to stop, Sharon scurried to the dirt shoulder to shoo the birds out of the road, but the stubborn turkeys remained, shifting their gaze between her and the oncoming vehicle. The Explorer slowed then came to a stop.

Sharon recognized the driver. It was Zach. She stared briefly then tipped her head as he opened the door, stepped out, and removed his dark sunglasses.

"Hey there. Have you met your neighbors?" Sharon started, pointing over to the tractor in the field. "That's Mr. Palmer. He's a real sweetheart. And that's Esther. She keeps him in line."

Zach waved to Esther, who had returned to her knitting. "Haven't met them yet. I was thinking of taking a walk tomorrow to explore — if this sinus headache will ever go away." He pinched the bridge of his nose.

"They're nice people. In fact, I think all of your neighbors are friendly once they get to know you."

"I see." Zach leaned on his car, trying not to stare at Sharon, but failed.

"By the way, there is some chamomile with lemon mint in the cupboard. Good mix for a sinus headache. A shot of cider vinegar could help, too."

"Thanks."

"You could have called this week, you know."

"I . . . I was thinking about it." Zach lowered his eyes.

"Too many raucous parties at night?" Sharon tilted her head and slipped out a smirk.

Zach sighed. "Well, I do remember why I called you last week. I went walking around the yard after you left and for the life of me, couldn't figure out what all the plants were. I was hoping that maybe you might be able to give me a little tour and some tips so I wouldn't kill anything that shouldn't be pulled out."

"I could, but I can't do it now. I've got to get back to the store," she pointed to the Barrett's truck pulled off the road.

"I couldn't remember anything today, anyway. Tomorrow?"

"That would work. I have to work the rest of the weekend, so I have to get a few things done first thing. I think I could swing over for a couple hours in the morning, though."

"That would be great. Can I make you dinner, as a thank you?"

Sharon wasn't sure what to make of the offer but it stirred something in her. "Let me think about that."

"That's fair," Zach slipped his sunglasses back on. "So, any more animals I need to watch out for before I get home?"

Sharon looked over her shoulder, then briefly over to Esther as she headed to her pick-up truck. Even at that distance, she could see the approval on the old woman's face. "I think you're good," she called over to Zach. "See you tomorrow."

Chapter 15

Zach sat at his small dining room table, nursing his coffee as the sun worked its way up behind the tree line, splashing pastel colors into the Saturday morning sunrise. His sinus headache that had built to a disabling headache by week's end finally dissipated and its accompanying fogginess had cleared. Outside of the headache, his week was productive, which made him feel good about where he stood with his new position. Of his eight new clients, most were cordial. Then there was Carolyn Appleton. He had handled some eccentrics in Chicago before, but none compared to the likes of Carolyn. He sensed she was hiding something from him, but that was her prerogative, as long as it wasn't illegal or immoral. He took his coffee out onto the deck for some fresh morning air and sunk into one of the wooden and worn Adirondack chairs he had retrieved from the shed. A light breeze coaxed the leafed out branches into a gentle sway around him. A few birds chirped and sang along their bouncy flight paths as they crossed from one tree to the next. At some point, he would hang a bird feeder to bring them in closer.

When he finished his coffee, he realized he had sufficient time for a quick morning walk to get his blood moving for the day. At some point, he resolved to start jogging again, but he figured starting out with some brisk walking might ease him into shape. He put on his sneakers and headed out, downhill, past the small graveyard and toward Palmer's farm. Once he passed the tree line, a wide hillside field spread out. In the distance, a turkey flock lazily moved along the top of the ridge, moving in a zigzag pattern until they disappeared into the woods. Further down the hill was a swampy area, across from John Palmer's farm, and on a crisp morning like this, it could be the perfect spot to see his first moose. He heard that there were a few that wandered down to this part of the state, and since there were several swaths of swampland just down the road, the perfect habitat he understood. When he was back in Chicago, he never took the opportunity to head up to Minnesota for some moose gazing.

Just down the hill, John Palmer's grayish-blue clapboard house rested by itself, looking as if something out of the prairies, small rooms spurring off to the sides, a bench and chairs by the side door near the gate out to the fields. The blue metal roof added to the rustic, worn down, but clean and well-maintained appearance. There did seem to be more activity out in the field than he remembered from last night — chickens, geese, horses, cows and even a grazing large goat with a bell around his neck that dinged as she popped her head up and stared directly at him. She eyed him closely as he approached, but then returned to grazing with several dings from her collar. Four black and white spotted cows worked through the hay near a circular stanchion, tossing flakes of hay as if rooting for something even sweeter underneath, and when they noticed him, started a gallop toward him.

Zach froze, not sure why the cows were coming at him at such a rapid pace. As they approached the electric fence, they slowed, then stopped within a foot of the barrier. Zach stiffened, staring at the cows with wide-open eyes, wondering what he had done to spook them.

"Mornin'," a voice called out from the barn. An old, bent-over man stepped out the open door and with the help of a cane, hobbled toward Zach. "You the new neighbor?" He tipped his floppy brimmed hat back with his free hand and beamed a welcoming, yellow-stained toothy smile."

"Yes, sir. Some nice animals you got there." Zach couldn't remember if he had met the old man last evening, but figured he probably didn't. The cows had turned and moseyed toward the farmer. There was no mistaking his accent; local, several generations in the dirt, as he heard someone at work say. Careful not to shock himself on the electric fence, the old man reached over with an open hand.

The oldest animal marched right over to him and started sniffing at his hand.

"Jenny's the mother. Millie's her daughter." He pointed to the smaller one. The difference in size was not that noticeable to Zach since they were all large animals in his book.

"Milkers?" Zach was guessing.

"Oh, no. Pets."

Zach was baffled. Pets?

"Watch this." Palmer motioned toward the house just as a kerchiefed older woman stepped out of the house with a plastic grocery bag full of something that caught the animals attention. The cows broke into a full gallop her way just as she emptied the bag. Zach wasn't positive but he thought he saw the youngest one breach a smile.

The woman rolled up the plastic bag and stuffed it into her plaid jacket as she carefully walked toward Zach. "Nice day," she said before mumbling something at the older fellow. He remembered her face from yesterday. "I seen you up at Sarah's house. And last night with Sharon, right?"

"Yes, Ma'am."

"I guess then you're the new neighbor, right?"

"Yes, Ma'am."

"Where you from?"

"Chicago."

"You like it here?"

"Very much, thank you. It's comfortable," Zach replied.

"Esther." She extended her frail hand toward Zach, who took it gently and shook.

"Zach Fields." He released her hand and looked toward the old farmer.

"That's John. He's a bit deaf. Don't see well, neither, but good enough. Can still take a deer when he wants. You hunt?"

"No, ma'am"

"He can manage a bow pretty well. He's a good man, though. I think I'll keep him a tad longer."

"I see."

"Sarah was quite a gardener, you know, but I guess you already saw that."

"I did." Zach was having trouble keeping up with Esther's thoughts jumping from one thing to another, but he still started to feel comfortable with her.

"It's so sad she passed at such a young age, you know."

"I've read about her."

"Quite a musician, you know. She used to come down here and serenade the cows. They sure liked that."

"Really. I didn't know that."

"And she'd come to watch the lights," Esther wagged her crooked finger toward the clearing across the road. "Over there. She'd just sit up on her car with her sister and watch the lights dance over there," Esther carefully turned and pointed out over the northern horizon, over her pastureland. Beyond the land, mountains rose in the distance. Zach thought he could still see lingering spring snow up top of them.

"That is quite a view." Zach drifted off with an image of Sharon and Sarah on the hood of the red

Jeep, gazing off into the dark, starry skies, probably sharing a bottle of wine between them, huddled in a blanket.

"Ever seen them?"

"Pardon?" Zach realized he hadn't been listening.

"The lights. Ever seen the lights?" Esther tipped her head and looked at Zach through one eye."

"No, I haven't. Too far south or west." He wasn't exactly sure what she was talking about, but it didn't seem to matter. He figured she'd get around to explaining at some point.

"They're quite a show when they get going. You know, the girls used to watch them all the time. Sharon's a nice girl. Have you met Sharon?"

"I have." Zach struggled with that turn in the conversation, thinking the question very odd since she had seen that Sharon and him did talk last night.

"She's helped us out quite a bit. It's a shame her sister passed. So young.

"I was the one in the . . ." Zach started but the figured he should just stay quiet, listen and try to keep up.

"She's a nice girl. She's single, you know. You married?" Esther asked, rather bluntly. She twitched her eyebrows and inspected Zach from head to toe.

"No. Just me."

"Can't do much better than her. She's a real hard worker, you know." Esther leaned forward, then whispered, "Don't tell him that I think she knows tractor better than he does," as she winked toward the old farmer.

"Moose down by the swamp this morning," John Palmer nosed into the conversation, derailing Esther.

"I was hoping to spot one," Zach nodded toward John then shrugged his shoulders toward Esther.

"You boys go look. Your breakfast will be ready in a few minutes, old man." Esther waved back, then turned toward the side door of the farmhouse.

"They hide out over on the other bank, you know. They like swamps. A lot of swamps here." The old farmer perched his eyebrows and let his cataract-covered eyes drift up with them. He pointed out over the far south of the property.

"That would be a sight I'd enjoy seeing. Not many of them out in Chicago."

"Might need to be here earlier, though. Dusk and dawn, that's when they move. A little late now. Blackflies ain't so bad then, you know. Once those bastards come out, the moose head back into the woods. Eeh, don't blame them."

Reflexively, Zach swatted at something buzzing near his face. He figured he'd have to head back shortly to get there before Sharon showed up, but when he looked up the hill, he gasped, thinking that it had become steeper and longer in just the few minutes ago he visited.

"So, young fellah. You gonna take those pines trees down?"

"Pine trees?"

"The big ones out front. They just make a mess, you know."

"Been thinking about it." Zach didn't want to admit that he was unaware of the pine trees and get the old man off on a rant.

"They're too weak for the winter. Just make a mess," Palmer groused. "Take the power out and you're stuck. But I got some wood here if you need it." Palmer pointed out to a stockpile of cut and split wood larger than Zach had ever seen.

"I appreciate the offer. Well, I've got to get to the yardwork. It's been nice meeting you." Zach offered his hand, but the old man had already touched his slouch hat and turned around.

"I gotta get to cleaning the barn, myself," Palmer said over his shoulder as he hobbled back toward the barn. "And fertilizer if you need it," he added, pointing to a large pile of manure riddled with hay.

"Have a good day with the young lady," Esther called out as she stood up from her bench.

"How does she know?" If Zach was not mistaken, she also winked at him. As he started back up the hill, he marveled at how much the view looked as if directly taken out of a travel catalogue. His leg muscles, especially his calves started to burn, reminding him how out of shape he was. By the time he reached the graveyard, he sucked in air and was close to breaking a sweat. When he reached the crest, he saw Sharon's Jeep pulling into the driveway. He sucked in another deep breath and tried to will the burn out of his legs to finish his walk. Still out of breath as he reached his driveway, he saw that Sharon was leaning on the tailgate, watching him struggle the last couple of steps.

"Hey there." Sharon's voice sounded like she was holding back a chuckle. She looked fresh as if ready for a long hike through the mountains. Her long sleeved t-shirt accentuated her athletic, attractive figure, with an earthy, unpretentious assist from her cut off shorts and well-toned legs.

"Hey. Just spending some time with the neighbors. I didn't realize how much they could talk." Zach leaned over to catch his breath. Sweat dribbled off his flushed face and had soaked through his t-shirt as well.

"Aren't quite used to these hills, are you?"

"No, I guess not. Not making a good first impression, am I?"

"To be honest, no, but it's not my first impression anyway." Sharon smiled as she stood up and tossed Zach a towel. It was that same, sweet, inviting smile that caught Zach's attention when he first saw her at the gas station. "You look terribly flushed. Why don't you fix yourself something to drink?"

"No argument here. Something I can get for you while I'm at it?"

"Coffee would be good. Iced. If you don't have it made, iced water would do. I thought I left ice trays, didn't I?"

"You got it. Why don't you have a seat on the deck and I'll be right out with it. I pulled out the chairs from the shed." Zach said and then headed toward the fence.

"I like it black," Sharon reminded Zach as he opened the gate for her. She was immediately drawn to the honey scented, blossoming shrub on the west side of the house that surrounded a dwarf cherry tree. Zach could tell there was something more than just adoration for the fragrance. He continued inside to get the drinks

When he stepped out onto the deck, Sharon had already sat down in the chair he had abandoned for his morning walk.

"You know there are moose around here."

"Palmer told me"

"And bears. And coyotes." Sharon turned her head back to look out over through the woods.

"This is the country, isn't it?" Zach handed Sharon the mug of coffee and sat down across from her.

"Just saying. Didn't think you had wildlife like that back in the big city."

"Well, you're kinda right there," Zach noted and settled back in the chair. "It was wildlife, just not the four-legged variety."

Through the corner of his eye, he regarded his welcomed visitor from her flowing auburn hair down to her sandaled feet. She crossed her legs at her ankles and slowly circled her foot in the air. Zach caught a whiff of her perfume. At least he thought it was. That really didn't matter. It smelled good.

"This is good coffee. Did you add something to it?"

"You like it? I sprinkled in some ginger and cinnamon when I brewed it. I like to experiment with different flavors."

"That's interesting. Sarah did too. Did you know she studied to be a chef?" Sharon cupped her hands around the mug.

"I didn't know that." Zach leaned back in his chair.

"So I am curious. What brought you all the way out east?" Sharon gazed at Zach.

"I guess I just needed a change. I felt like my life was getting a bit stale."

"No family? Just hit the map with a dart and move?"

"Something like that. Had a good offer in Nashua. Same firm. I figured, why not?" Zach chuckled. "You?"

Sharon didn't answer right away. A wistful expression paled her face as she stared toward the tall trees in the distance.

"Sarah and I always loved the mountains and the seashore. She moved out here first. Music brought her out. Some good schools up here. Once she had a taste of this area, there was no bringing her back. It didn't take long for her to start working on me as well."

"You didn't move in with her?"

"For a little while I found a place of my own. This was just too far from work and I would rather have something I didn't have to clean all the time. No. Too far from work. We were close, but not that close. At least then."

"So you aren't originally from here, either?" Zach struggled to keep the conversation going, but reckoned that this was what small talk was all about — repeating the same stuff over and over again. He sat back down in his chair, and while he sipped at his drink, forced himself to gaze out into the woods rather than let Sharon catch him gazing at her.

"Indiana." Sharon took another sip of her coffee.

"Really? I'm from the mid-west as well. Illinois."

"I know."

"Do you ever miss home?"

"Not really. This is home now. Besides, not much left back there and work keeps me pretty busy."

"You know, some time ago, you had said that if I had any questions . . ." Zach started, but then stopped to think about where he was going.

"Sure." Sharon said as she tipped her head into the back of the chair.

"If it's too much to talk about, I understand and you might think this a little strange, but I have been curious about Sarah since I looked at this house."

"I think I'm all right. It was hard to let go at first, but things have worked themselves out. Besides, there was nothing I could do about it."

"I understand."

"Well, where to start? Sarah spent her last days here in the house. She said that since they couldn't do anything more for her, she wanted to be in the comfort of her sanctuary. That's what she called this place, you know. I helped her out as best I could the last few months, practically moved in. I tried to keep up with the gardens, since she was just not physically up to it. But even at the end, she seemed content. Something about just being here, I'm sure."

"Did you spend any time here after she passed?

Sharon didn't respond right away. She continued to look out over the railing toward the woods. Zach wondered if his curiosity might be digging a deep hole.

"Not for any length of time, but I did have to clean up some. I just couldn't bring myself to stay more than a few hours. That's why so much stuff was left here when you bought the house."

"I think she's still here." Zach said, more under his breath than aloud.

"Sarah?"

Zach cringed. That he had admitted seeing Sarah might not have been wise, especially if she thought he was a little off center. But the barn door was open now. "Remember when you found me out in the shed?"

"Oh, yeah. You looked like you had seen a ghost."

"Sarah was out there. She was playing her oboe. Or at least, that's what I thought I heard." Sharon lifted her eyebrows and her expression turned skeptical. "That's why I went out there in the morning. I found the glasses she was wearing in my dream, which I have to admit, spooked the living hell right out of me. Especially since I don't remember ever seeing them before."

"You aren't one of those ghost hunters, are you?"

"No. I don't believe in ghosts or spirits, but Sarah seemed so real."

"And I assume she was playing Adagio for Strings?"

"As a matter of fact, she was."

Sharon stiffened as she leaned back into the chair, apparently stunned at Zach's revelation.

"I had not heard that melody since seeing the movie, but I would know those haunting strains anywhere. That was her favorite one, you know. I remember her trying so hard to play that in her last few days. It was a struggle for her at that point, but she felt she had to. It was her comfort melody. Sad, but comfortable."

"That's one of my favorites, too. I figured I must have been reading something about Sarah when I went to bed each night I had seen her, but it was weird."

"I'd say," Sharon noted. Zach read skepticism in her face.

"So, what do you think?" Zach asked with a straight face.

"Think about what?"

"About Sarah. Have you seen Sarah, I mean since she passed?"

"I really don't believe too much in that spirit stuff either, if that's what you are asking," Sharon seemed defensive. Zach figured she might be hiding something — as if she had seen Sarah, but didn't want to admit it.

"I know this sounds weird, but maybe if you spent some time here, you might see the same things I have. That is, of course, she is really a spirit or ghost or whatever they are called." Zach started to think he might have been too direct.

"Now that's a line I've never heard." Sharon looked at Zach with wide eyes, scanning him from head to toe. She then tilted her head and squinted one eye. "No funny business?"

"No funny business. I swear" Zach held up his hand. "It would be nice to know if you are seeing Sarah too, or if I am just going crazy. I've had some experiences recently that I just can't explain."

"So let me get this straight." Sharon twisted her eyebrows and looked puzzled. "You are having visions of my sister. Not dreams, actual visions."

"I'm not really sure what they are."

"And you want me to stay overnight to see if I have the same dreams?"

"Well —"

"You do realize that this is a bit out there, right?" Sharon straightened up before reaching into her fanny pack and pulling out a couple bags of trail mix. She handed one of the bags to Zach as her lips creased into a smile. "You sound like you're hungry. Have a healthy snack. We can take a walk and I'll think about it."

Really? He thought, stunned at her rather calm response. He wasn't sure if he had heard her correctly, but was not ready to push his luck any further. It was more than he could have hoped.

Chapter 16

Zach wasn't at all surprised that Sharon knew every planting around the house. She led him on the grand tour, starting with the lilacs at the front of the house. She explained that this distinctive strain of French Lilacs needed to be special ordered for her sister. Sarah had insisted they plant the shrubs next to the driveway, so she would be greeted by the fragrance when the panicles were in full bloom.

"You really need to do something about these." Sharon moved toward the roses that listed over the weathered cedar fence. Shoots of green from a vine tangled with the prickly rose branches, almost looking like the plants were symbiotic.

"Where do I start? It looks so tangled." Zach shrugged his shoulders and showed Sharon a puzzled, helpless look.

"Too late now. Pruning is a spring chore. You really need to give them a good trim to brighten them up some."

"I've looked pretty closely and those thorns are as sharp as knives."

"Oh, no worries," Sharon smiled enough to narrow her eyes. "I can show you how later, but then I get to watch. You do have pruning shears, don't you?" Her devilish grin warned him it was bound to be somewhere between brutal and masochistic.

"I don't think so."

"We've got them at the store. Next time you are in, I can fix you up." Sharon said as she stepped away from the roses. She maneuvered to an open area near the fence, then stopped and stared. Without a word, she turned back and headed toward her Jeep. "Stay here."

Zach watched her open the tailgate and pull out a partly filled out shrub about a foot tall in a gallon container. The leaves were a gleaming emerald.

"I thought so. This will be perfect right here," she said as she returned with the plant and a trowel. She knelt down and started digging, moving aside soil effortlessly.

"That looks like it's pretty rich. Could I ask . . .?"

"Clethra. Consider it a housewarming gift," she said as she caressed the plant and carefully extracted it from the dark green plastic pot.

"Thank you," Zach mumbled as Sharon set the plant down into the hole, then worked the soil in and around the shrub, tamping it down with her open hands.

"You will really thank me when this blossoms. The fragrance is absolutely heavenly." She rearranged the partly decayed oak leaves to cover the base. As she looked up, she brushed off her hands.

"I just hope I don't disappoint you with my brown thumb."

"You won't. I'm a good teacher." Sharon stood up on her own before Zach could offer her a hand. She dropped the trowel into the empty pot, moved it behind the shrub, then headed toward the mounds of mint.

"This lavender is exquisite, don't you think?" She bent over and weaved her hands through the branches of lavender at the end of each row, as if bathing her long, narrow fingers in the shrubs before effortlessly pruning a few scraggly branches away. She patted the stand as if it were a pet, then brought her hands to her face and inhaled the aroma deeply. An inviting smile graced her face, pushing up her eyes into smiles as well.

"Sure. Lavender." Zach made a mental note of the grayish plant with tiny purple blossoms. He wondered if he needed a notebook rather than rely on memory, which was getting a little defocused because of Sharon.

"Did you know that lavender is one of the essential oils for aromatherapy?" She stepped closer to Zach and invited him to smell the oil on her hands. With her standing less than an arm's length away, Zach inhaled as she brushed her fingers across his nose. Her palm moved close enough to his lips that he could have kissed it, but rather he just allowed the aroma of the plant to waft into his sinuses. She tipped her head, smiled, and added, "Relaxing, isn't it,"

It wasn't relaxation that Zach felt at that particular moment, but before he could say anything, Sharon moved away toward the next planting, skipping like a kid through a candy store. She squatted down next to the planting of peonies, set in an "v" shape, then explained it was Sarah's whimsy to have a garden that literally pointed true north. The blossoms were nothing more than golf-ball shaped emerald globes with a hint of pink peeking out near their centers. Sharon weaved her hands gently along the stand of forest green leaves, then bent over and inhaled the fragrance that seeped out of the buds and seemed to be hovering in the area.

"These little girls should be staked, you know."

"I'll keep that in mind." Zach tried to focus and take mental notes, but Sharon's presence was making it nearly impossible to concentrate.

"When these blossom, they'll be the size of dinner plates, and if you don't prop them up, they'll certainly make a mess. It's an old gardener's tale — there's a storm brewing when they open up. You are lucky this last one didn't roll in later than it did," she commented as she moved on, leading Zach toward the tentacle-like vine covered round trellis that stood like a grand entrance into the back yard where she detailed even more of what was planted. A series of raised gardens lined the back cedar fence, sadly choking under a healthy set of weeds. Yet amidst the weeds, Sharon pointed out a pomegranate bush Sarah so wanted that Sharon had special ordered for her, and a set of four Crandall black current shrubs, already filled with a thick cloud of yellow blossoms.

"There is one more spot that I'd like to visit," Sharon noted as they finished perusing the gardens. There was a sparkle in her eye when she mentioned it.

"I'm game. Where?"

"It's out in the woods. Not that far. Through that gate and over toward the right. Sarah enjoyed heading out there to play her oboe for the animals."

"Boots?"

"Yeah, you should. It's not a clear path."

Zach retreated to the garage to change into his hiking boots and caught up with Sharon just outside the fence. As she dodged the low hemlock branches and deftly stepped over protruding rocks, exposed tree roots, and ruts in an old sunken logging road, Zach followed. She finally stopped at a clearing and froze for a moment beneath an opening in the forest canopy. Sunlight shimmered down and through onto a U-shaped stonewall that enclosed a floor of thick pine needles. When Zach caught up, Sharon took one more step forward, turned her head up and looked through the boughs of the trees, but then groaned and started to fall backwards.

Zach reacted. He leaned forward, opened his arms and caught her. He closed his arms just in time to catch her armpits in the crooks of his elbows. Straining to keep her from falling onto the forest floor, he tried to hoist her up gently for better balance, but her t-shirt rode up along his arms and his hands slipped up and rested squarely on her firm breasts.

Sharon's nipples stiffened in his hands. Zach froze. Moving methodically forward as he cradled her armpits, he lifted her to vertical, all the while straining not to move a muscle in his hands.

"I didn't mean . . . are you alright." he asked, blushing as he felt her regain her footing and lift the weight off his arms. As Sharon slowly turned in his grasp, her breasts brushed across the inside of his arm. She stopped turning when her nose touched his and looked him squarely in his eyes.

"Uh-huh. But I thought you agreed to no funny business." Her voice was breathy and low.

"I . . . I was just . . ." Zach struggled to find the words. "I was just reacting. I didn't want you to fall. It was not intentional, I swear."

"It's okay, Zach. Really." Sharon laughed weakly. She touched his nose with her finger, then slid it down and pressed it against his lips for a second. She placed her hands against his chest and drew closer for a brief closed-lip kiss. "Thanks for catching me."

"You're welcome," Zach said softly voice, continuing to hold Sharon close as he stared into her eyes. She stirred a feeling that he thought lost. He knew that he should let her go, but holding her felt comfortable. Very comfortable.

"I guess you just swept me off my feet," Sharon whispered as she dropped her head onto his shoulder. She then slowly pulled away, adjusting her t-shirt to cover her bare midriff.

"I didn't expect you to be the one to fall out here. You were about to show me?" he asked as he slipped his arms down to her hips.

"Over here." She tilted her head, cracked a grin, and took Zach's hand, pulling slowly. Hand-in-hand, they walked into the clearing where three stumps stood, centered between the three walls. Sharon let Zach's hand go before she seemed to dance toward the middle stump. She then spun like a ballerina and sat down.

"This is where Sarah liked to sit and play for the animals." Sharon shrugged her shoulders and beamed as she looked about the treetops. "Sometimes she would bring her flute instead to play to the birds. They would come and sit on some of those branches as they listened. Some of them sang with her."

"Did you ever come out to listen?" Zach moved closer and sat on the stump next to Sharon. He scanned towards the pine trees where a blue colored bird started to warble.

"Sometimes. Most of the time she wanted to be alone. She said she needed time communing with nature to let her creative juices flow."

"I've heard artists like to do that." Zach heard a couple of chickadees join the warbler as he placed his arm around her back and his hand on her shoulder. Without resisting, she leaned into his shoulder again.

"Did you know she wrote poems as well? There was one that I still remember that sums up how she felt out here."

"No, I didn't."

"Lean back and close your eyes and listen," Sharon insisted. Zach complied.

> "I meant to do my work by three,
> But a passerine sang in the apple tree.
> And one by one, as if by cue
> More melodies then filtered through
> My open window, to my ears
> I thought how I have wasted years
> Just sitting in my sterile room,
> Silent, as in a mother's womb.
> Yet out there majestic symphonies flow
> So what could I do but laugh and go?"

While Sharon was reciting the poem, Zach heard a rustling nearby. He looked up and saw a doe and a pair of spotted fawns ambling toward them, ears perked forward, as if listening to Sharon.

"Well, I'll be," Zach whispered. Sharon carefully sat up and reached out with her open hand. The doe stalked toward her, one step at a time, its tail twitching. It stopped and looked carefully at Zach, then continued toward Sharon until she could reach the doe's muzzle. She stroked the doe's face for a moment before it lifted its head and gazed into Sharon's eyes. The mother then slowly turned around, ambled back to her babies. The fawns grew curious, but the mother nudged them back, and as a family, they moved on, back into the woods from where they came.

"That was quite a poem. You said Sarah composed it out here?"

"Yeah. She shared it with me last year, just before the cancer metastasized. It holds a special place in my heart to remember how her expression mellowed as she recited it. It reminds me about how we always seem to be in a rush all the time but need to slow down once in a while." Sharon's face relaxed and her eyes hooded. She leaned back and let the afternoon sunshine spill onto her face.

"How's your ankle?"

"It's fine. No twist, I just slipped off the rock. Seems odd, though. I've never had that problem before."

"Well, I'm fortunate to have been there to catch you." Zach felt his face flush. "I really appreciate you showing me this. I don't think I would have stumbled across all of this out on my own. I surely wouldn't know the story behind it all."

"The pleasure was mine. It's nice to reminisce." Sharon worked herself back vertical. A playful expression grew on Sharon's face as she stood up, close enough that Zach felt her warmth again. "I think I've thought about it."

"Thought about what?"

"Dinner. I think I'll let you make me dinner. It's the least you could do after groping me."

Zach wasn't sure how to take her comment, but her smirk hinted that it was meant more as a joke. "Is salmon to your liking?"

"It is, but it all depends how you make it. I have very discriminating taste." She extended her hands and pulled Zach up to her.

As Zach worked in the kitchen preparing dinner, Sharon monitored closely, perched on a tall stool, a concerned expression growing on her face. She cocked her head each time Zach glanced over for approval; first as he seasoned the fish, then as he prepared the pan and finally as he cut the lettuce for the salad. When the fish started to sear, he sensed her consternation, turned, and asked, "Okay, I give up. What am I doing wrong?"

"I would do it a little differently, that's all."

"It's not too late. What do I need to do differently?" Zach questioned.

"Let me taste." She vaulted up from her chair and stood next to Zach as he forked a small piece of the fish out from the pan and offered it to her. She wrapped her hand around Zach's, then pulled it to her waiting mouth, closed her eyes and evaluated the taste.

After a minute of looking at the ceiling, as if paging through a recipe in her mind, Sharon said, "Needs turmeric. But just a sprinkle." She reached toward the spice rack, uncapped the unlabeled bottle with orange powder and gently tapped it on the bottom. "Like that."

"Okay. And the salad?"

"Tomatoes?"

"Yup."

"And celery?"

"Got that too."

"And you really should add some snow peas. That would sweeten it up some."

"In the fridge. Believe it or not, I think I have all of those." Zach realized he was starting to sweat from the pan's heat. He pressed down on the fish with a spatula as Sharon opened the refrigerator door and squatted down to the crisper. Zach noticed her shirt start to ride up again, exposing the smooth small of her back.

"You aren't staring again are you?" Sharon obviously caught his glance.

"No. Just watching to make sure you didn't fall again. You seem to have a bit of a balance problem lately." Zach chuckled as he went back to the pan and turned the filets over.

"Funny boy," Sharon stood up with the vegetables in her hands. On the counter next to Zach, she quartered the tomatoes and long sliced the celery, added the snow pea pods, and then mixed the salad together before sprinkling a film of Italian dressing over the top. She finished setting the table, then sat down and waited to be served.

Zach scooped out the salmon onto a separate plate, turned the gas off to the stove, added sprigs of parsley, then brought the dinner over and set it down in front of Sharon.

"Doesn't look too bad. Decent start," Sharon noted as she slipped a filet onto her plate. She scooped up some salad and placed it next to her entrée.

As Zach sat down, he watched as she split off a flake of salmon and slipped it into her mouth. He let her swallow before asking, "Well? Does it pass muster?"

Sharon nodded. She took a sip of the white wine she had poured for the two of them, then waved her fork at Zach as she swallowed. "It'll pass. I think I'll let you cook for me again."

When they were done with dinner, Zach cleaned up as Sharon stepped out onto the deck. Through the screen, he could hear her singing an aria he thought unfamiliar. Her gentle, melodic voice rose and fell gracefully, and he caught himself thinking about holding her warm body close as they made love through the night. He imagined brushing his hands over her curves as she lay in his bed, gently at first then more firmly massaging her back.

He wondered if he might be wistfully thinking ahead of where they really were, but startled as he realized Sharon had come back into the house, slipped in behind him and had stopped by the stove. Making herself at home, she started the burner under the teakettle, then started looking through the cabinets. "You do have some chamomile tea up here someplace?"

"I don't know," Zach wiped his hands on a green dishtowel, then turned to help.

"Found it. And, by the way, you should really consider cleaning up this stove a little better if you are going to invite people over for dinner. Especially if you want to impress them."

"Does that mean you are going to stay?"

"Maybe." Sharon just tilted her head and flashed a thin-lipped smile as the teakettle started a shrill whistle. "I need to get some things from my car. Would you be a gentleman and pour my tea?"

"Sure." Zach wondered if she had planned to stay all along and was just being coy. As Sharon headed out to her car, he finished placing all the dinner plates into the dishwasher, then dropped the tea bags into the cups, and let them steep after pouring in the boiling water.

"It's such a nice evening," Sharon said as she came back into the house. She had slipped on a navy blue St. Anselm College sweatshirt. "What do you say we take this out onto the deck?"

Zach handed her one of the cups, then followed her with his eyes as she sauntered out toward the deck. Once Zach started the dishwasher, he took his cup and joined her.

"Sarah loved these evenings you know." Sharon had already reclined into one of the Adirondack chairs by the time Zach stepped out onto the porch. "The peepers over there in the swamp. The whippoorwills chattering in the distance. You know in a month, lightning bugs will be dancing in the sky, their flashers out to awe us with their streaks. And the bats. They really are quite intriguing to watch at dusk."

"Bats?"

"Harmless." Sharon shook her head and tweaked a grin.

"You spent a lot of time out here with Sarah, didn't you?" Zach sipped at his tea.

"All the time. Sometimes even in the winter."

"Really?"

"Not in a blizzard mind you, but when a light snow is falling it's really quite relaxing."

"I see." Zach looked up at the stars that started to emerge in the twilight. He could feel the chamomile start to work its way through his muscles, as if extracting all the tension that had built up through the week. Once the tea worked up his spine, he could feel his mind start to fog and his eyes grow heavy.

"So let me see if I have this straight," Sharon sat up in her chair and stared at Zach. "You have been seeing my sister over these past two weeks. My dead sister."

"I don't believe in ghosts, but I have to admit, they have been quite interactive."

"Really? Interactive?"

"Yes."

"So you've been more than just talking with her?

"Let me clarify, the conversations have been lively. Nothing more." Zach hoped the evening's darkness hid his embarrassed blushing.

"Hmm. And you said you don't believe in ghosts," Sharon cracked a wry grin as she sipped on her tea.

"Your sister is making it difficult to maintain that thought. Very difficult."

"My sister? You do have quite an imagination." Sharon smiled broadly, eyeing Zach while she finished her tea.

"So if you have not seen her, maybe I'm just dealing with some pretty vivid dreams then."

"Maybe so. By the way, you do have a spot for a guest, don't you? I think the small room in front would be fine."

"I've got a pullout in there, but it hasn't been opened in a while."

"You at least have a sleeping bag, don't you?"

"I may be batchin' it, but I'm not that crude. I can fish out some sheets for you," Zach said as he got up and slid open the screen to the French doors. "I think I might even have a pillow."

Sharon tilted her head back and smiled. "You didn't expect more for a first date now, did you?"

"I guess not," Zach mumbled as he stood up, stretched and headed into the house and upstairs to prepare Sharon's room.

Once Sharon had settled into the guest room, she closed the door and wished Zach good dreams with an impish grin. Disappointed, Zach moped down the short hallway, closed his door, undressed and slipped under his covers. He folded his hands together underneath his head and stared up at the ceiling. He accepted that he really shouldn't have expected more than what happened, even if the day seemed to be headed that way. He wondered if revealing that he thought he had seen Sarah was a little too open, but he figured they could talk more in the morning, especially if Sharon did have a visit from her sister. His eyes drooped closed as he rolled over on his left side, then over on his stomach, before fluffing up his pillow and drifting off to sleep.

Zach woke up on a sweat soaked sheet as the sun peeked through the sheer curtain covering his east window. When he heard bacon sizzling downstairs, he realized that Sharon must have woken before him and had already started breakfast. He rolled out of bed, threw on a pair of running shorts and a t-shirt and headed downstairs. As he stepped into the kitchen, he saw that Sharon was already dressed for work, cooking at the stove, with coffee already brewed.

"Oh, hi there." Sharon turned and cocked her head enough for Zach to see her smirk.

"I thought that you wanted me to cook?" Zach rubbed the sleep from his eyes. Sharon had already stuffed her sweatshirt into a leftover plastic grocery bag.

"I did, but I couldn't wait for you to finally wake up. You certainly didn't look like you were getting up any time soon I need to get going."

"You didn't."

"I'll never tell," She winked and turned back to the frying pan, slipped out the bacon from the pan onto a paper towel covered plate, then replaced the strips with a bowl full of lightly beaten eggs. The eggs sizzled immediately. "But you do look rather cute while you are sleeping all cuddled up with those pillows."

Zach didn't know whether she meant to be complimentary or critical. He slipped in behind Sharon, back to her back, and poured two cups of coffee. He could hear Sharon humming Adagio while she mixed sautéed onions into the congealing eggs. He thought he brushed Sharon as he passed, wondering if she would recoil or respond. She did neither. Setting the cups onto the table, he turned and leaned into the corner of the wall to watch Sharon finish preparing their plates.

"Did you see Sarah last night?" Zach asked, not sure if he really wanted an answer.

"You saw her again last night?"

"I guess that means you didn't."

"How about this —" Sharon avoided the question as she scooped out a large helping of scrambled eggs and ladled it onto a plate. She glanced at Zach as she topped the eggs with three strips of bacon and an inviting helping of home fries. "Why don't you take these plates over to the table and we can talk after we have something quick to eat, okay? You do remember this girl works on weekends."

Zach complied, taking the plates from Sharon. As he set them on the table, he noticed the bacon was crispy, just how he liked it. The eggs were fluffy yellow and speckled with an aromatic spice that he couldn't place. The red potato home fries looked like they had been scraped right out of his mother's pan, as close to blackened as they could be without being burned. He took a quick sip of coffee as Sharon sat down and forked some eggs for herself.

"Not bad. What do you think?" Sharon asked. She flipped her hair back over her shoulder.

"I have never complained about breakfast being made for me." Just the aroma of breakfast had already started his stomach juices churning. He took a fork-full of the eggs and recognized the rosemary tang she had used. He took two more. They were a perfect texture; neither runny nor dry. "This is good. I know this is cliché but it is just like my mother used to make."

"So tell me. You did or did not see my sister last night?" She swirled her fork in Zach's direction.

"Not last night. I think the chamomile did me in. Listen, I don't believe in ghosts, nor do I have any answers as to why I keep dreaming about your sister."

"I see. Are you thinking I might have some answers?"

"Yes, I do. Especially since she mentioned that you might be interested in me."

"Really? Then tell me, Sherlock. What makes you think that?" Sharon cracked a wry grin as she sipped on her coffee, then continued eating, unable to remove the grin from her face.

"Your sister told me. So, are you interested or is it just a figment of my imagination that you are?"

"Let me think about that," she winked and finished eating. When done, she got up then set her dishes into the deep sink. As she did, Zach leaned over and opened the French Doors, where just outside clusters of lavender flowers as tiny as pinpricks were blossoming and oozing a cloud of sweet fragrance.

"I do need to get moving. Busy weekend at the nursery, you know." Sharon turned around and tipped her head back to let the aroma of the lilac fill her nose.

Zach plopped into his chair. He wasn't sure if it he had been too direct, or if Sharon was just playing hard to get. He sipped at his coffee and stared out past the French doors and into the cluster of lavender flowers on the blossoming lilac bush. He secretly hoped she was just playing hard to get and his best Eeyore would convince her to stay.

"It's like perfume when the Miss Kim is in bloom, isn't it," Sharon commented, She moved closer and hovered over him. As she placed her hand on his shoulder, Zach stood and they were face-to-face. Leaning into him, she laid her head on his shoulder for a moment, then locked her gaze into his eyes.

"Do you really have to go? Don't you need help with anything?" Zach stammered, trying to extend the moment.

"I'm good, really." She leaned into him and kissed him deeper than before, then turned and headed toward the door. "Thanks for dinner. Keep in touch, okay?"

"Sure," he replied, half-heartedly as Sharon closed the door behind her. In a minute, she was gone, leaving Zach in the house, alone, with dishes that needed attention.

Chapter 17

Julian sat nervously in his tiny practice room at the Conservatory, slowly disassembling his clarinet, setting each of the pieces into its respective red felt padded location in the case. He inspected the reed on the mouthpiece and noticed the chips in the thin wood that must have been the reason why this session was so difficult to finish without squawking an off-tone note. He closed the case, sighed and buried his head in his hands, until he sensed someone looking at him. As he secured the small locks on the case, he looked toward the doorway.

"Hey, Julian. Tough practice, huh?" Liza Schumann asked as she stepped into the small beige room. She sat down in the metal folding chair next to him,

"Yeah. Tough practice. I think I need to change out these reeds."

"How are you doing?" Liza slipped her arm around his narrow shoulders.

"Not well. I talked with Katie yesterday."

"You were able to get hold of her, then?"

"It wasn't easy. Seems she's found herself a new flame in Philadelphia, and it was rough getting through him. The jealous type, I guess."

"I know it was hard, but we have to get to the bottom of all this."

"She finally admitted she was the one Vincent had come to see that night. She sent him away since he was so drunk he could barely walk."

"I'm sorry, Julian." Liza felt torn between elation for Sharon and grief for Julian.

"I couldn't believe it myself. I could hear her sobbing when I told her it wasn't for me, but that Carolyn was accusing Sharon. She liked Sharon."

"Have you spoken to Carolyn yet?"

"Couldn't get to Carolyn, so I talked with Judith. Something gnawed at my soul about what Carolyn had put together as a sequence of events. It made me think more about when Katie left. It was just before that when she wanted to break up with me, so I had to ask her."

"I know it hurts, but I'm glad you did. I think that was the missing piece we all needed."

"I have another appointment with Carolyn the day after tomorrow to discuss my resignation. I can finish up talking with her then."

"Resignation?"

"I'm thinking of heading out west. Chicago. Maybe even Denver."

"Why?"

"I can't stay here. Not with this hanging over my head."

"But it's not your fault, Julian." Liza dropped her arm and skootched in front of Julian. "She left you even before this all happened."

"It was because of him she left me. I'm thinking that she left mostly because I confronted her when I found a pill bottle with cocaine powder in a coat that she was trying to hide from me. At least I think it was. I should have been more attentive to the signs and maybe taken more action. Maybe I should have been a bit more understanding."

"How could you have known?"

"The signs were there. She was spending more nights away from home, and always seemed to be hiding things from me. She said a girlfriend was having a rough time and needed some consoling. I thought it might be Sharon or Sarah, but never followed through. And she seemed more paranoid by the day. He probably offered her more than a second chair clarinet could ever dream of giving her."

"We're all with you Julian. You don't have to leave."

Julian looked up at Liza with tear-filled eyes. She could see his heartbreak ripping at his usually cherubic face. "I appreciate that, but I'm a wreck. I can't seem to focus on the music and it seems like

I'm always feeling a bit melancholy over losing her. Nothing seems to help."

"I'm thinking once you talk to Carolyn, you will feel better. It will be off your chest."

Julian bent his head back and wiped the tears from his cheeks. Liza offered a tissue from her pocket to help. "I certainly hope you're right. I've been chewing on my reeds so much because of my nerves that I'm about to go broke." Julian cracked one of his infectious smiles that drew a tear to dribble out onto Liza's cheek. More tears rolled down his cheeks and soaked his shoulders.

"That's the Julian I know. Now give me that resignation letter before I have to physically rip it out of your pocket."

Carolyn Appleton glared at her business advisor, her jaw shaking more than the iced tumbler half filled with rye whiskey. She took a long draw on her glass and set the glass on the polished end table next to her high-backed chair. Her hair was askew around her blanched face and there were dark rings under her eyes, which fit the mood of her dimly lit parlor.

"You really believe that it was Julian's girlfriend chasing Vincent? You really believe it was her?" Carolyn's bloodshot eyes were wide in amazement.

"I talked to Julian today. That child is such a wreck over this that he wanted to resign and go hide out west somewhere."

"And pray tell, what was her name?"

"Katie. It was Katie."

"Katie. And what was Katie like?" Carolyn pried. After a week under a psychiatrist's care, Judith thought that Carolyn was worse off —worse than she had ever seen her. The excessive drinking was surely not helping, but keeping Carolyn out of the bottle at this point was proving futile at best. Even in the days following Vincent's accident, she did not look as close to death as she looked now.

"Small, blonde, not much for boobs as far as I remember."

"And you want me to believe that Vincent went chasing after her? A skinny little whore?"

"It's not whether you want to believe it or not. I could tell by the look on that boy's face that he was telling me the truth."

"And is there any corroboration to that story?" Carolyn grew agitated as she downed the rest of her drink then slammed the glass down on the table. She rolled her head back and stared at the chandelier that hung gaudily from her high ceiling. "Oh, Vincent. How could you?"

"There are others in the school that had mentioned he was seen with her several times."

"What was this gold digger's attraction to Vincent?" Carolyn lifted the framed photograph of Vincent she kept on her end table and stared absently at his thin, black mustache.

"She left Julian for Vincent," Judith swallowed hard as she tried to explain what Julian had revealed. "Drugs were a part of it. Julian found some powder in Katie's things. He thought it was cocaine, but Helen told me that the police sergeant you had sent her to talk to indicated that he was not only drunk, but also had traces of Vicodin in his blood. But I don't recall him using Vicodin, Carolyn, do you?"

"No." Carolyn withdrew.

"Did you have Vicodin?"

"So where did he get the Vicodin?"

Carolyn remained silent. Judith could see that she was growing more angry with her questions. Finally, it struck her that she remembered an empty bottle in the oboe case.

"It was Sarah. He was stealing it from Sarah, wasn't he?"

Carolyn slammed the picture hard enough down on her end table that the glass in the frame shattered. Judith jumped and immediately cleaned up the glass chards.

"How could you do such a thing, Vincent? How could you hurt me so?" Carolyn dropped her head to her chest, then curled up into her chair and sobbed openly. After dumping the glass into a wastebasket, Judith grabbed a box of tissues and consoled her client.

By the end of the month, Zach felt like he was finally on top of his workload. There were long hours and some weekends, but he felt it was worth the sacrifice. He had developed good relationships with most of his clients and felt that he understood the details of each portfolio so he could keep providing timely and useful information. It was more work for him, but since the economy had tanked, and so many people had lost a good portion of their investments, he had to provide the right focus for them.

He had felt appreciated by most of his clients with one exception. Carolyn Appleton, Director of the Music Conservatory. Zach was starting to think that there would be no pleasing her regardless of what he did. She had kept her thoughts and intents close to her chest, especially her operation of the Conservatory, leaving him to guess at what she expected from him. Even when his guesses were close, he couldn't tell since she was so stone faced and unresponsive. When she was there. The past two meetings he had were with Judith Rhodes rather than Carolyn, which seemed strange. It was all legitimate, power of attorney and all, but he found the discussions rather stilted since Judith seemed even more furtive than Carolyn had been.

He wanted to discuss some of the odd transactions directly with Carolyn, relatively large payments to 'cash.' But there was no cracking Judith. Although it wasn't his place to drive that either. All he could do with his position was raise the concern. When Judith simply acknowledged that she would relay the message to Carolyn, he felt pressing would be fruitless.

Even though he did all he could legally, his questions would go unanswered until Carolyn was feeling better. It still bothered him that something, possibly something borderline illegal, was going on. He closed up the Appleton file, then file it in the vault. For some reason, his sideward glance was drawn to the "T" file.

Tanchak. Sarah had not visited for over a month. No, she was just a dream, he thought. All of the encounters had a logical explanation; not noticing things on the walkthrough, fever spikes, reading her obituary before heading to bed. And since he hadn't dreamed about Sarah for a few weeks, and he hadn't thought about her in that time period, it made sense. Maybe it was just the final purge of Brenda's memory.

He hadn't seen much of Sharon either since that one day a few weeks back, although the thought did cross his mind to head to the nursery and just browse through and hoped she would notice him. She hadn't dropped by, but that was understandable since he figured she had probably been working long hours like him, including weekends. After all, it was prime gardening season. He did drop by Barrett's a couple of times on the weekend, but the place was crawling with so many people that it was hard to catch Sharon's attention long enough to even wave, no less suggest dinner after work.

He wondered if their relationship was nothing more than casual. After all, when she did spend the night, it was in a separate room. Yeah, it was only after a couple times of seeing her. Maybe he was just destined to remain single and searching for the right person. Rather than struggling with his feelings any more, he walked by the file, scanned out and let the vault door seal behind him.

"Hey, Zach. You look pretty beat. Too much partying on the weekends?" Natalie caught his attention as he walked by her cube.

"No parties, just working," Zach stopped in mid-stride, then stepped inside Natalie's space and collapsed into a chair against the partition.

"Hmm. Been burnin' the candle too much then?"

"I guess just focused on getting my feet on the ground."

"Maybe obsessed rather than focused," Natalie noted as she started to flip through her phone registry.

"Maybe," Zach sensed where Natalie was headed. "You know, I was thinking. Some time ago, you mentioned the Tanchak file."

"I believe it was the other way around," Natalie mumbled as she stopped at a page in her registry and started writing down a phone number.

"You handled that case, didn't you?"

"Not totally correct. Actually, I only tied up the loose ends when I took it over from Carl, the guy you replaced."

"Is there something more I should know about Carl and Carolyn Appleton? After all, I am struggling with her portfolio. She's sending Judith Rhodes now, who seems a little spooky to me."

"So Appleton's got your knickers in a twist?" Zach nodded.

"Well, I'm not sure if there is much to tell about her portfolio, and I think we need to be a little more open here. It's not her file that you are struggling with, is it?"

"Well, I tripped across something last weekend that seemed odd."

"In the file?"

"No, at home. I was tidying up some books at home and noticed that there was an odd connection between Appleton and Sarah Tanchak, more than just working at the Conservatory. A couple of cryptic notes, a couple of letters. Nothing that made much sense. The dots were too random for me to connect, so I thought you might be able to help."

Natalie stopped what she had been fidgeting with and faced Zach directly. Her expression was icy cold.

"Let me put it to you this way," Natalie started, narrowing her eyes until they were almost closed. Her voice dropped to a whisper. "Your project, that old battle-axe Appleton, owns the Conservatory where Sarah Tanchak taught and spent her last performing years, kind of like a contractor to other music groups, if you don't mind the analogy. Carl and I tried to convince her to do something Sarah's twin sister Sharon, since otherwise the house would have to be sold to pay off debts. That's simply the way probate works here. Instead, the frumpy old coot wouldn't budge."

"There seems to be something more, though." Zach leaned back in the chair and sighed. "Was Carl involved more than just professionally?"

"Oh, no. Carl was old enough to be Sharon's father," Natalie noted.

"No I mean with Appleton," Zach deflected.

"Oh, God no. It got to the point where Carl didn't even want to deal with her."

"So you know Sharon?"

"Poor girl was devastated by selling the house. She agonized for months about it. I wished I could have helped her more, but I was bound by rules, you know. I think she did finally buck up and come out of it." Natalie's eyebrow twitched.

"I see," Zach noted as his thoughts drifted toward Sharon. He wondered if there was something more that he could do to help her out. Or should do.

"So let's talk. You settled in enough at this point?" Natalie asked as she fondled the index card in her hand.

"Pretty much."

"Here. Take this and give Amelia a call. You look like you would welcome a distraction." Natalie handed Zach one of her business cards with Amelia's phone number on the back of it.

"I don't think it will work." Zach handed the card back.

"Really?" Natalie smirked as a knowing expression grew on her face. "You're seeing somebody, aren't you?"

"You might say that."

"It's Sharon, isn't it?"

Zach was silent.

"I see." Natalie winked.

"It's not like that."

"Don't get me wrong, Zach. I'm happy for you. Amelia might be disappointed, but she'll get over it."

"Thanks," Zach mumbled as he headed back to his cube. He dropped into the seat at his desk and looked at the day's mail had been dropped in a pile on his desk. Most of it was advertisements for training sessions on the new tax laws. He swept those aside, logged back into his computer and checked his calendar for his afternoon appointments.

Zach left work early for a change. He grabbed the mail when he got home and headed into his house. As he fumbled through the mail, he saw three bills, a flyer from Barrett's , and a flyer from the local real estate agent listing all the houses that had been sold in the area over the past month. Not that he cared, although he did take the time to examine the prices and noticed that most of the houses sold for a little less than what he'd paid for this one. The Barrett's flyer listed a host of garden supplies; rakes, shovels, hoses, bird seed. And shrubs. Three pages of shrubs, all in full bloom.

Once inside, he dropped the mail on the table, then turned on the burner under the teakettle to let the water boil while he headed upstairs to change into more comfortable clothes. The kettle started its obnoxious whistling just as he got back into the kitchen. He dropped a teabag into his Chicago Bears mug and let it steep for a couple minutes. On the table next to his mug sat the pile of mail, the Barrett's flyer still on top. He flipped it over and noticed that there was a group picture of all the Barrett's employees. Sharon was right in the middle, standing in the back, her inviting smile, slightly cocked head, and hair tied back in a ponytail. No note on the back. It didn't matter. It was probably wishful thinking on his part that they had hit it off that weekend a month ago. He looked again more closely at the flyer. From what he had heard about Sharon from the neighbors, it wouldn't be out of character for her to pen him a note on the flyer, but there was nothing. Just the group picture with Sharon smiling like she did when she was showing him the gardens.

Nothing to lose, he thought and dialed the phone number for Barrett's. After the phone rang several times, Sharon's voice came on, but it was a recorded message that listed their hours and that they would be open this weekend for all of your farm or garden needs. Disappointed, Zach hung up, finished his tea, turned off most of the house lights and headed out onto the deck. He leaned back in his chair just as a second meteor streaked by. He took another sip of his tea and ran through the different meteor showers in his head, trying to remember the name of the spectacular one that appeared late July and early August. After a minute, he remembered.

Perseids.

He sat back and watched the sky for another hour. It was a bit early for the more spectacular shows, but some of the smaller showers could be spectacular while others were just duds. He did see a single tiny fireball streak across the sky though, something he hadn't seen for years.

Chapter 18

"Can I get these in pink?" Liza Schumann
stepped up to the counter at Barrett's and placed a
flat of blue petunias on the counter.

Sharon looked up and saw Liza's face beam
from under her floppy-brimmed hat. Huge, round,
sunglasses covered half of her face.

"Oh my God, Liza?" Sharon almost jumped at
seeing Liza with her broad smile that creased her
face between deeply set dimples. Her long,
spaghetti strapped floral print sundress would have
dragged on the floor had it not been for her high-
soled sandals. "It's so good to see you."

Sharon scanned the greenhouse to see if there
was anyone else waiting to be checked out. There
wasn't, which was surprising since it had been such
a hectic day with what seemed droves of customers

gathering up plants and supplies for the weekend. She slipped out from behind the counter and hugged Sarah's old friend.

"Do you have a few minutes?" Liza spun around, glancing over the plant and supplement racks, then turned back to Sharon.

"It looks like a lull in the action." Sharon noted as she hailed Rhonda with a shoulder shrug and raised hands. A quick head nod confirmed the Rhonda would cover her for a break.

As they started back toward the pond, Sharon stopped and reached over and brushed off soil she must have rubbed onto Liza's sundress. She looked herself over and when she found where the soil came from, she swept off her shirt sleeve to remove it.

"Oh, never mind that. How are you doing?" Liza said as she took Sharon's arm and started out toward the pond. Sharon lifted a radio and showed it to Rhonda before they left the greenhouse.

"I'm doing alright I guess. Busy, like I'm sure everyone else is." Sharon and Liza walked slowly around the building and out toward the pathway to the pond. By the time they were halfway to the pond, Liza had placed her arm around Sharon's shoulder. "You sound perky. Some good news?"

"You will be happy with this. Remember when you suggested talking to Julian?"

"He doesn't remember, does he?" Sharon's pace slowed to a crawl. She sucked in a deep breath and braced herself for bad news.

"Well, that's not really the case."

"What do you mean?"

"He didn't, but he reach out to Katie. She admitted it was her —"

"Really? You aren't just saying that are you?" Sharon stopped and grabbed Liza's arms, then started shaking them uncontrollably. A wide, eye squinting smile blossomed on her face.

"Yes, really."

"Did he tell Carolyn?"

"He told Judith and she told Carolyn, finally. It wasn't pretty either side, but he did. Sounds like Vincent messed Katie's head up pretty bad."

Sharon tried to contain herself enough not to start a happy dance around the store. She wouldn't have to hide her feelings any more. No more looking over her shoulder. No worries that someone watching her — someone that Carolyn had probably sent to stalk her. No more white van sitting in the parking lot, monitoring her every move. No more sizing up spooky men that probably smelled of stale cigarette smoke.

"And how is Julian taking it? That must have been hard on him."

"He's alright, I think, other than missing Katie. He was torn to pieces when she left back then. He felt even worse when Katie told him what happened now. We had to talk him out of quitting and going to be a monk out west somewhere."

"You did talk him down, right? He's such a good player."

"We finally did. He was shattered, but better now."

"And Carolyn?"

"Devastated. I think it was the last straw for her. I think she had a breakdown, but Judith says that she is 'convalescing'. Sounds like the truth was harder to accept than the fallacy she had created about you."

"Any idea why she started this witch hunt now instead of when Vincent killed himself." Sharon wanted to find it in her heart to forgive Carolyn, but the incessant persecution calloused over any hope for that. Maybe in a few days she might soften, but right now, she felt a satisfaction that vengeance had been served. She wasn't really sure if she wanted to know, since Sarah had to be involved somehow.

"I can't say for sure, but if I know your sister, I'm thinking she had some part in keeping Carolyn off your back. What I pieced together was that Vincent was stealing Sarah's Vicodin and was using it to drug up Katie, with a little on the side for himself. Carolyn must have called him out on it, but rather than hold him to account, she blamed Sarah. And when Sarah passed, the old lady's festering bitterness was set free."

Sharon was baffled why Sarah hid that from her, but what she heard from Liza pieced the puzzle together.

"Sharon. This is Rhonda. Needed up front," Rhonda's scratchy voice chimed over the radio.

"Duty calls." Sharon gazed at Liza and twitched another dimpled grin. "Thank you for letting me know. This has made my day."

"I'll come with you," Liza placed her arm around Sharon's shoulder. "By the way, do you have those petunias in pink? You were handling my request first, you know."

"Sure. I think there's a flat over here," Sharon noted as they detoured into the rear of the greenhouse. "Here they are. I rescued them from the compost heap, so we can discount them if you would like. They are a little leggy, but some extra attention will bring them back. Maybe some good fertilizer would help."

Liza split off to talk with Rhonda as Sharon turned the corner into the greenhouse and stopped to survey the floor, confused why Rhonda needed her at the checkout. She recognized the only customer at the checkout.

"Can I help you?" Sharon felt a flutter as she logged into the register.

"Sure. Hey, hi." Zach looked up as he groaned and placed a gallon container of Drylock onto the counter. He tweaked out a one sided grin. "Finally getting to the basement crack. Is this what you were saying I should use?"

Sharon could not help but stare at Zach. He may not have been the most elegant or masculine man she had ever met, but something about him made her feel squishy, and ready to risk opening up her feelings. With the specter of Carolyn's wrath sounding like it was about to vanish like a bad dream, visions of Sarah, Inga and the old maid, real or unreal, faded in and out of her head. She glanced up to the fuchsias and noticed that the lavender and pink hanging plant near the end was gone.

"This is the right stuff, isn't it?"

"Oh, yes, sorry. Drifting a little. Must be tired," Sharon fibbed. "Yes, that's the stuff, but you might want to just buy a quart container. I thought you said it was just a small crack."

"Good point." Zack grabbed the handle and started back toward the hardware section.

Sharon watched him as he headed past Rhonda's checkout station and back into the store. She noticed that he tipped his head and weakly said hi to Liza, who craned her neck as if trying to catch a glance of his backside as he passed.

Liza glanced back at Sharon, twitched her eyebrows and nodded in approval before squaring up with Rhonda. Sharon wagged her finger at Liza as she headed out to her car, a lingering smile creasing her face. She was right. His jeans fit him very well. Zack returned with a smaller can and placed it on the counter next to the red crossed petunias, then pulled out his wallet and offered Sharon his credit card.

"These look nice," Zack pointed to the flowers as Sharon processed the cement paint. "You think these would look good in front of the roses?"

"Might add some color."

"Did someone else buy them?"

"They were but then decided on something else. I didn't have a chance to get these back on the racks, yet. Do you like them?" Sharon waited for Zack's answer before she swiped the card.

"Sure." Zack looked around the greenhouse while Sharon punched away at the computer register. When she stopped to let the total compute, he asked. "Do you know where the potted plants are coming from? It seems like every Saturday, another one shows up?"

"Oh, my word." Sharon giggled as she slipped the paint into a plastic bag before swiping the card and handing it back to Zach.

"It's not you, is it?"

"Oh, no. They're probably forget-me-nots. I think Esther Palmer is just giving you some welcome gifts. She used to do that for me and Sarah."

"Oh, okay. That makes sense then. Her version of Welcome Wagon then?"

"Yeah, she's a real hoot."

"I was wondering," Zach started, tentatively and with measured words. "Do you have any plans for the weekend?"

"Just working. It's one of our busy weekends. You?"

"Oh, nothing big. I'm planning on a traditional Fourth cookout. I also heard there were some fireworks in town tonight. It's like — brats and blasts," he chuckled at his lame quip. "Should be able to see them from the deck. Interested?"

Sharon heard Sarah's words to give him a chance. She quickly thought through her schedule for the weekend and remembered that her real early day was Sunday. Tomorrow she could arrive a little late if the night lingered on. "I should be able to swing by tonight after work. If I may ask, what's your traditional Fourth cookout?"

"Brats and German potato salad. I think I have some pickles if the salad is a little thin. And I think I have some beer."

Sharon rolled her eyes. "Should've known. I'll swing by after work, but we can't make it a late one."

"Great. See you in a bit then." Zach smirked.

Sharon arrived at Zach's house as the sun started to set over the hay field. Rising smoke from behind the house betrayed Zach's location. She sauntered around the flagstone wall that encircled the Daphne, weaving her hand through the leaves, left fragrant by the tiny pink and white blossoms that had passed. After climbing the stairs to the deck, she stopped and watched Zach roll six brats around open hot dog rolls laid out on a smoking kettle grill. Paper plates sat on the top of a closed cooler, which she figured had the balance of the traditional Fourth he had mentioned; the potato salad and the beer.

"My word, the Miss Kim is making quite a statement," Sharon mentioned, drawing in a full breath of the heavily perfumed, lavender like aroma that the late blooming lilac wafted into the air.

Zach glanced over his shoulder, then returned to his cooking, trying hard to carry the tune from the music selections on the boom-box he had set up just inside the door. Phil Collins. Must have been the oldies station out of Concord, she thought. As he worked over the grill, with his dark hair tousled while a swath of perspiration wetted down his t-shirt, she had to admit to herself that there was something about this mid-western boy that seemed to spark feelings to life — feelings that warmed her and scared her at the same time. She hadn't felt this way since her first couple years of college when she met Colin, an environmental engineering major who swept her off her feet, then broke her heart when he moved back to England before her senior year.

But this time things were different. Zach arrived when she was vulnerable. Instead of taking advantage of her vulnerability though, he consoled her. Not often, but it seemed he was there just at the right times. No rushing, no pushing, no wham-bam-thank you ma'am. Just there with a warm shoulder and a soft voice. With the weight of Carolyn's vitriol hopefully past, she felt that she could be a bit more open and more herself, and not have to drag anyone else through that emotional nightmare.

"Oh, hi there." Zach glanced over his shoulder. "Didn't hear you."

"It was probably that croaking I heard that drowned out my steps." Sharon chuckled as she stepped toward the kettle grill. She leaned over into the smoke and inhaled the aroma from the brats. "You know the Hannaford's carries a sweet turkey sausage with chunks of apple? They are rather tasty."

"You like them?" Zach turned toward her, grilling fork at attention.

"I do. You should try them sometime." Sharon noticed that his relaxed appearance and demeanor — t-shirt, jeans and flip-flops — fit his body very well.

"I'll keep that in mind. Salad and beer in the cooler." Zach pointed to the large blue cooler with his grilling fork then went back to poking at each of the brats on the grill, before announcing, "Done.

Can you hand me one of those plates and we can eat?"

Sharon complied and handed Zach a plate for the brats and rolls. She retrieved two Michelob bottles and the potato salad buried in the crushed ice in the bottom of the cooler and set them on the small end table Zach had set up on the deck. Zach piled the meat and bread onto the plate while Sharon spooned out the potato salad on two others.

As she expected, the brats and beer brought back memories of the cookouts her family had while she was in high school. The potato salad had just the right amount of tang, complete with small round mustard seeds, as if it had been homemade. Without much more said, they sat in their respective Adirondack chairs and ate. By the time they had finished eating, evening had darkened the sky enough that as Sharon leaned back, she could see the stars glinting above.

"If you don't mind me asking, who's Brenda?"

"Brenda? You know about Brenda?"

"Sarah told me to ask."

Zach understood. He took a pull on his beer. Sharon could see his eyes glassing over. "Brenda was my girlfriend back in Chicago. Maybe a little more. Musician. Like your sister. In fact, she looked a bit like your sister."

Sharon could tell by the waver in Zach's voice that he was uncomfortable. "I'm sorry. Do you want to talk about it?"

"I don't mind. She was part of my life for a year or so until we drifted apart. A friend of mine at work matched us up. We were quite the opposite

personality, but seemed to do okay for a while.
Then it unraveled. Let's just leave it that she was
having an affair and that ended us." Zach eased
himself up out of his chair and walked to the rail,
then looked out over the yard and into the woods.
"There was a terrible car accident that killed her
before we could iron out our differences in a civil
manner."

"I'm sorry," Sharon atoned. "I didn't mean to
bring up bad memories."

Zach leaned back and drew on his beer again as
Sharon let his words sink in. He turned back to
Sharon and she could see a tear twinkle in his eye.
Out over the yard, fireflies sparkled in circles while
the glow on the horizon pulsed with each explosion
in the distance.

"So let me get this straight. Sarah told you to
ask me about Brenda? Sarah?"

A smile crept onto Sharon's face as she stood
up and walked toward Zach. "Yes, I have seen her
too."

"So Sarah is real." Zach stammered a bit as
Sharon shook her head in agreement. "I mean, as
real as a ghost can be?"

Sharon shook her head.

"And we've both seen her."

Sharon shook her head again.

"And she's the one who told you about
Brenda?"

"She told me to ask." She felt a chill in the air,
which drew her closer to Zach, close enough to
wrap her arms around him and drop her head into
his shoulder. It was as comforting for her as it had

been before. She could hear Zach's heart mellow out and sensed it was for him as well. "It doesn't matter to me, Zach."

In the distance the fireworks display at the fairgrounds had started and a faint glow emanated from the horizon as rumbles shook the ground around them. For the moment, they stood on the deck, arms wrapped around each other, swaying ever so slightly to the faint strains of Phil Collins' In the Air Tonight playing through the radio. Through her shirt, she could feel Zach's warmth and it was as comfortable as she had ever felt.

"Why don't we pick up and head inside before it gets too cold," Zach stopped and whispered into Sharon's ear. She didn't want to let go at this point, but she did. Once the deck was cleared and the kettle grill closed, Zach turned the armchair in the great room toward the deck and set a bottle on the end table. Sarah drew closer; facing him as she gently descended onto his lap and wrapped her arms around his neck. She leaned into his shoulder again and let his warmth comfort her while the radio station continued working through a playlist of Genesis love songs.

There was no need to go back to her apartment tonight.

Chapter 19

Sharon finished with her last customer in line and noticed a familiar face nuzzling the blossoming red and yellow tea roses. She slipped out from behind her computer at the register and sauntered toward Liza Schumann.

"Make sure they get plenty of water if you are planning on heeling them in now." Sharon said as she came up beside Liza. "Mid-July is a rough time to plant."

"These are beautiful, aren't they?" Liza turned to Sharon and smiled under her wide brimmed summer hat. She had lost a few pounds since Sharon had last seen her just a week or so back, but enough to be noticed.

"These stay compact as long as you keep up with them."

"That reminds me. I passed by Sarah's house the other day and noticed how everything in the yard had finally come to life. Not quite what I am used to. Maybe the new owner might need to pay a little more attention. A gardener's hand would surely help."

"I've talked to him and provided a little coaching." Sharon's eyes sparkled. They are his gardens now, but I will keep an eye on them. He seems to be doing alright at this point, doesn't he?"

"So you know who bought the house?"

"He's been in a few times. He's a little rough around the edges with the plants, but he's learning."

"The one with the nice buns?" Liza raised her eyebrows.

"Yeah, that one," Sharon blushed, hoping Liza didn't notice. She didn't want to reveal much more about her and Zach, since she figured that Liza would beg her for even details — details that she was not ready to divulge, since there were so few.

"So you've been over to see him then?"

"It's been busy this season, you know. I've been working quite a bit and I really haven't had much time to work with him. He does stop in at times to ask for some help, so I guess he's learning."

"Work with him?" Liza leaned forward and dropped her sunglasses so that Sharon could see her deeply set blue eyes. "Sounds like you are hoping for something more?"

"Time will tell. Don't want to rush things. Just starting to right my own emotional ship, you know." Sharon tried to dodge the conversation. "We talk a bit on the phone, but he's pretty busy with a new job and all. Maybe when things slow down a bit here we'll talk a bit more."

"He's not putting you off, is he?"

"No, nothing like that. Slow is good for now for both of us."

"You aren't having one of those open relationships and he's got someone else on the line."

"Doesn't seem the type."

"Well, does he like good music?" Sharon sensed a sly undertone to Liza's voice.

"I think so."

"This might help, then. Perhaps nudge things along?" Liza took out an envelope from her oversized purse that looked more like a crocheted book bag and handed it to Sharon. "I know it is a little short notice, but we were finally able to work out the details for a benefit concert."

"Tickets? Tanglewood?" Sharon recognized the envelope.

"With Appleton convalescing, Judith Rhodes agreed to let Julian and me work the back door with Director Ozawa and set aside a weekend up there."

"Oh my God, that's great. You said Julian helped set this up?"

"Uh-huh. I wanted to keep him involved."

"How's he doing, anyway? I hope he's back to his own self again." Sharon stared at the envelope, speechless. She enjoyed the evenings at Tanglewood with Sarah and Liza, especially the ones in the late summer, when a slight mist would roll in, trapping the music close to the ground to savor rather than it drifting out and singing to the hills. When the skies were clear and the mist didn't roll in, the music made the meteor shower that much more spectacular, like celestial fireworks.

"He's doing much better. Katie's back up here with Julian and they seem to have worked things out, Sounds like she had a falling out with her friend down in Philly."

"I'm glad that worked out." Sharon tried to hand the tickets back to Liza. "But I don't think I can take these. There is so much to wrap up here and get ready for the fall season that I just couldn't take the time."

"Nonsense, Sharon. We're as slow as molasses in January." Rhonda Barrett squawked. Sharon jumped and spun to the voice. "I think it would be good for you."

"Did you know about this?" Sharon scowled at Rhonda.

"Well, yes. And just to clear the air, I suggested to Carolyn Appleton that she arrange this concert months ago. Then I started working on Judith when Carolyn had her meltdown. Once Liza, Julian and I made Judith understood we would underwrite the concert, doors opened and things started happening."

"Really?" Sharon stared at Rhonda, slack-jawed in disbelief.

"It just took a while to get through."

Sharon looked at Liza, who simply cocked her head. "Did you know about this when we were up in Franconia?"

"Not completely. It was more a hope than anything else. It took Rhonda's coaching to push this past the finish line."

"Maybe you and Mr. Barrett should go then." Sharon tried to hand the tickets to Rhonda. "Aren't sponsors supposed to be there? I can watch over the store for that weekend."

"I'll hear nothing of it. It is in honor of your sister and besides, you always went there when Sarah was playing. This will be good for you." Rhonda looked sternly at Sharon.

Liza cocked her head inquisitively and winked at Sharon. "Besides, it gives you another excuse to see your boy."

Sharon regarded Liza closely with a frown, then shifted her glare toward Rhonda. "Were you two conspiring against me?"

"Conspire is such a harsh word, Sharon," Liza and Rhonda giggled like schoolgirls. "What we had to do to get Judith to agree to doing this would probably be considered the conspiracy."

"I would prefer to consider this as cooperation for the well-being of Barrett's employees. A benefit of working here," Rhonda added, wagging her head confidently. "Besides, I have that weekend already covered. All of your co-workers jumped at the thought of filling in so you could enjoy a long weekend."

"But I've taken so much time off recently —"

"You know my thoughts on excuses." Rhonda interrupted and hoisted her hands onto her hips. She scowled at Sharon. "Things are slowing down some now and it's a good time to start getting some rest and relaxation before the fall planting season."

"But —"

"Do I sense insubordination?"

"I guess I don't have much choice, do I?"

"No, you don't," Liza and Rhonda said in unison.

"Love you guys." A tear welled in Sharon's eyes as she looked over the tickets again, then smiled broadly at Liza. Sharon held the envelope close to her chest as she noticed a customer rolling up to the counter with a full wagon of annuals. After a quick hug for both Liza and Rhonda, she headed back to her station and slipped the envelope into her modestly small backpack she used as a purse, smitten.

Sharon leaned back in her wicker chair on her balcony and debated if she should ask Zach to go with her or if she should just go alone. It wasn't so much that she didn't want him to go, but it was more that she was thinking about his feelings. A night with musicians for him could bring back bad memories of Brenda. She could tell it was still painful when he talked about her, even if it was a year or two back.

For her, though, relaxing in the mountains while a live orchestra played outdoors, with only the pines as their acoustic shell, was something she missed. It had been years since she had spent time in Tanglewood. It was not just the pleasure of the experience, but it was also getting there that she missed. She had special memories of the nearby little towns, and one special eclectic coffee shop along the way. It would be nice to see Dottie from the Coffee Shop if she still owned the corner store. And the Perseids meteor shower was to peak this weekend as well, and with clear skies expected, the show could be that much more spectacular. Ozawa would certainly select Holst's The Planets as a finale while the Perseids provided the light show above. And the day at the Briarwood, nestled nearby in the Berkshire Mountains, where her old friends Amy and Steve had set up a bed and breakfast, was an ambiance that was as fit for reflection. And possibly romance, if things worked out.

She thought about Liza's comments concerning Zach. She was right. Amidst the encounters she had with Zach, this would be an opportunity to get to know him much better. He enjoyed classical music, or at least he mentioned that once or twice. On the other hand, she reckoned, if she discovered that they really weren't as compatible as she sensed they could be, she could always mingle into the all-night party that the orchestra players typically held after the concert and let the evening fade away at an arm's length. No harm, no foul. Just a night of further exploration, to be sure what she was feeling with him was real. She could also help her friends Amy and Steve, the owners of the Briarwood Inn, since keeping the wine and food going for the party was always a challenge.

Sharon leaned forward and stared at the hundreds of flickering stars, progressing through a logical sequence, as she always did for decisions. It would have been nice to talk with Sarah, but she had not appeared lately. She was probably just one of the many people that Zach had met in the past few months. He could have met someone else by now, which could answer why he hadn't called or dropped by more often than he did. He did work in the higher dollar circles than she did, and the possibly that he met someone at work, where he was probably spending so much time, was high. Maybe one of his co-workers matched him with a friend. Someone he worked with would surely have more in common with him than she did. After all she was just a sales clerk at a garden shop.

Maybe he was still being cautious about getting too deeply involved, still wary of deep relationships after his problems with Brenda. Maybe he needed a bit more time. She thought she could just drop off a ticket at his house, leave her phone number and leave it for him to decide whether to call her or not. That would work, she thought, but good plan or not, she still had to do something.

There was still a week left to work through additional details, but if there was even a remote chance he was interested, she would have to act sooner than later. Throwing caution to the wind, she slipped on her sandals, grabbed her keys, and headed over toward Pleasant Hill.

With doubt about her place still nibbling at her mind, she turned off the four-lane, then turned right onto Birch River Road, and finally onto Pleasant Hill. As she reached the top of the hill, she cringed. There were no lights on at the house and it was already past dusk. She slowed down and pulled off to the side to let the pick-up that was tailing her rattle by before continuing to creep up and turn into the empty, dark driveway. Biting her lip, she sat in the driveway and thought more about how long of a drive Tanglewood would be from here.

That didn't matter, Sharon thought. One way or another, she would go. She would prefer Zach come along, but leaving the ticket here was a good start to the conversation. She flipped on her overhead light, scribbled a note with her phone number on the ticket to give her a call. Leaving her car lights on, she got out and went directly to the flat stone where she left a spare key. It was gone. She scratched around in the dirt but could not find the key. It was definitely gone.

She figured that she could wedge the ticket into the doorjamb, close enough to the lock that he couldn't miss it. The storm rolling in wasn't due for a few more hours, and he couldn't work so late that the ticket would be blown away with the winds. Before heading back to her Jeep, she checked how secure the ticket was in the doorjamb, and still set so that it would be obvious.

Satisfied, she left. As she slipped back into the driver's seat, she started to wonder more about Zach, and whether this was the right thing to urge along their relationship. She wondered if he was missing her as much as she was sensing that she was missing him. For a moment, she thought about waiting for him so she could talk to him directly, but concern tweaked the thought that he might misread her intentions. She assured herself that her plan to leave one ticket was subtle enough. Without knowing how long he would be and needing to be at work early to open, she had to leave.

At this point, though, only time would reveal where she stood with Zach. If he called, she would have an answer. If he didn't, the story could be different, but she would know something as well. and she could catch up with him next week. She really didn't need to wait around to find out, and she was already pushing past the time she needed to get to bed. Tomorrow would be soon enough to find out.

"Alright, Sarah, wherever you are, it's up to you," she mumbled and started her engine. As she backed out into the road and shifted into gear, lights appeared, coming up the road from the other direction. She slowly drove in first gear to the top of the hill, where Lake Road turned off to the right and waited, hoping it was Zach. Then she could go back and personally invite him.

False alarm. It was the same old pick-up truck that rattled by her before. It drove by, not even slowing down. She sighed as a slight gust of wind kicked up, which it usually did this time of year before rain rolled in. Sharon hopped out and quickly pulled up her ragtop over top of the seats, secured the plastic windows, and climbed back into the driver's seat just as large raindrops whacked onto her windshield. Rather than waiting any longer, she pulled back onto the road, and headed back to her apartment, alone, and with one unanswered question.

Later that night, Zach turned into his driveway as the rain continued to pound on his car. He could not believe that the mandatory dinner meeting Joshua called lasted as long as it did. On a Monday, no less. Then again, he didn't realize that Joshua could talk that long about something as bland as derivatives and what it could mean to all their customers. It sounded more like a shell game, which is why he steered his clients away from them in the first place. But theoretical discussion over a marginal dinner of baked, stuffed scrod, whatever that was, just made his head ache and his stomach churn.

He knew he would get drenched in the ongoing downpour if he used the side door to the garage as he usually did. The inevitable puddle in front of the latchkey gate would soak through his shoes as well. Instead, he pushed the clicker, turned his engine off and waited until the overhead door completely opened. It was a little sluggish, something he figured he could work on to loosen up, but it was not going to be tonight. He decided he could wait until the morning to grab his mail on the way to work and dipped his head before dashing into the garage, trying not to get soaked. Dripping from just the few feet to the bay, he shook off most of the rain, then pressed the close button and headed inside.

He lit the burner under his red kettle for some tea, figuring a beer at this hour would just make his head pound even more, then dropped his portfolio bag on the table and ferreted around the cupboard for one of the homemade blends Sarah made and

Sharon left for him. Chamomile. That had to be it. He dropped a bag into a tall cup, then dropped his head into his arms on the table and waited for the kettle to whistle that it was ready. It wasn't long.

He set the cup at the table and let the tea bleed into the hot water. A single envelope had slid out of his open portfolio bag next to the cup. It was a letter sent to him at work that he simply didn't have time to open before rushing out to the dinner meeting. The return address was the Conservatory but it was from a Liza Schumann, someone he didn't know, or at least didn't think he had. The Conservatory stationery piqued his interest, since otherwise he would have just thrown it out as junk mail. He slit the end open and noticed a letter folded around two tickets. The tickets were for a benefit concert at Tanglewood, a benefit for Sarah Tanchak and the American Cancer Society. "An evening in memory of our colleague who fought valiantly through her illness," the heading on the tickets read. The concert date was the coming weekend.

He then opened the letter and realized that Judith Rhodes had penned a personal note on the Conservatory letterhead of the Conservatory. Not the Liza Schumann that was on the envelope, and not Carolyn. She was complimentary of the work he had done for Carolyn, and since she understood that he enjoyed classical music, she thought that he might be interested in attending. She went on to say he could provide donations at the gate if he wished, but these tickets were intended as complimentary.

Sharon would like this, he thought as he took a sip of his tea. It could be a nice weekend in the mountains, just the two of them, enjoying a bit of outdoor music. They would have plenty of time to talk on the way out and the way back. Three hours each way if he remembered where he saw the Tanglewood exit sign on the Mass Pike.

An odd tingling crept up his spine as he looked over the tickets again. It had been a long time since he had been at an outdoor concert, when Brenda was playing. What he most remembered was being uncomfortable since there were so many musicians there, especially at the after-party, and he was just a tag-a-long spouse that didn't quite understand the nuances of the jokes floating around. He sensed at times that he was the brunt of them.

But Sharon wasn't a musician, and with her, it would be different. He took another sip of tea and felt his eyes starting to slide closed. He figured it was too late to call though, so as he started up to bed, he pinned the tickets on the refrigerator and resolved to give her a call either tomorrow or the next day to work out the details.

Chapter 20

When Sharon parked in Hannaford's crowded parking lot, she was reminded why Friday was not the best day to pick up groceries for the weekend. She had hoped that Zach would have called sometime during the week so that they could work out the details of the trip to Tanglewood, but he didn't. She probably should have tried to talk with him directly. Each time she called him to see if he got the ticket, he was out. The week had slipped away and now was too late.

She had resolved that she was going regardless. Sliding out of her Jeep, she locked the door and headed toward the store. As she walked inside, she remembered his reaction to her question about Brenda, and obsessed that he actually did find the ticket but didn't want to go. He could have at least called and said it was just not right. She wondered if the venue had turned him off. But he did say that he was over Brenda.

I guess I should have thought of that before, she muttered as she grabbed a basket and started down the aisles. Whether Zach was going or not, she was. She owed it to Sarah. She could catch up with him next weekend. In the back of her mind though, as she peered down each aisle she passed, she secretly hoped that she would see Zach mulling over which snacks or wine to pick up to surprise her. But after working through each of the aisles, including a second time through the wine section, her hope faded into disappointment.

She escaped the chaos in the store and drove slowly home along the back roads. Wilting when she finally parked just outside her apartment, she felt exhaustion from fighting through the shopping free-for-all overcome her. After weeks of trepidation, she felt safe that there was no white van parked in the lot waiting to watch her every move. Catching her breath before unloading, she felt the slight chill of the sweeping northwest wind that mussed her hair, odd for this time of the year, but not uncommon. She could bring an extra blanket and jacket tomorrow, just in case, since the gown that she had her heart set on wearing would definitely not be enough to keep her warm.

Locking the door behind her, she headed into her condo, set the groceries on the counter, then quickly checked the phone. No messages. No calls. Not even a cryptic "See you there." Disappointed again, she sighed, kicked off her sneakers and riffled through over what she had picked up. The wine was a nice blush — Atwater Sweet Catawba — the same wine that she shared with Sarah when they hunkered down during snowstorms. She remembered one storm in particular that Sarah decided to master a new Mahler piece while the storm raged outside. Her sister was a sight even before they started; her auburn hair in a tangled Medusa-like mess, her red terry cloth robe wrapped around her and oversized fuzzy slippers bouncing in time with the clicking metronome. They took turns pouring each other's drinks, and by the time they had worked their way through half of the bottle, Sarah's fingerings were so far off that her rendition sounded more like a jazz improvisation rather than a classical piece. Sharon remembered singing in a gravelly and sexy voice, as if she was imitating Aretha Franklin before they both dissolved into laughter and tears.

"No, not tonight," Sharon mumbled as she packed the bottle away into her designated outdoor concert picnic basket, and instead poured herself some peppermint sun tea. During her college years, early morning drive hangovers had convinced her that it would be best to keep the wine for parties or quiet evenings alone. She carefully wrapped the blocks of cheddar and Monterrey Jack cheese, added a log of smoked sausage, and then two sleeves of Ritz crackers. She left the browned French bread loaves in their plastic bags, already being bundled with waxed paper to hold in moisture and keep it fresh. She wouldn't need anything else.

Amy and Steve, the innkeepers, always took care of her and Sarah.

She then placed her jacket and a rolled up blanket next to the basket near the door, before tiptoeing in bare feet over to her bookshelf for a nightcap read. Most of the books dealt with gardening and soils, with the exception of one small section of a shelf where she hid her steamy romances. She settled for one by Nora Roberts, and although she had read it several times before, she always found it as warm and bittersweet as the first time she worked through the pages. She giggled to herself as she headed into her bedroom and dropped the book in her bed. With all the lights dimmed except for her reading light on her bed, she undressed and sat on the edge of her bed. She picked up her lavender scented lotion, warmed dabs in her palms, then smoothed the cream over all of her body, savoring the feel on her bare skin. Putting on her nightgown, she then slid under the comfort of her mother's down filled quilt, and flipped to the dog-eared pages that marked the juicy parts.

Zach welcomed the end of the day Friday, even as late as it was, since the entire week turned into a never-ending, exhausting hell. There wasn't a day without a five o'clock crisis. Missing file escapades, hastily called meetings to discuss another banking fiasco, and fire drills. They had a fire drill just when he started to call Sharon on Wednesday, so he had to hang up quickly and exit. Somebody had actually twisted an ankle in the stairwell on the way out, and he had to help call an ambulance. Joshua, his needle nosed boss, relentlessly called evening team meetings that droned on for hours. Zach knew people were in trouble with the recession and Y2K just around the corner. It wasn't as urgent as Joshua made it out to be. People just needed to remain calm, listen to his researched advice, and not obsess about the volatility of the market.

And now it was Friday night. Late on Friday night. The week had vaporized without touching base with Sharon. Opportunity lost, he resolved. It would not be an issue if he didn't go. It was not as if he had spent a fortune for the tickets. There were plenty of things around the house needing attention. He still hadn't fixed the cracks in the basement and he did want to do some organization in the garage so he could park his car in it before winter rolled in. He could always just relax on the deck, maybe even indulge in a self-effacing drunken stupor. It wouldn't be a wasted weekend if he chose not to go.

It was an evening concert, so he figured he could delay thinking about what to do until the morning. His head hurt so much now that even sorting socks would be a challenge. He swallowed a heavy dose of aspirin, slogged up the stairs, soaked a washcloth in cold water and crawled into bed, fully dressed. The wet cloth on his forehead and the aspirin eased the pounding in a few minutes, enough that he could sense himself drifting off to sleep.

A bright light in the corner of the room was the first thing that caught Zach's attention. Then a tinny voice called his name and he felt himself drifting upward to a sitting position on the edge of his bed.

"You are going to the concert, aren't you, Zach?" The voice mellowed. Zach opened his eyes and saw Sarah sitting in a folding chair, like the ones that he remembered from the outdoor concerts when Brenda performed. She was a foot off the floor, as she was in the shed, with her oboe set cross-wise in her lap.

"I don't know. I figured I lost the opportunity."

"Now that is as confounding an excuse as I have ever heard. The concert is tomorrow. How is that a lost opportunity? You are overthinking this." Sarah cocked her head to the side and twisted her lips. Still seated, she started to drift about the room.

"I wasn't able to call Sharon and ask her if she wanted to go."

"Really. Weren't able or just didn't? There is a difference you know." Sarah's image had moved behind him. His shadow on the wall in front of him wavered, provoking vertigo.

"Okay, I didn't. But it's been a hell of a week. I don't think there was one day I got to bed before midnight." He turned his head to catch up with Sarah as she moved about the room. "And I've got such a head ache right now —"

"I don't buy into excuses, Zach. You don't have a headache right now. You had a headache. It's gone now."

She was right. His headache was gone. "I haven't had a chance to even figure out how to get there."

265

"You don't always need a plan, Zach. Plans don't always work out. Sometimes you just need to improvise."

"It's a long drive. I don't think I can drive all night back home, and I haven't . . ."

"Taken care of. Amy will have a room for you."

"Who's Amy?"

"She runs the place where you should stay."

"And how am I supposed to find this place and this Amy?"

"You'll know when you get there. You know, Zach, I am starting to wonder what Sharon sees in you. Maybe you should think more about her feelings if you want things to blossom than feeling sorry for yourself because of Brenda."

"Brenda?"

"Your problem is Brenda. You're still not over her, are you?" Sarah's drifting about the room, like she was on a string, mesmerized Zach. "Well dear, I've taken care of that for you."

"Huh?"

"I've talked with Brenda. Let's just say, we walk the same concert hall now. Things happened that you had no control over. Like I said, plans don't always work out. She wants you to move on. It's been long enough."

"Will Sharon be there?"

"That is something you need to find out for yourself." Sarah settled down to a spot in the corner as her image started to fade. "So will you come see me?"

Zach nodded his head as he watched Sarah's image dim into a wisp, then disappear.

Chapter 21

Zach woke early, just before the rising sun's light fully subdued the darkness of the night and brewed up a quick cup of coffee. Looking out through his east-facing door, he nursed his coffee and started having second thoughts about traveling all the way to Western Massachusetts for an outdoor concert by himself. Not being familiar with the roads, it would have been at least tolerable if there was someone he could have shared the drive with — like Sharon. He sucked down another mouthful of coffee, and wondered how brutal the traffic would be on a summer Saturday, headed toward the mountains with everyone else. Perusing the brochure from Tanglewood that had been included with the tickets, he noticed some road directions on the back. Opening it, he saw a map of the grounds, but that was confusing. He wasn't sure which building the concert was being held in, but he figured he could probably stumble around when he got there if he just followed the music.

He finished his coffee, warmed up a bagel in his small toaster oven, and as he waited for the bread to brown, realized his eating habits would need to improve before he turned into a pear shaped man. In the back of his mind, the lingering thought that he would be wandering around on unfamiliar grounds in unfamiliar woods with a troupe of unfamiliar musicians spooked him a bit. He could not help but think about the times he was lost at Brenda's concerts, but Sarah did tell him it was time to get over her.

Sarah told him, he thought. The oven dinged. He slipped the bagel halves out onto a paper plate, buttered them before lathering the tops with cream cheese. As he chewed his first mouthful, he realized that he was arguing with a ghost last night — a ghost who said she was taking care of everything and all he had to do was go.

Really? A ghost? A real ghost, he thought working through the first half of the bagel. As he finished, he heard Sharon's voice in the back of his mind, "So what could I do but laugh and go?"

It wouldn't hurt to explore, he figured, let his hair down, so to speak, and see what was out there. It may have been more a whim than a convincing argument, but he did indicate to Sarah that he was going. And if he didn't, she would probably haunt him for a long time. He took his smaller blue and white Igloo cooler down from the cupboard, packed a few peanut butter sandwiches for the concert, some Gatorade and a sleeve of Ritz crackers. Figuring he could grab a burger along the way, or even a doughnut or two at one of those Dunkin Donut shops that seemed to be everywhere, he loaded his Explorer and headed out before the sun fully rose above the horizon.

Zach stopped at the end of the driveway and checked the time on his dashboard. Six-thirty. He wondered for a moment, then decided to detour past Barrett's, just in case someone had come in early to set up who might know where Sharon's apartment was. If he was lucky, it might be Sharon, especially if she wasn't going to the concert. Then he could set up a nice evening here with a little Phil Collins or even Jim Croce. The drive along Route 23 was quick for a Saturday morning, but then, he wasn't usually on the road this early.

Reality, though, set in as he slowed down at the entrance to the nursery. It was closed as tight as he had ever seen it; canvas drawn down over the no-walled shrub sheds, displays had been rolled into fenced open barns, no cars in the parking lot and the long metal swing gate crossed and locked at the entrances.

"It was just a thought," he mused and headed toward the interstate.

Sharon woke to bright sunlight spilling through the sheer curtains of her bedroom. She realized that the week must have exhausted her since she was usually an early riser. Slipping on her summer bathrobe, she saw the book she was reading last night, still open to the teary part, where the main characters were saying their bittersweet farewells to each other. She looked at the pages for a moment, then closed the book and headed downstairs.

When she stepped onto the cold bare floor in the kitchen, she checked her phone for messages, but there were none. None from Zach directly and none from work that said he had called. After dropping the book on the table, she flipped on the coffee maker, then poured a half-full bowl of shredded wheat. She dropped in a handful of blueberries and walnuts, added milk and let it soak in. After loading the toaster with two slices of wheat bread, she poured herself a cup of strong black coffee.

Once the toast popped up and she added a smear of pear butter, she settled in at her small table. She stared out through her window wondering if she should have done more to reach out to Zach. When she called him at work, the message on the answering machine was still Carl Edwards, which concerned her a bit. Carl dealt with Carolyn, which probably meant that Zach was dealing with her now. Maybe Carolyn or Judith convinced him that she was a problem and he should stay away. But she also could have taken some time on Thursday and driven down to Nashua to surprise him at work. Waiting for him to make the next move was probably too hopeful and too much to expect.

She took another swallow of the coffee. As she set the cup down, she stared out through the window and wondered if she had hurt Zach more than he was willing to admit when she brought up

Brenda. Or maybe he was just comfortable being a bookish single nerd and there was no hope they would amount to anything more than a weekend or garden help. It just seemed that there should be something more between them, especially since she kept remembering how he had gazed at her that day in the woods. And then that night they held each other for so long. Sarah thought there was something there as well.

Right now, though, it didn't really matter. She was content being who she was; single and doing what she wanted to do. Carolyn was off her back and she felt freedom to be herself again. She could always true up with Zach after the concert to see where their relationship stood. As she finished her breakfast and quickly rinsed out the dishes, she resolved that she would enjoy the weekend as she had other weekends in the Berkshires when Sarah was alive. This weekend was supposed to be a celebration of Sarah's life, not an obsession of her love life. And she was sure that her sister was counting on her being there.

She set everything outside her door, then locked it before loading up the Jeep with her small overnight bag, hiking gear, and the picnic basket. She took a moment to inspect the evening gown she had picked out, remembering that she had worn it for Sarah's last concert at Tanglewood. Careful not to fold it, she laid it out across the back seat.

The weather report was for sunny skies, warm daytime temperatures that cooled off slowly at night. With vacationers headed to the mountains, she figured the interstate would be a bear to wrestle with and decided to take the long way, which was the way she and Sarah had always travelled. There were more scenic pull-offs that extended the travel time, but otherwise she would miss the special stops along the way.

The winding road to Keene was spectacular, passing swift flowing streams and slipping through fresh smelling pine forests along the way. Once into Keene, she detoured through Main Street to stop briefly in front of the Colonial Theatre, where she had watched Sarah and her wind ensemble perform a few years back. After another hour, she drove on through Brattleboro and into the Vermont mountains on Route 9. The views from the switchbacks along the route through the mountains were as breathtaking as she remembered, with overlooks that enticed her to pull off and view the Green Mountains in their summer glory.

There was one particular switchback halfway through Vermont, at the top of one of the mountains that she didn't remember the name of, but it had a wide parking and viewing area with an unobstructed view. It was where Sarah always insisted they stop so she could get one last quick open air rehearsal. Her insistence became almost a pre-concert rehearsal when she convinced a few peers to stop and join in. Sharon recognized the landmarks, slowed and pulled into the parking area.

After turning off her engine, she stepped out of her Jeep, hopped up on the hood, the sat cross-legged as the warmth of the engine seeped through her shorts. Cottony clouds drifted along on a sparkling clear blue sky. Pines undulated in the distance with the topography. Whether she was dreaming or actually did hear the echoes from the last few years still resonating through the hills, Sharon sensed Sarah and her companions work through their melodic renditions of Handel.

The music stopped. Thank you, she thought.

"You're welcome." Sarah's voice echoed in her head. Sharon popped her eyes open. Even though she sensed Sarah being next to her, no one was there. She slipped off the hood, straightened her shorts that had crept up her thighs, and then climbed back into her Jeep. As she headed out of the rest stop, she maneuvered around the stares of the few dawdlers in the lot, and worked her way back onto the highway. She needed one more stop to make this journey complete.

Ten miles up the road in Wilmington, she slowed and pulled off the road that had narrowed considerably on its way toward town. She parked as close to The Coffee Shop, a small shack on the side of the road, a place Sarah had discovered five years before. Since then, it became a ritual to stop, whether it was heading back home or coming to a Tanglewood event, just to chat with the owner.

Inside the quaint corner store, a line of carafes with several aromatic blends, stacks of cups, both paper and ceramic stood next to a bowl full of bills and change she remembered as the Karma cup. It was something that Dottie, the owner who seemed to be still living in the sixties at her commune, maintained as her way of keeping her customers coming back, regardless of the time between visits.

Pay forward, pay back, enjoy the coffee, welcome back, Sharon remembered Sarah always chanting when they left. She drew a cup of coconut flavored coffee, rolled up a couple of bills and stuffed them into the Karma cup just as Dottie emerged through her beaded curtain separating the small kitchen in the rear from the main room.

"Hey, sweetie. Been a while, eh?" Dottie smiled broadly. She was a bit older than Sharon and looked like a genuine throwback to Woodstock. She had put on a few pounds since the last time Sharon had seen her, but she was still nowhere near filling out her kimono-like, Hawaiian print gown. Her hair was long and a bit wild, with thick bleached streaks weaved within the reddish-brown hair, bundled in a loose rough braided ponytail that reached her waist. Her earrings were as gaudy as she remembered, beaded and dangly with no recognizable pattern, similar to the strands of beads and silver necklaces around her neck.

"It has been some time, hasn't it?" Sharon tried to pay for her coffee.

"Some of your friends already stopped in a bit ago. They told me about your sister and it sounds like it will be a wonderful concert. Anything I can do for you?" Dottie's eyes were wide ovals of sincerity. She handed Sharon a small bowl full of dark chocolate espresso beans, then handed her money back. "On the house."

"Just the coffee, but thanks." Sharon returned a warm smile.

"It's a nice gesture. You know, the concert and all." There was an elfish sparkle in Dottie's steel blue eyes. "Oh, you know how those musicians are. Once you get the instrument out of their mouths, they babble like a bunch of teenagers."

"They can be pretty chatty at times, can't they?"

Dottie's eyes rolled back in her head for a moment, as if she had a flashback. When she returned, she casually asked, "Would like to meet this boy you've been pining about."

"Huh?"

"Zeke, Zach, something like that."

"How did you know? Did Liza tell you?"

"No dear, I can read it in your eyes. And a little birdie is telling me you want to talk a little about him." Dottie giggled with a contagious chuckle as her eyes gleamed.

"Sometimes, Dottie, I wonder if you are clairvoyant, a shrink or a bartender."

"Maybe a little of each. Maybe in previous lives. Or maybe I'm practicing for the next one. I'll figure it out one of these days, as long as they don't catch me and burn me at the stake."

"That won't happen. You're in Vermont." A wide smile creased Sharon's face.

"You know, that coconut aroma is telling me to visit for a piece, and it looks like a gorgeous day out there. Why don't you have a seat out at the table and I'll come and chat with you." Dottie tapped Sharon's hand, then reached down under the counter for her handwritten sign that read, 'Honor system 'til I get back. $1.00 for a small, $1.50 for a large, If you need me, I'm out back.' She then drew herself a cup of the coconut coffee and headed out with Sharon to chat a bit.

After another hour on the road, Sharon pulled up the narrow driveway of the Briarwood Inn. The distinctively Victorian mansion had not lost any of its storybook charm since the last that she had seen it. She remembered how Sarah would always invite Liza and her closest orchestra companions for an after concert wine and cheese get-together, which Amy and Steve, the owners always accommodated. Sometimes they even joined in when it just the musicians stayed at the Inn. It was like a class reunion, and by the time everyone had a few drinks, especially if the weather was good, the party would spill out onto the grounds.

She shouldered her overnight bag and evening gown, then strutted through the parking lot, bounced up the steps and stepped into the lobby. For a moment, she was drawn back years — the plush, patterned chairs convened around a polished, large coffee table, and the fireplace was stacked with white birch, waiting for evening conversation over coffee or wine. Sharon drew in a deep breath and noticed the slight scent of lavender in bloom wafting about the room. And something baking.

"Welcome back, Sharon. We're glad you could come," a voice drifted out from the kitchen. "I'm just finishing up some oatmeal cookies."

"Oh, my word, you remembered." Sharon squeaked like a little girl when she caught the aroma. She dropped her bag and draped her dress over the nearest armchair, then headed toward the propped open door to the kitchen, but stopped when Amy, who she knew had called out to her, appeared in the doorway holding a silver tray mounded high with Sharon's favorite oatmeal cookies. If she remembered correctly, the cookies would have a perfect blend of sweetness, nuts, raisins, and decadent chunks of dark chocolate.

"How could I forget you two?" Amy set the tray down on a serving table and greeted Sharon with a friendly hug, even though Sharon's attention was drawn to the tray. As she held her tightly, she whispered, "Rhonda told me you would be coming, I'm so sorry about Sarah. Is there anything I can do for you?"

"I'm fine, Amy, really. It was a struggle at first, but things have worked themselves out." Sharon snitched one of the cookies from the bottom and smirked as she closed her eyes, took a bite and let her head drift back, reveling in the chewy sweetness.

"Well, if you do need to talk a bit after the show, Steve has assured me we can get some girl time in."

"I think I would enjoy that," Sharon said as she swallowed her first bite. It was just as decadent as she remembered.

Chapter 22

After six hours travel through horrendous traffic, Zach pulled into the visitor's center just off the Lee Exit from the Mass Turnpike. With the late evening concert time tonight, he knew he would need to find somewhere to overnight nearby rather than risk an early morning accident, or serve as a target for the State Police with out of state plates and traveling in the wee hours of the morning. Once inside the travel center, he recognized the display cases that held tourist brochures for hiking trails, ski resorts, sugarhouses, and bed and breakfasts. He randomly pulled one out that seemed to look nice, and after he read a few of the enticements and noticed it was nearby, decided it was worth a try. It even looked a bit on the posh side and it was close enough to Tanglewood that they would know how to get around the expansive grounds.

He opened his flip-phone and saw that the battery was almost dead. He had forgotten to charge it before he left the house. He noticed a payphone, dropped a quarter into it and dialed the listed number for the Briarwood Inn. A chill ran up his spine when the proprietor answered the phone and identifying herself as Amy.

"Taken care of. Amy will have a room for you," Sarah's words resonated. And she did have one room left.

He got back on the road and followed Amy's directions precisely, working his way through Lee and then Lenox. Just outside of Lenox, he saw the driveway for the Briarwood Inn, and turned off the access road into the small, packed parking lot. He tussled with his haphazardly packed overnight bag for a moment, then stopped before stepping onto the wrap-around porch.

The Inn was a rather quaint Victorian mansion, and from the outside, it was charmingly beautiful. The grounds were as expansive as the brochure had described, and in the distance, he could see the Tanglewood concert grounds. Music coming from that direction confused him for a moment, remembering that the concert wasn't supposed to start until much later, but then he realized the musicians were probably just tuning up.

Turning back to the inn, he walked up the staircase to the sprawling porch where a foursome in rather formal attire lounged in cushioned sitting chairs near a round glass topped coffee table, sipping from goblets of red wine. He avoided eye contact despite them all raising their glasses toward him and kept moving through the large oak double doors, inlayed with ornate stained glass, and into the rather comfortable looking inner foyer.

"Welcome to the Briarwood. Am I safe to assume you are Zach Fields?" a cordial voice greeted him. A woman about his age and average build tipped her head and smiled. Her dark blond wavy hair sat loosely cropped close to her rounded face. There was a hint of color to her cheeks, as if she had spent a few more hours than she should in the sun with her pale skin.

"Yes, ma'am. I was the one that called about an hour ago. Zach Fields. I really appreciate you accommodating my last minute call." He glanced back over his shoulder at the gathering on the porch that seemed to be studying him as well.

"Oh, not a bother at all. I'm Amy and I'll be your host for your stay."

For real, Zach thought, then started to wonder what else Sarah had set up for him.

"Steve, my husband and I run the Inn. He's out back in the garden. Let me check you in and give you some information about us."

"Thank you," Zach mumbled and moved toward the counter, which looked more like a converted high-class, old fashioned bar. He could not help but eye the mound of oatmeal cookies on the platter in front of him on the counter.

"Feel free to take one. They should still be warm. I just made them a few minutes ago." Amy noted as she accessed the files and electronics tucked within a roll-up desk. "And over there in the carafes are coffee and hot water. We have a pretty broad selection of teas."

"Thank you very much. I appreciate the hospitality." Zach set his overnight bag down, fished out a credit card, and then took one of the cookies. As Amy indicated, their aroma was enticing and they were still warm. They tasted even better since the quick McDonald's burger he grabbed along the way now felt more like a rock in his stomach.

"Let me get some information and check you in," Amy noted as she sat down in her computer chair and started typing. "You said you are from Edenton, New Hampshire, if I remember correctly. We've had a few visitors from out that way."

"Actually from Chicago. I just moved here a few months back."

"It is such a lovely area, isn't it? It reminds me a bit of where I grew up in Pennsylvania. Address?"

"153 Pleasant Hill."

Amy typed in the address. When she pressed enter, she froze at the computer's response. Zach could not help notice her surprise. Or horror.

"Sarah …" Amy mumbled under her breath.

"Oh, yes," Zach realized what surprised Amy. "I bought Sarah Tanchak's house. One of my clients gave me a pair of tickets to this benefit concert earlier in the week. It was a little late to really plan out, so I do appreciate you being able to accommodate me."

"I see," Amy noted, took a deep breath, then continued processing Zach.

"I guess that means she stayed here before?"

"Right, right," Amy mumbled as she carefully typed his credit card numbers on the keyboard. When she was done, she switched her focus between the screen and the card to ensure correctness. She then turned back toward Zach and inspected him while slipping a key into an envelope. "Per chance, do you know her sister?"

"Sharon?" Zach sensed something strange about Amy's questions. No, not strange. Secretive, perhaps.

"Yes, Sharon."

"I do, but not as well as I would like to. She did help me move in. Well, sort of. She drove me back to the house when I dropped off the U-Haul. We've had a couple of short visits. I think she would have enjoyed coming up here for this."

"I would think so, too." Amy inspected Zach more closely as he remained silent. "I see. Well, Room 15, through the double doors, and it will be on your right. It's an East facing room, so you will get the sun in the morning, if that's not a problem." While Amy was explaining the layout, Zach noticed that she seemed nervously looking over her shoulder as if she had been expecting someone.

"Well, thank you very much." Zach could not help but look back himself, but all he could see were the musicians jabbering amongst themselves, goblets of wine quivering in their hands.

"It's our pleasure. Anything else?"

"Could I bother you for some tips on Tanglewood itself? It's my first time up here and to be perfectly honest with you, I have no clue where I am supposed to go to get in, or even where to go when I do get in."

"Sure," Amy said, her face returning to normal. She pulled out a large paper map of the Tanglewood grounds and pointed out the main entrance, the major buildings and in particular, the band shell, where the concert was being held. She also pointed out how close the Briarwood was in relation to the grounds, and a shortcut from the backside of the inn.

"I don't need to wear what they are, do I?" Zach nodded over his shoulder to the porch where the more formally dressed had gathered.

Amy perched her eyebrows, cocked her head, then circled her finger like she was spinning a ballerina. Zach complied and slowly turned around, feeling a bit silly.

"You don't need to go that far, but a step up from what you have on at this point would be warranted."

"Casual?"

"Should be okay with a blazer."

"Thanks," Zach noted. As he turned away to head to his room, he poured himself some coffee and grabbed another cookie, all the while feeling like Amy was watching him very closely. He was sure there was something Amy wanted to tell him something but was holding back for some reason. When the double doors closed behind him, he felt less conspicuous.

"So was that our wayward guest?" Steve stepped into the great room through the frost framed French double doors. Each of his hands held a wide wicker basket overfilled with fresh vegetables from the garden. He had always had a prolific green thumb, which added a special flavor to the evening meals, something their bed and breakfast had grown a reputation for the region. He was tall and thin, but with broad shoulders. His square face betrayed his coal miner's roots, as did his wavy dark hair.

"Yes, he was. He has some very interesting details as well," Amy noted as Steve removed his well-worn garden clogs.

"Should I be worried?"

"Oh, no, not those kind of details, dear." Amy waved him off as he ferried the produce toward the kitchen. As he passed, he nodded for her to follow him, which she did, passing through the white swinging doors. As Steve set the baskets onto the counter, she continued, "I was thinking. Let's just imagine you were single, and I was as well, but we knew each other."

"I can imagine where this is going." Steve absently listened as he started to sort through the greens he had laid on top of the pile. Amy leaned into the counter.

"And let's imagine we both ended up in the same place to go to the same show, but didn't know it at first."

"It would be rather —"

"Romantic, don't you think?"

"I was going to say spooky. What scheme are you planning on hatching and what's our part in this?" Steve dug down to a large bunch of dirt-covered carrots and carefully set them into the deep sink. He started the water spray before he cut them down to an inch of the tops, then rinsed them down, one-by-one, revealing their bright orange flesh. Amy watched silently as a smirk twitched into place.

"I've seen that look before. Should I ice down some wine for someone's room?" Steve finished with the carrots, dried his hands, then leaned toward his wife. Inches away from her face, he could see a sparkle in her eyes.

"Room temperature might create a bit more ambiance, don't you think?"

"A nice Cabernet? Or were you thinking something a bit more subtle?"

"That's the ticket. Cabernet. I knew you were a romantic at heart," Amy laughed softly, then headed back out to the great room to accommodate patrons.

Refreshed from her afternoon hike on the nearby trails, Sharon stepped inside the foyer and noticed that the collection of musicians in the great room had grown, some standing some sitting, but all of them relaxing in preparation for the evening's performance. She quickly glanced through the faces, hoping to recognize at least one or two of them, but none looked familiar. It would be nice to see Julian at this point, but she would catch up to him later, she was sure. One younger looking man did wave to her and she did wave back, but she didn't recognize him either. She changed her glance back to the reception desk and spotted Amy standing behind the counter, looking out toward the parking lot as if she was waiting for someone.

"Hey, Amy. Looks like you have your hands full this weekend. Do you think you might need some help?" Sharon wiped her face with the towel she had slung around her neck. "You know I did a short waitressing gig over this past winter."

"I think Steve and I can handle it, but I'll keep that in mind. But my gosh, it has been quiet most of the season, until now. It just exploded this week. You know, I've actually turned people away today. And I had to find the 'No Vacancy' sign. It was buried so deep in the closet that I guessed I never thought I'd need it."

Sharon noticed that the collection of musicians had moved on. The young man continued to eye Sharon as they walked through the front doors, leaving the lobby empty.

"So, it looks like you had a nice walk?" Amy nudged toward the armchairs near the cold, empty fireplace. Sharon complied and when she reached one of the plush chairs, melted into the cushions.

"The air is so fresh up here. It's like the White Mountains back home. Must be all the pine trees."

"Sharon, I need a favor." Amy leaned over her back.

"Sure. What do you need?" Sharon leaned forward and turned back toward Amy. "Do you need me to run into town and get something for you?"

"No. Not that kind of help."

"Oh?"

"Well, the last guest came in about an hour ago and said that he had never been to Tanglewood before."

"It can be intimidating," Sharon agreed.

"Do you think you might be able to help him out?"

"Depends." Sharon narrowed her eyes at Amy. They narrowed even more when Amy grinned. "He's not a dog faced boy, is he? Or some hard luck case from Jersey?" Sharon turned skeptical.

"Oh, no. Not at all. He just doesn't want to get lost and be wandering around the mountains and valleys by himself for the next three years trying to find the way out."

"Still depends. He's not a letch, is he?"

"Oh, no. Nothing like that."

"Okay, on a scale from one to ten, what is he?"

"If ten is dreamy, he's about a seven or eight, I'd say."

Sharon thought about it for a minute, then asked. "And where would you put Steve? Be honest now."

"Oh, he's busy tonight."

"Where is Steve right now?" Sharon frowned and vaulted up from her seat.

"The kitchen."

Sharon strutted toward the kitchen, bounced open the doors and saw Steve working his way through the lettuce he had picked. He stopped what he was doing, tilted his head and weakly smiled.

"Hey there." Sharon waved quickly and headed back toward Amy, who had followed Sharon and was standing next to the counter again. "Where do you rank Steve?"

"Huh?"

"On a scale of one to ten, where's Steve. I need to know what your scale is so I know what to expect."

"You know I'm partial. We've been together for some time, you know."

"On a scale of one to ten?" Sharon perched her eyebrows, hoisted her hands onto her hips and glared into Amy's eyes. She leaned over and whispered, "I've been set up with some real cavemen in the past. I just need to know, and be honest. I promise I won't tell him."

"He's an eight."

"Ok. Deal then. You can let dog-boy know I'll meet him here at six."

"You got it." Amy clasped her hands together in glee. Steve, standing at the kitchen doors, clearly overheard the girls and just rolled his eyes before slinking back into the kitchen.

Chapter 23

Zach slipped on a decent pair of khaki slacks, and a reasonably clean white shirt. He grabbed his navy blue blazer, remembering Amy's advice that a step up from the little less than casual dress that he arrived in was expected. Primping just a bit in the mirror, he brushed his hair back and resigned himself to the fact that there was not much more he could do and he didn't have much more to work with. He headed out, locking the door behind him, more out of habit than need. A well-used bag without cash or a computer didn't leave much worth taking anyway. Trying his best highbrow swagger down the hallway, he froze in mid-stride when he spotted Amy glaring at him with a disapproving scowl. Embarrassed, he cracked a sheepish grin then moved on with a more normal walk.

"That's better." Amy came over and inspected him from head to toe. She brushed off a piece of lint from his jacket. "I was able to find someone who was willing to help you out tonight."

"I don't remember asking for help, just directions." Zach hand-pressed his shirt nervously.

"No, Zach. Just a guide. Someone I know who's been here before that can show you around."

"I'll trust your judgment. Am I presentable enough, then?" Zach opened his arms and slowly turned a full rotation. He stopped, faced Amy, opened his blazer and propped his hand on his hip. Amy cocked her head for a moment, until an apparent thought seemed to have popped into her head.

"Wait here." She pointed to one of the armchairs next to the fireplace. Zach complied and Amy headed into the kitchen, almost dancing in cherubic glee.

Sharon slipped on her maroon formal and pressed it as close to her skin as she could before examining herself in the full-length mirror. It wasn't too revealing, she thought. Just elegant. Her shoulders were exposed, but her farmer's tan was not too obvious. The neckline didn't expose too much. She felt that she looked good in it despite having lost enough weight that the dress hung on her a bit on the loose side. The weather prediction was a plus; just as it was that night; a little warm at the start, but dry enough to stay comfortable when sunset cooled the field at the pavilion.

It felt good to primp again. Her hair was a little wild and few inches shorter than it was back then, but it was still long enough to rest teasingly on her almost naked shoulders. She twisted her hips one side to the other, considering if her dress might be a little over the top for a dog-boy, especially so if Amy had read him wrong. Noting the time, she realized that at this point, it was probably too late to change, so it was this or a smelly t-shirt. She preferred the evening gown.

"You're fine." Sharon thought she heard a voice behind her. She glanced up into the mirror and for a fleeting moment, thought she caught a glimpse of another image next to her. When she turned fully around, there was nothing but the white folding closet doors, propped open with her empty clothes hangers on the closet hook.

"Well, this is it," she mumbled as she opened the door and stepped out into the hallway. She turned to close and lock her door, bumped into someone as she backed into the hallway.

"Oh, I'm sorry. I didn't see you." She turned around and saw Amy.

"No worries, dear. Here. I think your escort needs this. I think he was expecting to go alone." Amy handed a Sharon a pink peony bud that hinted a kiss of maroon at its center, then leaned over and whispered into her ear, "By the way, you look gorgeous."

Sharon smirked, then hugged Amy tightly. "You know you didn't need to do this."

"Is there something you know that I should know? Your mothering is making me very suspicious."

"You'll be fine. Now scoot. Your dog-boy is out there waiting and I wouldn't want you to be late."

"Not too much?" Sharon asked as she waved her hand over her calf-length dress."

"You're fine. Enjoy your evening, dear."

Sharon scrunched up her nose and wagged her finger at Amy in a friendly tone. As she headed into the great room, she noticed someone sitting near the fireplace, where she had sat before. When he turned his head slightly, she immediately recognized the face.

"Zach?" she mouthed. Their eyes met and locked. She tried to think of something to say, but instead she just stood stunned, staring and speechless. Her emotions swung from happy to angry as if she was bi-polar. She was pleased that it was Zach, that he was here and he had come even though she didn't ask him to come. Then anger rushed in, cajoling her to believe he didn't want her to know that he was headed here for the weekend. Then comfort. Then disappointment. Then —

"Sharon?" He said as he slowly rose to his feet and stood frozen in place.

She reveled at his voice for a moment then turned back to Amy, who was now leaning against the entrance to the great room, a smile beaming on her face. She closed one eye and wagged her finger at Amy before turning back to Zach.

"Turn around," she ordered.

Zach complied.

"Seven at best," Sharon said over her shoulder. She then stepped toward Zach and worked the stem of the peony into the small buttonhole on his blazer before patting him on the chest. "That's better."

"Seven?" Zach stood, confused at the discussion.

"On a good day. Com'on. We can talk about that on the way. We don't want to be late." Sharon grabbed Zach's hand and pulled him toward the exit.

"You've been here all along?" Zach stammered, pointing to her Jeep.

"You know you could have called?" Sharon continued leading Zach toward her Jeep.

"All I had was the number at Barrett's. And when I did call, there was no answer."

"I put my home number on the ticket," Sharon let go of Zach's arm, opened the hatch of her Jeep, and pulled out her wicker picnic basket.

"What ticket?"

"The one I left at your house."

"You did what? When? Where?"

"The ticket in the garage door. I left it there Monday night."

"It was pouring. I know I got home a little late, but I swear there was no ticket in the door." Zach took the basket.

"It wasn't raining when I was there." Sharon closed her Jeep and glared at him before taking the basket back from him.

"Are you kidding? It was pouring. I . . . I went in through the overhead that night."

"So, where did you get the ticket, then?"

"Tickets. Two tickets. At work." Zach reached into his pocket and pulled out two tickets. He looked over both sides of both of them before shaking them near his face. "I wanted to you to come here with me, but when I couldn't get hold of you . . ."

"Well, you should have tried harder. You could have asked Rhonda." Sharon snapped around and started toward the field at the rear of the Briarwood. She stopped and scowled at his empty hands. "So were you planning on meeting someone or were you really all alone?"

"Alone. I was hoping to meet Sharon here since I wasn't able to get hold of her." Zach snarked back.

"And what were you planning on snacking on? You know they don't serve food there. At least anything that's edible."

"No I didn't and I guess I forgot my snacks in my room." Zach just stood, slack-jawed at Sharon.

"I guess I could share mine." Sharon's ire tempered a bit as she turned and walked into a trimmed pathway alongside of the Inn.

"Wait, we're walking?" Zach caught up with Sharon, trying to keep stride with her.

"It's a quick walk and actually easier to get in since we don't have to fight parking."

"Ok, then. We're walking." Zach shrugged his shoulders and followed as closely as Sharon allowed.

"And you want me to believe that cockamamie story you laid on Amy?"

"What story?"

"That you requested someone to show you around, like a lost little puppy?"

"This was all her idea, Sharon. All I asked for was directions."

Sharon stopped suddenly and stiffened. She spun around and glared at Zach, then looked over his shoulder to the Briarwood garden where she saw Amy and Steve standing at the edge, their inside arms entwined, waving their free hands.

"Why that little imp," she mumbled under her breath. Even though she knew Amy couldn't see, she winked back and wagged her finger.

"Listen, Sharon," Zach gently took her arm and pulled her close enough that Sharon mellowed as their eyes locked. He sucked in a deep breath. "When I got the tickets in the mail, I thought about whether I really wanted to go."

"You got these in the mail? From who?"

"Lisa, Liza, I don't remember. It came from the Conservatory. Then I thought it would be nice if you could come with me, but for whatever reason, we never connected. Then Sarah —"

"Whoa. Sarah?"

"Yes, Sarah. Last night."

"She didn't?" Sharon widened her eyes and covered her mouth with her open palm.

"Not what you're thinking. She told me I had to go. I even stopped off at Barrett's this morning to see if I could catch you or someone who knew where you lived."

"You did?"

"It's not like I was stalking you all the way here to pounce when the moment was right. Look, if you don't want to be with me, that's fine. No problem. Just drop me off on some remote spot on the lawn, gallivant off with your friends and poof, you are done with me. Deal?"

Sharon cocked her head, backed away a step, and regarded Zach from head to toe, stopping for a brief moment to gape at his sandals. She then moved her gaze up until she saw the sincerity in his face.

"And let's be clear. It was your matchmaking friend's idea to hook us up this way. It was sheer luck that I picked up the brochure for this place. And looking at the parking lot, I have no clue why there was still one room available. Never having been here before, all I did was ask her if she could give me some directions and tips on how to navigate around this place."

Sharon let Zach rant defensively as she held her laugh inside. She knew it wasn't, as he said, pure luck that he picked up the Briarwood's brochure. And it wasn't Amy being the matchmaker. Sarah was meddling again, but this time, Sharon was fine with it.

"So, truce?" Zach opened his arms.

"Don't you want to be with me at the concert?" Sharon's eyes gleamed.

"I'd be a fool not to. Look at you. You are absolutely gorgeous, even more than I thought a couple weeks ago," Zach's voice lowered a bit.

"Then maybe you should ask me." Sharon propped her hands on her hips, tilted her head and twitched her eyebrows.

"Really?"

Sharon crossed her arms and scowled.

"Okay. Will you go with me to the concert, Sharon?" Zach smiled weakly.

"Hmm, let me think about it." Sharon placed her forefinger on her cheek, side glancing at Zach.

"Not too long. I hear it's starting soon and I wouldn't want to be late."

"Alright. I'll go with you. But no funny business." Her eyes sparkled.

"Alright. No funny business."

"Then lead on. We don't want to be late." Sharon stood still and waited.

"You know I have no idea where I am going. Would you mind showing me the way?"

"Sheesh. Six." Sharon allowed Zach to slip his arm in between hers and her torso. Their fingers met then laced together as they moved closer to the grounds.

Once inside, Sharon led Zach through a tunnel of overhanging oak boughs along the expansive yard and toward the massive shell that caressed the orchestra as if searching for a particular location. She pointed out a spot just underneath a canopy of spreading oak branches, insisting that this was the best spot. Without argument, Zach spread out the blanket and set up their island in the sea of the crowd. Sharon sat down at the center of the blanket and settled in, propping herself up from behind her with her arms and slipping off her sandals before crossing her legs at her ankles. She could tell he noticed the slight breeze teased away the slit on her evening gown, exposing her well-toned legs up to her thighs.

"You could offer me some of that wine." Sharon stroked her hair back away from her face. He complied, filling two goblets partway. As he handed her the glass, she caressed the glass at its stem, swirled the contents, and then gently sipped at it. "This was one of Sarah's favorite wines, you know."

"No, I didn't." Zach absently noted as he started cutting through the brick of cheese, piling up the slices onto a paper plate that he carefully placed between them. Applause rose from the crowd as Philippe St. Claire, the symphony conductor strutted onto the stage, tuxedo tails flapping as he approached. He stepped onto the podium, faced the crowd, and waited for the applause to settle before speaking.

"We have a special night here at Tanglewood," St. Claire started. "Tonight we honor a talented musician who was taken from us too soon. Sarah Tanchak was a commanding presence, with a voice of beauty, grace and harmony that emanated from her oboe during the number of concerts I had been blessed to be her conductor. She was a colleague and friend for many years and never hesitated to help advance the fine art of musical performance. We leave her chair open for tonight, for no one can truly replace Sarah in the orchestra or in our hearts."

Sharon slowly sipped at her wine and listened intently as St. Claire finished his thoughts. Through the corner of her eye, she could see that Zach was dividing his attention between her and the conductor, then felt his hand cover hers just as St. Claire finished and struck his music stand with three baton taps. Silence settled over the mountaintop until one swoosh of his baton coaxed the orchestra to explode to life with Tchaikovsky's Symphony Number Four.

Chapter 24

As the orchestra worked through their second piece, Beethoven's Pastorale under Director St. Claire's direction, Sharon and Zach had consumed more than half of the wine and most of the sausage and cheese. When the musicians transitioned into Vivaldi's Four Seasons, Sharon inched closer to Zach, leaving only a narrow sliver between them. She leaned back, fully consumed by the music; sometimes closing her eyes and weaving her head in rhythm with the more fluid passages of the movement and sometimes just gazing at Zach as he absorbed the passages. She absently stroked the outside of his legs, feeling comfortable with him being next to her. Very comfortable.

She leaned into Zach, then slipped her hand up his back and behind his head. Zach moved closer, turned toward her, and twitched a weak smile on his face. Thoughts raced through her mind about the man now in front of her. Did he want her as much as she wanted him right now? Would this be just one night and then they would drift apart again? Was she expecting too much out of this boy from the Midwest? Rather than stare and debate what might be, she drew him in close and pressed her lips into his, then kissed him deeper than she had before. As their tongues met, she felt her blood surge. She pulled him even closer, and his arms responded in kind. She released him, quietly asking, "You know Sarah is watching?"

"Really?" Zach stiffened a bit, withdrew a bit more, but remained close enough to sustain a dreamy gaze into Sharon's emerald eyes.

"You didn't see her?"

"The empty chair?"

"Why don't you look?"

The orchestra had already moved into the final movement before intermission as Zach turned his head and squinted, trying to see over the sea of candles that flickered in the slight breeze of the night. "I'm not seeing her."

"Well, I know she's there. Maybe you need to believe a bit more." Sharon ran her hand through Zach's tousled hair, then leaned into him again.

Applause rose from the field when the orchestra completed the first part of the concert. As he applause died down, the stage emptied and the chatter of the crowd rose. Sharon sat up and gazed back at Zach with hooded her eyes.

"You know, it is kinda creepy that you dream about my sister all the time."

"I can understand that, but there is a reason, although you might think it convoluted."

"Try me." Sharon tipped her head.

"Do you really want to know?"

"Well, I do."

"To be perfectly honest with you, I can't say for sure." Zach chewed on his lip. "When I was buying the house, I wanted to know more about her. The more I learned, the more she reminded me of Brenda. I was actually thinking of withdrawing my offer because they were so much alike."

"I don't think it is convoluted at all," Sharon covered Zach's hand and held it firmly. "I'm sorry, Zach. I didn't mean to drag that memory out."

"It's alright, Sharon. I think Sarah helped me reconcile with Brenda. And she brought me closer to you, and you helped me feel again."

"I can understand."

"Maybe I just needed to obsess a bit longer, you know, to wash away the memory."

"It's okay." Sharon turned away, and lowered her head to her chest. A coy grin tweaked to life. "You know, back when I kidded you about seeing Sarah?"

"I know. You think I have a very active imagination."

"I have to confess. I've seen her too."

"Really? Like the night you stayed?"

"No, not then. Some other times, though."

"Like tonight?"

"Yes. She is here." Sharon edged closer to Zach, and leaned into his shoulder as she noticed that the orchestra regrouped and started the mournful phrases of Barber's Adagio for Strings. The music swelled through crescendos and diminuendos like waves at the seashore. It was a very fitting piece since it was Sarah's favorite.

Sharon leaned back and scanned the orchestra, focusing on the chair that had remained empty for her sister since the start of the performance. For a moment, Sharon thought she heard an oboe, distinctly Sarah's timbre, work through the quiet passages, much in the same way she had practiced at home. Her playing was as unique as she was, vibrant, giddy at times, but always loud enough to carry over an entire orchestra when she needed.

The orchestra transitioned into their finale, Holst's Planets as Zach and Sharon leaned back, absorbed in the music. Zach removed his blazer, then covered Sharon's bare shoulders before both of them reclined to their backs and laid together, staring off into the clear view of the deep purple sky. Sharon rotated her head from right to left, scanning the sky, until she saw a shooting star flash to life, streak for a couple seconds, then flare out.

"Did you see it?" she asked.

"Perseids? It's that time of year, isn't it?"

"Did you ever do this as a kid? Just go out into the yard and watch for the shooting stars?"

"Zach rolled onto his side and propped his head up. "I did. Just wish I had more time to do it now."

"We do have all night, you know, and I know a great place to watch them," Sharon noted as she turned to Zach. Before she could move any closer, the finale's last raucous phrases pounded the concert to a close and the field burst out with a standing applause punctuated with "bravo's" that echoed through the valley. The tall, dim field lights started a yellowing glow as the crowd of concertgoers coalesced as a mass headed for the exit.

When the crowd thinned and the lights at the band shell gleamed brightly for the musicians to collect their things, Sharon stood and stretched toward the sky while Zach packed away what was left of their picnic dinner. She watched the sky for a bit longer, hoping to catch a shooting star or two while they waited for the crowd to thin out, then let her gaze come back to earth. As she glanced up toward the stage, her face beamed.

"Oh my God, it's Liza. Com'on, you need to meet her," she encouraged Zach to follow as she headed upstream of what was left of the crowd. He did.

"Liza?" Her voice squeaked as she came within calling distance of Sarah's longtime friend. She had already wrapped her long, crocheted sweater over her concert dress. Her high-soled sandals strapped to her legs with a weave of thin leather straps seemed out of place, and almost dangerous in the rolling hills.

"Oh, Sharon, dear," Liza's surprise was genuine. She smiled broadly, excused herself from her conversation with another horn player, then opened her arms for Sharon. "What did you think?"

"It was simply fabulous. Sarah would have enjoyed playing this concert."

"She did." Liza smirked as she pulled out a tape player from her sweater pocket and handed it to Sharon. "That was her playing the solo in Adagio. We couldn't fathom playing that piece without her."

Liza's attention turned to Zach for a brief moment, then back to Sharon. There was recognition in her expression as she craned her neck and inspected Zach, head to toe again, "So, is this a new friend? I don't believe we have met." Liza lifted her hand toward Zach, then twitched one eyebrow up.

"This is Zach, Liza," Sharon's eyes twinkled as an impish grin grew on her face. "Amy pulled a fast one on me. She said he just needed some help getting around. You know how much I'm a sucker for lost puppies."

"Zach Fields. Pleased to meet you," Zach nodded politely as he weakly waved. "You must be the Liza that sent me the tickets?"

"Oh, my word. You? You are the fiduciary that Judith insisted I send a pair of tickets?"

"That would be me." Zach tipped his head politely, then side glanced to Sharon, smitten that someone had corroborated his story.

Liza scanned down to Zach's backside for a moment, then looked up to Sharon and winked before twitching her eyebrows in approval. "Well, I am pleased to finally put a face to the name." She leaned over to Sharon and whispered in a hushed voice, "He's kinda cute. Nice buns."

"I'm glad you approve. Just a six and working up to seven," Sharon giggled as she squeezed Zach's arm. "And Julian? Did he make it?"

"Oh yes. Julian and Katie are here."

"I'm so happy for that."

"Dear Sharon, I hate to be rude, but I do need to be sure my instrument doesn't fall into the wrong hands. These grounds people are like Neanderthals with our gear."

"Oh, no worries. Maybe see you back at the Briarwood?"

"Does that mean you both will be joining us for the closing party tonight? Amy has promised us some of her fabulous hors d'oeuvres."

Sharon looked over to Zach. Her emerald eyes narrowed and smiled at him as she squeezed his hand. "I don't think so. I believe someone promised me some star-gazing tonight."

"I see." Liza winked again, clearly aware of Sharon's intent. She leaned into Sharon, caressing her face in her palms. "Well then, we'll miss you and your new beau, dear."

"And us as well. Maybe tomorrow?"

"That might be pleasant." Liza whispered in her ear before kissing her on the cheek, then strutted away awkwardly in her heels.

"Six working on seven?" Zach asked.

"Yeah, working on a seven." Sharon wrapped her arm around his waist and together they meandered back to the Briarwood, slow enough that by the time they arrived, most of the performers had already gathered in the flickering oil lamp ringed front yard, passing the first round of wine and champagne.

"I guess that puts a crimp in our star-gazing for tonight," Zach noted as they meandered by the party and onto the front porch. Some heads turned toward them, but with solely a smile, each of them turned back to the party and let Zach and Sharon continue undisturbed.

"That's alright. We can take a peak later when they are all asleep," Sharon purred as they walked through the doors and into the almost empty lobby. Sharon moved closer to the fireplace, where welcomed warmth emanated from the birch logs that Steve had piled and lit. She stood fascinated at the flames lapping around the logs while Zach sat into the loveseat in front of the fire, propping his feet up on the slate hearth. Sharon removed his blazer and laid it on the arm of the seat, then wedged in next to him, snuggling up to his shoulder. Her hand and fingers skimmed their way up his arm, finally resting on his chest. Zach responded in kind and rested his hand on her now naked shoulders.

Sharon closed her eyes and wondered if this was right to give in to her more base desires rather than running away from them. It would be a change, a drastic change from where she had been before. He inspired something inside that she had not felt before. And even more tonight. She fretted that she was actually living some fantasy that she would be waking up from, again alone with just a memory. For just a moment. She glanced up to Zach, his chest moving up and down slowly, calmly, his hands working her shoulder with a gentle touch, and his scent enough to make her want to let her inner feelings be known.

"Is this what you expected?" Sharon could hear her voice tremble as she spoke.

"To be honest, it's more. Much more. I thought I had scared you away."

"I thought it was me that scared you off."

"Well, it seemed touch and go there a few hours ago."

"Huh?"

"You seemed more than a tad angry with me before we left."

"I had already written you off, but I'm glad I didn't."

"I'm glad too."

"You know, when I fell in the woods, I suddenly felt alive again and I so wanted you to sweep me off my feet that night."

"I guess I was a little worried you might think I was taking advantage of you."

Sharon thought for a moment. "I might have then. Not tonight."

Zach reached over to his blazer and pulled out the wilted peony from the lapel. He gently slipped the stem underneath her hair so it rested on her ear. He then stood up and pulled her toward him into a tight embrace, tight enough that Sharon felt her breath escaping briefly. She looked up and gently stroked his face before turning and leading him to her room. Locking the door behind them, she then turned and noticed a small bottle of wine on the desk, with goblets icing in a bucket next to it.

"I don't think we need any more," she whispered, then gazed into Zach's eyes and started unbuttoning his shirt. She wondered no longer, thinking it could be a very good night.

It was.

As the sun broke over the horizon, Sharon worked herself more deeply into Zach's side, sleepily draping her arm across his chest. Her hands moved with his slow, steady breaths, rising and falling as he slept. Zach's eyes finally fluttered before he rolled into her and moaned pleasurably. His hands again worked slowly up and down her back until they rested comfortably on her curvature.

It was right, she thought.

"I guess we never got back out for sky watching." Zach said with a rather scratchy voice.

"Guess not. Breakfast?" Sharon breathed deeply, tasting his musk on the air that moved through her nose.

"It can wait," Zach whispered as sun beams broke through the veiled curtains and they made love again.

Zach would have preferred to drive back with Sharon rather than caravanning ahead of her through the Vermont mountains. The time together with only the winding road to distract them would have been a prime opportunity to talk and get to know each other better. And he would have a better sense of where he stood with her, whether it was just a quick fling at a concert in the mountains or if it was the beginning of something more. The latter made sense to him.

He was first to arrive back at the house, exhausted from all the driving. He rested his head on the steering wheel for a moment before stepping out on rubbery legs. As he stretched, he noticed that another potted plant had appeared close to the mound of forget-me-nots he had already planted. He found the trowel he had left near the fence and then worked the latest gift from Esther into soil, expanding the mound of lavender and yellow flowers just a foot more. As he finished, Sharon's red Jeep slowed down and turned into the driveway. He brushed off his hands and headed toward her car.

"Stay for dinner?" Zach leaned toward her open window.

"I really should be going. Morning comes early around these parts, you know."

"I might be able to work something up that you might like."

Sharon scrunched up her lips, debating the offer. Zach nodded back to the picnic basket.

"And maybe finish off that other bottle of wine in there?"

"Alright. If you insist." Sharon turned off the engine and sighed loudly. "That was a very long drive."

Sharon followed Zach into the yard and as he fumbled with his keys at the garage door, they slipped out of his hand onto the stepping-stones that sat just above the ground level. When he reached down to retrieve the keys that had wedged themselves between two of the stepping-stones, he noticed an oddly shaped piece of paper; long, thin and rectangular.

"Would you look at this?" He picked up the concert ticket, turned it over and noticed that in faded ink. Sharon had written her phone number. He showed it to Sharon as she walked through the gate.

"Well, I tried." She shrugged her shoulders and cracked a smile. "But things worked out anyway."

Zach even surprised himself with his rendition of rosemary chicken, especially since Sharon complimented him on his cooking and presentation. With the wine half done, Zach started to clean up the kitchen as Sharon showered. Through the wall, he could hear her gentle, melodic voice singing an aria he thought unfamiliar. Her voice rose and fell gracefully, and he caught himself thinking about holding her warm body close as they made love through the night. He imagined brushing his hands over her curves as she lay in his bed, gently at first then more firmly massaging her back.

Zach jumped when she opened the bathroom door and poked her head out, holding a towel loosely in front of her. "Would you be so kind as to let me borrow one of your shirts?"

"Uh . . . okay, I guess. Flannel?"

"That would work," Sharon noted as she started to wrap the towel around her.

Zach went upstairs and searched through his closet, but could not find a single flannel shirt. Instead, he grabbed one of his dress shirts and headed back downstairs. "Sorry. I guess I didn't unpack my flannel shirts yet."

"This will do," Sharon said as she slipped back behind the cracked open door. After a few seconds, she stepped out. She had only half-buttoned the shirt, top opened enough to reveal her shapeliness.

"I left my clothes hanging in there. I hope you don't mind," she noted rather casually, then brushed Zach as she walked in bare feet toward the stove.

"Not at all," Zach mumbled. He failed to keep his eyes from watching the beautiful, barely covered woman now reaching into the cupboard to get a pair of cups, the shirttail barely covered her backside. She turned on the burner beneath the teapot, and then worked her way through the coffee and spices in the cabinet. "Do you have some chamomile tea up here someplace?"

Zach started toward her to help look, but she quickly noted, "Found it."

The teakettle's shrill whistle came to life as Zach finished placing all the dinner plates into the dishwasher. Sharon dropped the tea bags into the cups, and then poured the steaming water over them to let them steep.

"It's a nice evening. Let's take this outside," Sharon insisted as she handed a steaming cup to Zach, then headed out onto the deck. Zach started the dishwasher, then took his cup and joined her.

"I had a great time at the concert," Sharon leaned back in her chair and looked up to the sky. "I'm glad you decided to show up."

"Do we have a chance?" Zach asked as he leaned back into his chair, feeling the exhaustion of the drive all over. As the chamomile worked up his spine, he could feel his mind start to fog and his eyes grow heavy.

"We might be able to work something out." Sharon turned her head toward Zach and twitched a brief smile. "You do have a spot for a guest, don't you?"

"I think I can make some accommodation." Zach rose from his chair and offered his hands to Sharon. As she slipped her slender fingers into his hands and stood, she leaned into his chest, then followed him upstairs.

Chapter 25

Zach arrived at work mid-day and settled in at his desk, set his coffee down and booted up his computer. He leaned back, laced his fingers together behind his head, and stared at the ceiling as he waited for the weekend updates to finish loading. He pulled a mouthful of coffee through the plastic cover of his Dunkin Donuts commuter cup and closed his eyes, unable to shake the sense that even though they had a great weekend, something was amiss between him and Sharon. She woke before him and left without as much as a good bye or a quick note to call him later. He wished he could have at least woken up and caught her before she left, but the excitement and exhaustion had caught up with him, leaving a nagging sense he had done something to chase her off.

"Good morning, stranger," a familiar voice broke into his thoughts. He leaned forward, opened his eyes, and saw Natalie standing at the opening of his cube. "You look as if you had a rough weekend."

"Just a lot of driving. Maybe I'm getting too old for road trips."

"So you went to the concert after all?"

"I did. The concert was nice. Wait, you knew?"

"It just made sense. I knew about the tickets. Some woman called to be sure you got them. I put two and two together."

"Who called?"

"Liza I think was her name. Is she the one you've been seeing?"

"No. Not Liza. Liza's friend."

"I see." Natalie perched her eyebrows and smiled for a moment until she added, "Joshua called for another meeting at five. I swear he's going to drive us all into the ground, Catch you for a late lunch?"

"Sure." Zach absently noted as he logged into his computer and started stepping through his calendar for the week. He spotted an opening mid-morning tomorrow where he could call Sharon if he couldn't free up some time later today.

Sharon worked through the invoices for the deliveries scheduled for the day, wondering how she could arrange the truckload of chrysanthemums for best exposure. The organic vegetables that hadn't sold had been picked through extensively and had grown leggy. She would need to shuffle them over to the bargain section, which opened up space on one rack. The same was with most of the annuals; their blossoms had wilted a bit, burned out from the sunlight and heat of mid-days. She also had noticed she would need to move some of the amendments to behind the building to make room as well.

"Hey Sharon, how was the weekend?" Rhonda Barrett slipped in behind the desk and opened the faucet to water the inside displays.

"It was nice," Sharon avoided the answer she thought that Rhonda really wanted to hear. "The weather was phenomenal. Not too warm in the day, and not too cool at night. And the sky was the perfect indigo for star-gazing."

"That's nice," Rhonda watched the hose uncoil as it filled with water. "And was the concert what you expected."

"It was excellent," Sharon marked where she was in the pile of invoices and set them down. "They closed with The Planets. I knew they would. Of course, they had to play Adagio. It was Sarah's favorite. Liza had a tape of Sarah to fill in for her."

"So did you go alone?" Rhonda prodded. Sharon knew the question was coming.

"Well, I went alone. The trip out was nice. I stopped off at several spots where Sarah and I used to stop. I was surprised that most of the shop owners along the way remembered me and Sarah from years back."

"So, did you meet anyone up there, then?"

"I did meet up with Liza. She was pleased that I enjoyed the performance." Sharon answered directly.

"Oh that's too bad. I was hoping that you were able to hook up with that young man you seem to be interested in."

Sharon thought for a moment about providing a few more details than what Rhonda was asking for, although she certainly was implying that it was why she was fishing. It was a very nice weekend with Zach. Even though she was disappointed when she headed out early this morning, overall, it turned out to be a very satisfying weekend. Zach had filled a void that needed to be filled for a long time, but she figured she needed some time to herself to let her head catch up with her heart.

So why am I having second thoughts, Sharon struggled through her cycling emotions. Zach was thoughtful and considerate of her quirks and playfulness. And he was gentle, unselfish, open and honest. She wondered whether he just happened to be Johnny on the spot, there when she needed a shoulder to lean into, and someone to hold onto because she was feeling lonely and missing her sister. Or was she finally satisfying her own needs.

Sharon noticed a touch of sadness in Rhonda's face. "I didn't mean it quite that way. I did meet Zach there. Not quite the way I would have thought it could happen. It was a pleasant surprise to see him,"

"Oh, dear. I am so happy for you." Rhonda tipped her head and gazed at Sharon for a moment. "Is he what you expected?"

"I don't know," Sharon replied as the panel truck full of mums turned into the parking lot and stopped.

"We can talk more later. Looks like we got some work ahead of us." Rhonda moved closer to Sharon, hugged her, adding, "You probably want to let everyone know the truck is here."

"I will," Sharon picked up the radio and called back into the store for some help to unload the delivery.

Sharon was amazed at how busy the day had become, especially for a Monday. There was an endless stream of customers since the delivery truck left, which was good in a way, since there was little time to obsess about Zach. Every so often though, when a couple ventured in and together surveyed the shelves of geraniums in the greenhouse, she could not help but fixate on their every gesture. She watched their eyes as they met. She watched their gentle touching. She watched their gentle exchange of soft words. She saw how they showed they were in love, and wanting to please each other more than getting something in return.

Then she could not help but think about how much Zach was like that. Their eyes met and he didn't look away. They touched softly and he didn't move away. He seemed to sense what she needed before she asked, as if he knew what she wanted. She couldn't understand why she had the sudden urge to leave this morning, especially since he had made her feel so good.

The afternoon's pace wasn't any slower than the morning had been and by the time six o'clock rolled around, Sharon remained alone to close up shop for the night. The busy day was a relief, since she wasn't really sure if she wanted to talk to anyone about her feelings. She wanted to understand them first.

Once the store was closed up for the night, Sharon headed out. A fleeting thought crossed her mind to just head directly over to Zach's house, but since he hadn't called, maybe he was just working late again, and he might not have made it home. She thought about heading over and surprising him when he walked in, but decided rather to sort out what she was feeling and what she was thinking. She stopped off at the grocery store, picked up a few things, and head back to her condo. She could quickly fix some tacos, wait for sunset to headed out into the courtyard and drink in the last of the Perseids. If she was lucky, she would make a wish to arrive at some answers.

Zach pulled into his empty driveway after an extended day, disappointed not to see Sharon's Jeep. He realized it was his own doing, since after deciding to call her from work, he got busy and never did call. With his appointment calendar booked solid for the week ahead, there would be limited opportunities to steal a few minutes and call during the day.

There had to be another way, he thought as he flipped off his lights and turned his car off. The thought he might be able to just leave work one day this week and head over to Barrett's for some trumped up reason. Maybe he could leave early to get something like mulch for the plants, but with his schedule as full as it had ever been, and with Barrett's over an hour drive one way, he'd have to cancel a whole afternoon of appointments to make that happen. He preferred not to wait until Friday night or Saturday to run down to the store, but everything seemed to be pointing to that being the solution.

Something had to be done now, he resolved as he headed into the house. He had to stop for a moment and look down to the rocks where the ticket had fallen that night. It was something he had to do now. The ticket. Once inside, he dropped all his things on the table, found the ticket, picked up the phone, and dialed. It rang. One. Two. Three. Four. No answer. He hung up, checked the number, and then dialed again. The sound of the ringing was the same. He sighed and hung up without leaving a message. Drained physically and now emotionally, he decided to just slap together a peanut butter sandwich and go to bed. Tomorrow would be another long day.

Exhausted, he barely finished his sandwich, washed it down with some water, and crawled up the stairs to his bedroom. He cracked open the window, set his alarm and collapsed in the bed, face down, still in his suit.

A heavy fog rested like a blanket over the back yard as phrases of Schubert faded in and out, as if swallowed by the tide of the surging and retreating mist-laden shroud. The melody was one of the pieces that the orchestra had played at Tanglewood, but now a single oboe sublimely turning the phrases carried the melody. Drawn to the music, Zach found himself at the tool shed in the far corner of the yard, again. The small four-paned window to the right of the door was cracked open. The door was not. The lock on the door was still there, open but in place.

He took off the lock and opened the door. Sarah was inside, playing again, dressed in a flowing white evening dress, which other than the color, looked very much like the one that Sharon had worn. He stood at the open door and watched Sarah's flowing auburn hair move with the music until she stopped and laid her oboe crosswise in her lap.

"Did you enjoy the performance?" Sarah's voice emerged, sounding more like wind chimes encouraged by a swirling, gentle breeze. She effortlessly turned toward him, still in her sitting position. Her auburn hair flowed and drifted over her shoulders, as if being teased by a breeze. Her face was the same one he saw that evening in the mountains, a gentle glow, and cheeks a bit higher than most that shaped her eyes into almonds that lay beautifully under thin, delicate eyebrows. Her curves were the same as the ones he caressed and found so pleasing. She was very much Sharon's twin.

"It was fabulous." Zach leaned up against the doorjamb and just stared at Sarah. Her image stood and floated to be close enough that Zach thought he should feel her warmth. He reached out to touch her, but despite how close she felt, she remained just out of reach.

"She loves you, you know." Sarah's mouth turned up at the corners. Zach didn't know how to respond. He felt the same about Sharon. "I think you should tell her how you feel."

"I tried. There was no answer," Zach reasoned. Sarah inched closer until he felt her nose brush his.

"She's just being playful. You know, hard to get."

"You think so? It's not that I disappointed her?"

"Not at all."

"How do you know?"

"I was there, Zach. In the chair that they left open for me. I could tell what Sharon was feeling. A sister can tell."

The alarm clock started pulsing with an arrogant, irritating tone. Zach lifted his head and squeezed the crust from his eyes before silencing it with a smack on top of the clock. A dim light worked its way through the half-drawn shades in the east window. Zach sighed and dropped his face back into his pillow, wanting just a few more minutes to understand what Sarah knew about Sharon.

Tuesday passed. Sharon hoped that Zach would drop by, or at least call and see how she was doing. But as each group of customers filed through the shop with no sign of Zach, she felt doubt creep into her mind. She found herself fighting off the sense that once his conquest was done, he moved on. Although each passing hour solidified that thought, her intuition told her otherwise.

She had read that there had been a large solar flare earlier in the week and the Borealis was due in tonight. And the weather was clear. Most of the borealis light shows seemed to be early morning in the recent past, but the timing of this one, as best as the scientists could determine, would start to be visible about an hour after dusk. She could head over to the best spot she knew, the logging road across from the Palmer's farm. There was no spot equal to marvel at the twisting glowing auras while wrapped in a blanket and sitting on the hood of her Jeep. With wine. It would be a good night for it, she thought.

Zach closed up his desk files, locked his desk, then logged off his computer. He was sure he was the last one on the floor, based on the darkness that hung over most of the cubes. He lowered his head to stretch his neck and started to feel the vertebrae start to expand. He helped them along with a slow neck roll.

"I think you need to think about getting' out of here." Ben Parker's gruff voice startled Zach.

"Yeah, just working on it at this point,"

"You were here awfully late every day last week and you aren't doing much better this week." Parker sat down in Zach's cube. "Lady problems?"

"Nah." Zach looked at Parker's badge and immediately felt guilty. "Well, maybe. Now that you mention it, that just might be my issue."

"Well, they aren't going to get much better burying yourself in your work. Seems to me, lady issues need to get resolved sooner than later. One way or another, put them to bed, in a manner of speaking, and move on. If you let it keep on eating at you, it's no good for your health, never mind your focus. It's almost as bad as booze."

Zach leaned back and thought about the guard's counsel. He was right. He needed to get his head out of his ass and go for it.

"And working late all the time. Maybe you need a dog. Ever think of that?"

"You're right. I'm leaving."

"I've seen a lot of good men fall into that rut. Next thing you know, they're drinking their life away on Friday nights, then Saturday nights, then late to work on Monday. It's a death spiral, you know."

"You're right, Ben," Zach stood up and grabbed his blazer. A lingering petal from the peony that Sharon had placed into the lapel last weekend dropped from underneath the collar and fluttered to his desk. "It's a good night to take care of this, I think. One way or another, it will be resolved."

Parker escorted Zach out the door, then locked up behind him. He slipped out of the parking garage on foot, went to the Seven-Eleven down the street, and picked up the last arrangement of flowers they had set up in a bucket at the counter. He figured it should last until the morning, just in case he couldn't catch up with Sharon tonight.

He set the flowers onto the passenger seat and headed home. The radio seemed scratchy, more so than he had noticed before when he drove out of range of the oldies station. As he drove up Pleasant Hill, the curtain of iridescent blue, green and teal weaving in the sky caught his attention. If these were the Northern Lights, they were as spectacular as Sharon described.

As he came around the last big curve in the road, he started up the hill just before Palmer's farm. His headlights swept by a car parked on the left side of the road, facing toward the farm and the open view to the north. He recognized the distinct shape of a Jeep and as he passed, he saw a person wrapped in a blanket sitting on the hood. He slowed, but then decided that since it was only a short walk down the street from his house, he could walk back.

He grabbed the flowers from his seat and then quickly started down the street, walking at first, then breaking into a dress shoe jog. Amazed at how bright the eerie glowing Lights were, he kept working his way closer. When he caught a glimpse over the crest, he slowed, relieved that Sharon was still there.

"Am I interrupting anything?" Zach continued his measured approach. He could feel his heart race, almost jumping out of his chest, as if reaching out to Sharon.

"Oh, hi." Sharon startled, then turned and gazed in his direction, Zach thought he saw her eyes sparkle, as they did at Tanglewood. "No, not at all. Just me and the Lights."

"You know, I've never seen the Northern Lights," Zach leaned on the Jeep's fender. "Are they always like this?"

"Up here they are." Sharon tipped her head and sent a sideward glance toward Zach. "You never called," she added, then turned away and stared out into the weaving curtains.

"I did. You never answered."

"I was out watching the stars. Why didn't you leave a message."

"I don't know. I guess I just wanted to talk to you." Zach presented the flowers to Sharon. "Would it be okay if I join you up there?"

"Com'on up." Sharon buried her nose into the center of the blossoms, then patted the hood of her car. As Zach climbed up, he skootched closer to Sharon, noticing the open bottle of wine nestled between her legs. It was open, but she had no glass. It looked like she had already tapped into it.

"If you finish that, I'll have to take your keys, you know," Zach said.

"And then what? How am I supposed to get home?" Sharon leaned into his shoulder, still gazing out to the lights. She slipped open her blanket and draped it over Zach. He moved closer and as he did, was able to feel her warmth.

"I know a place just up the road. You can stay there."

"I heard it was haunted."

"That's just a rumor."

❧End❧

327

Thank you for reading Sarah's Home. I hope you enjoyed the story. I would be grateful if you would take a moment to post a review at your favorite retailer and recommend Sarah's Home to your friends.

Thanks so much!

Connie Mikelson

About the Author

Sarah's Home is Connie Mikelson's first published story. When not writing, Connie enjoys gardening to classical music in the shadow of New Hampshire's White Mountains.